W9-BHQ-754

Inside the cafe, hamburgers were frying to a crisp while customers sat motionless in the booths; the cook had fallen onto the grill; he was frying too. Down at the service station a stream of gasoline trickled into the street as an attendant, leaning against a car as unmoving as the driver behind the wheel, continued to pump gas into a gank that had obviously been full a long time.

Boland, California; Hartley, North Dakota; Berwick, Maine: the litany of small towns wiped out overnight grows longer hour by hour. There is no help to turn to, no one to blame, in this

WAR OF SHADOWS

ANALOG BOOKS

—Series Editor: Ben Bova—

look for these and other Analog books from

ACE SCIENCE FICTION

SF

A WAR OF SHADOWS

Copyright © 1979 by Jack L. Chalker
Copyright © 1979 by The Condé Nast Publications Inc.

All rights reserved. No part of this book may be reproduced in any form or by any means, except for the inclusion of brief quotations in a review, without permission in writing from the publisher.

All characters in this book are fictitious. Any resemblance to actual persons, living or dead, is purely coincidental.

An ACE Book, by arrangement with
Baronet Publishing Company

Printed in U.S.A.

A WAR OF SHADOWS

by

JACK L. CHALKER

SF
ace books
A Division of Charter Communications Inc.
A GROSSET & DUNLAP COMPANY
360 Park Avenue South
New York, New York 10010

THE BOOKS OF JACK L. CHALKER

A JUNGLE OF STARS
MIDNIGHT AT THE WELL OF SOULS
AN INFORMAL BIOGRAPHY OF SCROOGE
  MCDUCK
THE WEB OF THE CHOZEN
DANCERS IN THE AFTERGLOW
EXILES AT THE WELL OF SOULS
QUEST FOR THE WELL OF SOULS
THE IDENTITY MATRIX
AND THE DEVIL WILL DRAG YOU UNDER
  WAR GAME
in preparation:
RIP SAW
NATHAN BRAZIL
DOWNTIMING THE NIGHT SIDE
FOUR LORDS TO THE DIAMOND
A WALK IN THE DARK

This book is for Eva C. Whitley,
so loving a completist that she
not only has all my writings, but she
married me, too.

ONE

The shadow of death passed through Cornwall, Nebraska, but it was such a nice day that nobody noticed.

The sign off Interstate 80 simply read "Cornwall, next left," and left it at that. If you took it you were immediately taken onto a smaller and rougher road that looked as if it had last been maintained in the days of the Coolidge administration. Avoiding the potholes and hoping that your own vehicle wasn't too wide to pass the one coming toward you, you finally passed a small steak house and bar and were told by a smaller sign that you were in Cornwall, Nebraska, Town of the Pioneers, population 1160, together with the news that not only did they have Lions and Rotary, but when they met as well.

The town itself was little more than a main street composed of a few shops and stores, an old church, the inevitable prairie museum, and a motel which had never seen better days, as much maintained by pride as by business.

There wasn't very much business in Cornwall; like thousands of others throughout the great plains states the town existed as a center for the farmers to get supplies and feed, and to order whatever else they needed from the local Montgomery Ward's or Sears catalog store.

It was stifling hot on this mid-July afternoon. The ancestors of these people had settled in inhospitable Nebraska because they had lost hope of Oregon; trapped with all their worldly possessions, they had made the land here work—but they had never tamed it.

Three blocks down a side street, a woman gave a terrified shriek and ran from her front door out onto the sidewalk, down toward the stores as fast as she could. Rounding the corner, she ran into the small five-and-ten and screamed at a man checking stock on one of the shelves.

"Harry! Come quick! There's somethin' wrong with the baby!" She was almost hysterical.

He ran to her quickly, concern on his face. "Just hold on and calm down!" he said. "What's the matter?"

"It's Jennie!" she gasped, out of breath. "She just lies there! Won't move, won't stir, nothin'!"

He thought frantically. "All right, now, you get Jeb Ferman—he's got some lifesavin' trainin'. Did you call the doctor?"

She nodded. "But he'll be fifteen, twenty minutes coming from Snyder! Harry—please come!"

He kissed her, told her to get Ferman and join him at the house. Jeb had once been a medic in the Army, and was head of the local volunteer fire department.

In a few minutes, they were all at the house.

It wasn't that the child was quiet; in many circumstances parents would consider that a blessing. Nor was she asleep—her eyes were open, and seemed to follow Jeb Ferman's finger.

She just didn't move otherwise. No twitching, no turning, not even of the head. Nothing. It was as if the tiny girl, no more than ten weeks old, was totally paralyzed.

Jeb shook his head in confusion. "I just don't understand this at all," he muttered.

By the time the doctor arrived from two towns over, Jennie was no better, and her eyes seemed glazed.

While they all clustered around as the man checked everything he could, the concerned mother suddenly felt dizzy and swooned almost into her husband's arms. They got her onto the sofa.

"It's just been too much for me today," she said weakly. "I'll be all right in a minute. I've just got this damned dizziness." Her head went back against a small embroidered pillow. "God! My head is killing me!"

The doctor was concerned. "I'll give her a mild sedative," he told her husband. "As for Jennie— well, I think I'd better get her into a hospital as quickly as possible. It's probably nothing, but at this age almost anything could happen. I'd rather take no chances."

Harry, feeling frantic and helpless now with two sick family members on his hands, could only nod. He was beginning to feel pretty rotten himself.

It would take a good forty minutes to get an ambulance, and the patient was very small, so the doctor opted for a police car. He and the father got in the back, carefully cradling the young and still motionless infant, and the car roared off, a deputy at the wheel, siren blaring and lights flashing.

Not far out of town the car started weaving a little, and the deputy cursed himself. "Sorry, folks,"— he yelled back apologetically. "I don't know what happened. Just felt sorta dizzy-like."

He got them to the hospital, pulling up to the emergency entrance with an abandon reserved for police, and stepped out.

And fell over onto the concrete.

The doctor jumped out to examine him, and a curious intern, seeing the collapse, rushed to help.

"Hey! Harry! Get Jennie inside!" the doctor snapped. "I got to take care of Eddie, here!"

The intern took immediate charge, and the two men turned the deputy over and looked at him. There were few scrapes and bruises from the fall, and he was breathing hard and sweating profusely.

"I'll get a stretcher," the intern said. He turned and looked back at the police car, seeing Harry still sitting in it, holding the baby.

"Harry!" he yelled. "I told you to get Jennie inside!"

There was no reply, no sign that he had been heard at all. The doctor jumped up swiftly and leaned back into the car.

Harry sat there stiff as a board, only his panicked eyes betraying the fact that he was alive.

The doctor ran inside the emergency room entrance.

"We got us some kind of nasty disease!" he snapped. "Be careful! Isolation for all of them, full quarantine for the staff. Admit me, too—I'll assist from inside, since I've been in contact with them. And get another ambulance over to Cornwall *fast!* I think we got a young woman there with the same thing!"

Tom Scott and Gordon Martin had driven ambulances over half the roads of Nebraska in the six years since they'd started, and were hardened, prepared for almost anything—but never for driving into Cornwall that late July afternoon.

There were bodies all over. A couple of cars had crashed, but that was only part of it. People lay all over the place, in odd positions. Inside the cafe, hamburgers were frying to a crisp while customers sat motionless in the booths; the cook, fallen onto the grill still clutching a spatula, was frying too. Down at the service station a stream of gasoline trickled into the street as an attendant, leaning against a car as unmoving as the driver behind the wheel, continued to pump gas into a tank that had obviously been full a long time.

"Jesus God!" Scott reached for the radio. "This is Unit Six to dispatch," he said, trying to sound calm and businesslike.

"Dispatch, go ahead Six." A woman's cool, professional tones came back at him.

"We—I—I don't know how to tell you. Get everybody you can over to Cornwall, full protective gear, epidemic precautions. Everybody in this whole damned town's paralyzed or dead!"

"Say again?" The tone was not disbelieving; it was the sound of someone who was sure she'd misunderstood.

"I said the whole town's frozen stiff, damn it!" he almost screamed, feeling the fear rise within him. "We got some kind of disease or poison gas or something here—and I'm right in the middle of it!"

Within minutes four doctors were airlifted to Cornwall by State Police helicopters; troopers blocked the entrances and exits to the town except for emergency vehicles. It was a totally unprecedented thing, and there were no contingency plans for it, but they acted swiftly and effectively, as competent professionals. Nearby National Guard vehicles were pressed into service as well, and a frantic hospital tried to figure out where and how to deal with the huge number of patients. It was a 150-bed hospital; they already had forty-six patients. Appeals went out to hospitals and doctors as far away as Lincoln, and the CAP was asked to provide additional airlift capability.

The state Health Department was notified almost immediately. Again, there was initial shock and disbelief, but they moved. The Governor mobilized appropriate Guard trucks and facilities, not just to aid in handling the patients but also to cordon off the entire area around the town.

Less than fifteen minutes after the network newmen had it, a report went in to the National Disease Control Center in Fairfax County, Virginia, just outside Washington. Field representatives were dispatched from Omaha and the University of Nebraska within the hour.

In a small but comfortable apartment in the city of Fairfax, a phone rang.

Dr. Sandra O'Connell had just walked in and hadn't even had time to take off her shoes when the ringing began. She picked up the phone.

"Sandra O'Connell," she said into it.

"Dr. O'Connell? This is Mack Rotovich. We got another one, Red Code, same pattern."

Oh, my God! she said to herself. "Where?"

"Small town in western Nebraska, Cornwall I think it is."

"Symptoms?"

"Catatonia, looks like," Rotovich informed her. "Things are still more than a little sketchy. It just broke a few hours ago."

She dreaded the next question the most. "How many?" she asked.

"Six hundred forty or so to this point," Rotovich told her. "Maybe more now. Hard to say. Got a few elsewhere, seemed to hit about the same time, and there's a lot of people out in the fields yet. We're sending the Guard in on a roundup."

She nodded to herself. "Have you sent the Action Team in?"

"Of course. That's the first thing I did. Blood and tissue samples should be coming within the next two, three hours. Want to be down here when they come in?"

She was tired; bone-weary, her father used to call it. It had been a long day and a long week and she needed sleep so bad she could taste it.

"I'll be down in an hour," she said resignedly and hung up the phone. She stood there for half a minute, trying to collect herself, then picked the phone up again. Carefully, she punched out a full twenty-two digits on the pushbuttons, including the * and # twice. There was an almost unbelievably long series of clicks and relays, then an electronic buzz which was immediately answered.

"This is Dr. O'Connell, NDCC," she said into the phone. "We have another Red Town. An Action Team is en route. Please notify the President."

TWO

Mary Eastwicke had thought that being press officer for the National Disease Control Center would be a fairly nice, easy job. Nobody was very interested in NDCC, most of the time, except for an occasional science reporter doing a Sunday feature, and the pay was top bracket for civil service. But now, as the trim, tiny businesslike woman walked into the small briefing room bulging with reporters, TV lights and cameras, and into the heat generated by it all, she wondered why she hadn't quit long ago. With the air of someone about to enter a bullring for the first time, she stepped up to the cluster of microphones.

"First, I'll read a complete statement for you," she said in a smooth, accentless soprano. "After, I will take your questions." She paused a moment, apparently arranging her papers but actually giving them time to get ready for the official stuff that would grace the news within the hour.

"At approximately 3:10 this afternoon, Eastern Daylight Time, the town of Cornwall, Nebraska, first began showing symptoms of an as-yet unknown agent, said agent causing most of the town to come down with varying degrees of paralysis. The symptoms showed first in the young, then quickly spread to upper age groups. We have been as yet unable to fully question any victims, but there appears from hospital and doctor records of the past few weeks to have been no forewarning of any sort, although the malady struck every victim within a period of under three hours." She paused to let the print journalists catch up and check their little shoulder recorders, then continued.

"So far there are fourteen confirmed fatalities—seven infants, two persons in vehicles which crashed, and the others elderly. Another forty-six are considered in critical condition. Federal, state, and local authorities are currently on the scene, and NDCC is at this moment running tests on samples from several victims, as well as two bodies of the dead. At the moment this is all we know. I'll take questions."

There was a sudden tumult, and she waited patiently for the mob scene to calm down.

"Please raise your hands," she said professionally when she thought she could be heard over the din. "I'll call on you." That settled them, and she pointed to a well-known network science editor.

"Have there been any signs of this affliction spreading to other localities?" he asked in his famous cool manner. "We have some reports of it hitting in other areas."

"So far we have had a number of cases outside the area," she said. "Twenty-six, to be exact. All but three are known to have been in Cornwall within the last few days. Except for four people in a truck stop on I-80 and two truckers in West Virginia who passed through there three days ago, no other victims. And, no, we can find no sign of any spreading of the affliction by these people to others with whom they've come in contact, except perhaps at the truck stop."

Another question. Did the disease affect animals in the town, and did it spare any people?

"Yes to both," she said. "That is, many people seem to have had such a mild case there appears to be no question that they'll recover with no serious effects. As to the animals, some pigs were affected, but not cows, horses, chickens, or other animals. Some dogs seem to exhibit slight signs, but there are no totally paralyzed ones that we've found."

"Is there any connection yet between this disease and those that struck Boland, California, Hartley, North Dakota, and Berwick, Maine, in the past few weeks?" That was the *Post* man.

She shrugged. "Of course, they are all small towns, and in each case the mystery ailment struck suddenly and with no prior warning. However, the symptoms were far different in those other cases, even from each other. If you remember, Boland's population went blind, Hartley's became severely palsied, and Berwick . . ." She let it hang and they didn't pursue it. Everyone in Berwick, to one degree or another, had become rather severely mentally retarded.

"It's almost like somebody's trying to kill off small-town America," a reporter muttered. Then he asked, "All of these maladies are related to attacks on various centers of the brain and central nervous system, aren't they? Isn't that a connection?"

She nodded. "It's the only connection, really. We are still running a series of tests on the earlier victims, you know. Our teams are working around the clock on it. If, in fact, it's a disease of the central nervous system and/or brain, though, how is it transmitted? There is no apparent link between the afflicted areas. And why hasn't it shown up elsewhere? Unless someone else is prepared to answer those questions, we must assume we are dealing with different diseases here."

"Or a new kind of disease," a voice said loudly.

It went on for quite a while, with even the crazies having their turn. Any flying saucers reported near these places? No. Is the Army back into biological warfare experimentation? No, not the military. Somebody who'd just seen *The Andromeda Strain* on the Late Show asked about meteors, space probes, and the like, but again the answer was no, none that had been found.

They left with lots of scare headlines and nasty suppositions, but nothing more. Page one again, to scare the hell out of the population, but the truth was that nobody really knew what was going on.

Mary Eastwicke made her way wearily back to her office feeling as if she'd worked ten hours in the last seventy minutes. Several staffers were looking over papers, telexes, and the like. She sank into her chair.

"I need a drink," she said. "Anything new?"

A young assistant shook his head. "Nothing more. The toll's 864 now, with eighty-six deaths. In a couple hundred cases they'd be better off dead, though. A hundred percent paralyzed. Stiff, too. You can bend 'em in any position and they'll stay that way. Most of the rest are nasty partials. That town was wiped out as surely as if you dropped a bomb on it."

Mary sighed, and decided she was going to get that drink no matter what. It was going to be a long night; no going home for them or anyone else this time.

She prayed that the folks upstairs would come up

with something solid on this one. She thought of that comment from that reporter to the effect that it was as if somebody was wiping out the small towns of America.

She wondered how the tests were going.

Dr. Mark Spiegelman was about fifty, and usually looked forty, but by 5:00 A.M. looked seventy instead. He sank wearily down in Sandra O'Connell's office and gulped his thirty-sixth cup of strong black coffee as she read the reports and looked at the photos.

"Did you ever dream of a nice little VA hospital job someplace?" he asked her. "You know, the kind where they give you some patients with known ailments and ask you to do your best to help them? I do. Lord! I'd settle for a nice bubonic plague someplace. But *this!*"

She nodded. "Same sort of thing as the others. These motor areas of the brain were *burned,* actually *burned!* It's as if some nice, normal cells just suddenly decided to stop producing the nice normal acids they need and suddenly devoted their time to producing sulfuric acid or something. How's it possible, Mark? How's it possible for just a few cells in a particularly critical spot, all in a group, to suddenly produce a destructive series of chemicals for a period, do their damage, then let the surviving ones return to normal? Even cancer, once it starts, keeps doing what it's doing. *This* was triggered only in a few centers of the brain, critical centers, within a couple of hours in just about everybody in that town, then stopped. How is that possible, Mark?"

He shrugged wearily. "You tell me. You know

LSD, though?" She nodded, wondering what he was getting at. "It's a catalyst. Does just about nothing itself. You take it, it goes through the brain, trips a few wrong switches, then leaves, either in body waste or skin secretion. It's almost out of the system by the time you get the full effects."

She frowned. "You think we're dealing with something like that here? A catalytic agent?"

He nodded. "It's the oddballs that give it away. Remember in every case we had not only the town zapped, but also a number of people in other places who'd merely been in that town? Well, the magic number is three days, and maybe with a little more work we can pin it down to certain hours within those three days. At least we have a couple of people who were in Berwick in the early morning and left and didn't come down with their disease, and we have a few more from Boland who were in town three days earlier, getting there late in the day, and didn't get it, either. I bet we find those truck drivers who were in Cornwall were there within certain hours."

"I'll go along with the catalytic agent," she said, "but how does that explain those truck stop people? If we're dealing with a chemical, whether natural or artificial, how'd those others far from the town catch it?"

Again Mark shrugged. "If any of them pull through, and we can establish any sort of communication with them, maybe we'll find out they sipped some of the driver's coffee or something. Back in the late sixties—before your time, I know— the young crazies who thought LSD was the greatest thing since sliced bread often dumped it secretly in cafe coffee urns and the like."

Sandra smiled slightly at the flattering "before your time" remark, and wished it were so.

"So what do we have?" she asked rhetorically. "We have a catalytic agent that is somehow administered to an entire population within a few-hour period, sends a signal somehow to the brain to have certain vital cells malfunction for a short period three days later, after it's too long gone for us to trace. A nice chemical agent, but show me a coffee urn, *anything,* that a whole town uses!" She had a sudden thought. "You checked the municipal water supplies?"

He nodded. "We checked *everything,* and we'll do it again. A lot more chemicals than there should be in some cases, but nothing unusual, and certainly nothing to cause this. No, it has to come from something they all touched or consumed. I'm positive of it."

She slammed the stack of papers down hard on her desk. "Then why haven't we found it, damn it!" she snapped angrily. "If it's a chemical it's common to all the towns, and it should still be there!"

"They're taking everything apart piece by piece and brick by brick," he said wearily. "If it's there, we'll find it. But *I* won't, at least not tonight—er, this morning. I, my dear, am going to go down the hall, enter my office, stretch out on that couch of mine, and if ten more towns go under I will not awaken until at least noon." He got up slowly, with a groan, and stopped at the door. "Care to join me?" he asked with a leer.

She smiled weakly. "Some pair we'd be." She chuckled. "Asleep in ten seconds."

Mark returned the smile. "Shame on you for such dirty thoughts," he said, and walked out. She didn't see or hear him go.

Dr. Sandra O'Connell was sound asleep in her big padded chair.

THREE

The alarm clock woke them. He reached out, fumbled for the stud that would silence it, and finally succeeded. He opened his eyes, still holding the clock, and brought it in front of him so he could see it.

He stared at it in wonder, trying to figure out why. He held the clock for the longest time, looking at it curiously, as if it were some strange new thing. He felt confused, adrift, wrong somehow.

He looked around the room, and it didn't help. Nothing was familiar, nothing looked like something he'd seen or known before. He felt a shifting next to him, and for the first time he was aware that he was not alone in the bed.

She was still asleep. She was middle-aged, a bit dumpy, with a few touches of gray, in an aquamarine-blue nightgown.

Who the hell was she?

He strained, tried to remember, and could not. He was a blank, a total blank—it was as if he'd just been born.

He got out of bed slowly, carefully, so as not to wake the woman. He felt odd, giddy, light-headed, but with a dull ache that started in his head and spread throughout his body.

He walked dully out into the hall, an unfamiliar

hall still masked in shadow, and looked up and down. He tried one room, then another, before finally finding the bathroom. He had to go, he knew that much.

He walked in, searched for and finally found the light switch, and turned it on.

He almost jumped. A man's face stared at him, and he started to address it, to apologize or whatever, when he realized suddenly that it was his reflection.

His? Someone he'd never seen before?

He stared at it until he just had to go, and did. After, he didn't flush for fear of disturbing the quiet and that woman in the bedroom.

He switched out the light and stood there in the semi-darkness, wondering what to do next. Get dressed and get out of here, he decided. That first of all.

He crept back into the bedroom, but stepped on a loose floorboard, and the woman awoke with a start, sat up, and stared at him, an expression not unlike that on the face in the mirror's on her own features.

"Who—who are you?" she asked timidly, a bit fearfully.

He shook his head. "I don't know," he said helplessly. "Who are you?"

Her mouth was open, and she shook her head slowly from side to side. "I don't know," she said wonderingly. "I can't remember."

The sound gonged at her from beyond her subconscious, beating in, like a lot of little hammers. It seemed to be demanding entrance. She struggled against it, but it kept on, insistent, and slowly turned from a series of poundings into an insistent ringing.

Dr. Sandra O'Connell awoke. Like a contortionist, she was twisted and bent in the chair, and she'd obviously slept hard for quite some time. Her right arm and upper calf were both asleep, and she could hardly move them. She tried shifting, and pain shot through her.

Cursing, using sheer willpower, she managed to get both feet on the floor and somehow grab the ringing telephone, bringing the receiver to her.

"Hello?" she answered groggily, still half asleep. There was no reply, and it took a few seconds before she realized she had the thing upside down. Turning it right, eyes still only half-open, brain only partially there, she tried again.

"Dr. O'Connell," she mumbled.

"Sandy? This is Mark." It was the voice of Dr. Spiegelman. "Better wake up in a hurry. Another town's been hit."

This brought her mentally awake immediately, although the rest of her body didn't seem to want to cooperate.

"What? So soon? Where?"

"Little town on the Eastern Shore, not seventy miles from here," he told her. "We're getting a team up from here and Dietrick now. Want to come along?"

Her mind raced. "Give me a moment," she pleaded. "My god! How are you getting there?"

"Choppers. One's here now. Two more due any minute. Get yourself together, grab your kit, and get up to the roof. I'll bring you some coffee in the helicopter."

"I'll be right there," she said, wondering if she could really do it.

She managed to get up, almost falling on the tingling leg, but worked it out as best she could. The wall clock in the outer office said 9:10; the light coming in from the windows said it was in the morning.

Four hours, she thought, resigned. *At least I got four hours' worth of sleep.*

Four out of forty.

It would have to do.

She knew she looked a mess, but whatever repairs could be made in the helicopter would be all that would be done. She got her purse, reached inside for some keys, and unlocked the right double drawer of her desk, removing a doctor's bag. Her smaller purse fitted into it on clips, and she hoisted the whole thing and put the strap over her shoulder.

She was almost to the hall before she realized that she was going barefoot. With the carelessness of someone in a hurry she knocked over a couple of things getting back, unlocking, getting in, getting the shoes, and leaving again. She put them on while waiting for the elevator, which seemed to take forever to come.

Speigelman was waiting for her on the roof, along with a number of technicians, lab men, and some other department heads. A "hit" this close to home was irresistible to them.

She had little time to get any details before the second helicopter swung into view and came over the roof, blowing dirt, dust, hair and everything else around it as it settled gently onto the large painted cross.

They lost no time in piling in; it was a large craft, but it already carried a number of people from Dietrick and a lot of technical gear. She scrunched into a hard seat next to her fellow NDCC doctor and had barely fastened the seat belt when they were off.

It was tremendously noisy, and she strained to be heard over the *whomp! whomp! whomp!* of the overhead rotors and the whine of the twin jets to either side.

"What have we got?" she screamed at Spiegelman.

He shook his head. "McKay, little town on the Chesapeake Bay in Talbot County. Just about everybody seems to have woke up this morning with total amnesia."

She frowned. "How big's the town?" she yelled.

"Twenty-three hundred," he told her. "Pretty much like the others. First reports said it wasn't a hundred percent, either, as usual. Bet we find out most of the exceptions weren't in town during some period about three days ago."

"You think it's the same thing, then?"

He nodded. "Remember our talk last night? A catalyst that struck a particular and very limited part of the brain, creating an odd sort of stroke. You know most total amnesia victims have some kind of clotting cutting them off."

She nodded. It wasn't her specialty, and she had been more administrator than doctor anyway these past few years, but she'd heard of rare cases. It made sense. It matched with the others.

Which meant it didn't match at all.

The agent, whatever it was, was pretty consistent, though. She wouldn't take Spiegelman up on his bet. But what sort of agent could appear in such widely separated communities, rear its ugly head for only a brief period, then vanish without a trace?

Suburban Washington vanished quickly beneath

them, replaced by the sandy soil and dense forests of southern Maryland, a place curiously little changed from its earliest beginnings, geographically or culturally.

As she checked herself out in a mirror and tried to become as presentable as possible they crossed the ancient Patuxent River and the fossil-strewn cliffs of Calvert with its incongruous nuclear reactors and LNG docks stuck somehow in the middle of wilderness, and out over the broad, blue bay.

Within twenty minutes they were angling for a landing. The town was a pretty one, almost a picture-book type. The families here were old and deep-rooted, mostly involved in the shellfish trade as their ancestors had been for centuries; the town was neat, almost manicured, with a strong eighteenth century look to it.

But now there were helicopters landing, and swarms of vehicles on the ground, while Maryland State Police on land and sea blocked access to the curious.

They touched down with a slight jar, then quickly unloaded personnel and gear.

"Joe Bede got here ahead of everybody and he's coordinating," Mark Spiegelman told her, their ears just starting to readjust to the lack of steady noise.

Sandra nodded approval. "Joe's a good man. But how did he get here ahead of us?"

Spiegelman chuckled. "He was on vacation, on that boat of his, just up at St. Michaels The call came over for any and all doctors, he smelled what it was, and got somebody to drive him down. I'd say he was here inside of thirty minutes from the first reports."

That was good, she thought. A trained NDCC

doctor on the scene almost from the start. In a way she almost pitied poor Joe; he was not only going to lose the rest of his vacation, but stood the awful chance of being debriefed almost to death in the next few days.

They had the people out in the town square; somebody had set up folding chairs procured from various restaurants, the church basement, and who knew where else? It was a shock to see them; they just sort of sat there, seemingly at a loss to do or say anything. But their expressions weren't blank; there was tremendous fear and tension there, so thick you could smell it.

Several men and women had set up tables and were interviewing the townspeople one by one. After the interviews, they were taken gently off by troopers to waiting busses. A few would be flown out to Bethesda and Walter Reed; the rest would be placed temporarily in every local hospital from Norfolk to Wilmington, and probably a lot more, too.

Dr. Joseph Bede, in a tremendously loud sport shirt, jeans, and sunglasses, a three-days' growth of beard on his face, hardly looked like the supervising doctor in a medical crisis. He looked up, saw her, and waved.

She went over to him. "Hello, Joe," was all she could say.

"Sandy," he said. "Hey! Get a chair. This isn't gonna be too pleasant, but you should be in on this."

"At least no one died this time," she tried.

He frowned, paused, sat back a moment and sighed. "Well, depends on how you look at it. You'll see what I mean in a minute." He turned back around, nodding to a nervous-looking State Police corporal. "Next one," he ordered softly.

The next one was a middle-aged woman, over-weight, face lined and weathered. She stood there, looking nervous and bewildered.

A young man in casual dress leaned over toward Joe Bede. "Holly Troon," he said. "Lived here most of her life. That's her old man, Harry, second row, third one in over there. Part-time cashier, drug store. Three kids—we took 'em on the first bus."

"Education?" Bede asked.

The young man shrugged. "High school. Nothin' odd, nothin' special, neither."

Bede nodded, then turned back to the woman. "Please have a seat," he urged in his most calm, soothing manner. She sat, looking at him expectant-ly.

"I'm Dr. Bede," he told her. "What do you re-member about yourself?"

She didn't say a word, just shook her head slowly from side to side.

"Tell me the first thing you *do* remember," he prodded, gentle as ever.

"I—I woke up," she stammered. "And—well, I didn't know where I was. I *still* don't know. And then this old man came into the room, and we kind of stared at each other."

The kindly interrogator nodded sympathetically. "And this man—you had never seen him before, either?"

She shook her head. "I can't remember anything at all. Nothing." She looked at him, almost plead-ingly. "Why can't I remember? Why can't any of *them* remember?" She gestured at the waiting towns-people, her voice rising slowly and quivering as if bordering on hysteria. He calmed her with that charismatic gentleness he had been born with.

"Take it easy," he said. "You—all of you—caught a disease. It has this effect—loss of memory. We're working on it."

She clutched at the straw. "You mean you can *cure* me?"

He put on the number twenty-three smile, the one reserved for terminal patients.

"All of your memory's still up there. It's just that the rest of you can't get to it right now. That's what we'll be working on. Like a telephone that's out of order because a wire is broken. Fix the wire and you can use it again."

It seemed to make her feel better, and she relaxed.

"Now, tell me," he continued. "When you saw this strange man you weren't afraid of him? I mean, a woman sees a strange man . . ."

That brought back a little of it. "You just don't understand," she said, shaking a little. "When I woke up I didn't even *know* I was a woman."

His eyebrows went up. "You thought you were a man?"

"No," she said in frustration. "I wasn't *anything*. Then he said, 'Who are you?' and I asked him the same thing, and we found neither of us knew. And then we found this closet mirror and looked at ourselves and neither of us recognized ourselves." She half-pointed to herself. "I never saw this woman in my life before. You understand that?" The hysteria was rising again.

"Just take it easy," he told her. "Now, I don't think we'll pester you any more. We want to get you to a hospital, where they can start to find out how to bring you back."

The corporal took her arm, genuine pity in his

face, and she went meekly with him to the bus.

All around the square the same scene was being repeated, with slight variations. Spiegelman was already handling some.

Joe Bede sighed and turned to Sandra O'Connell. "See what I mean?"

She did. "My god! And they're *all* like this?"

He nodded. "There are some gradations, of course. Most are total. Some are so far beyond total they can't even remember what a telephone *is*," he told her. "Even some basic skills have disappeared or diminished. Even the ones with some vague concept of identity can't remember their pasts." He turned, looked at the still considerable numbers of people waiting patiently on the chairs. "Notice something else?"

She thought a minute. "The docility," she asked as much as said.

He nodded. "You can lead 'em anyplace. Not a one of 'em in a rage, or yelling and screaming, or resisting. Almost like sheep. Even if they get close to hysteria, like that poor woman, they are easily diverted. Worst they do, men or women, old or young, is cry softly and hopelessly. And suggestion! Just on a hunch I asked a woman who was still wearing a nightgown and nothing else to disrobe for me, and damned if she didn't do it, right here in front of everybody!"

Sandra shivered and decided to slightly change the subject. She looked quizzically over at the young man who had provided the identification. Bede got her meaning and both her intents.

"Jim Shoup, this is Dr. Sandra O'Connell, the coordinator for the National Disease Control Center Action Teams," he said. "Jim's from Hartley, about ten kilometers down the point here, closer to the main drag. He knows almost everybody."

Shoup nodded. He appeared to be in his middle twenties, lean and athletic.

"Anybody in Hartley come down with this?" she asked both of them.

Shoup nodded. "A dozen or so. So far," he added worriedly.

"I wouldn't worry," she reassured him. "This thing only strikes once, it seems, like lightning. If you didn't get it within an hour or two of everybody else, odds are you won't."

He scratched his chin nervously. "Well, I hope you're right. This is really givin' me the creeps."

"If I could wake up twenty-four, tanned, and muscular I'd surrender every damned memory I got," Bede mumbled, and it relaxed the other two. It was almost a miracle that he'd been the first here; he was the best field man NDCC had.

The light, warm wind shifted slightly, and Bede's pipe smoke blew toward Sandra. She coughed and he tried to shield it. As luck always had it, no matter where he put it the smoke aimed at her.

"I'll put the damned thing out," he said apologetically, and knocked it against his foot.

The odor didn't quite vanish, but seemed to reveal another tobacco smell, fouler by far than his pipe.

"That's all right," she said. "I've got to go check on the other groups, make sure all the spaces are reserved, and get the labs set up again." She stood up. The odor persisted. "Lord! This—agent—whatever it is, it gets increasingly bizarre, doesn't it?"

"Increasingly closer to perfection," said a sharp, Brooklynesque male voice just behind her.

She turned in surprise and saw a man standing

there with a monstrous black cigar in his mouth. He was slightly shorter than she, about 175 centimeters or so, with a pitted, blotched complexion and a nose at least four times too large for his face. Although he was neatly dressed in suit and tie, the clothing hung wrongly on him, and looked like it had been worn by someone completely different for a week before he got it. He was mostly bald, with incongrously long shocks of gray-white hair on the sides and back.

He looks like a mad scientist from an old and bad movie, she thought.

"What do you mean, 'increasingly closer to perfection?' " she asked him irritably. "And who the hell are you, anyway?"

He smiled, and in back of the cigar she could see that his obviously false teeth were stained and yellow. He reached into his coat pocket, pulled out a little leather case, and flipped it open. It contained a picture of him on an ID card that managed the impossible task of making him look worse than he did, and a very fancy embossed metal emblem above it.

"Chief Inspector Jacob Edelman, Federal Bureau of Investigation," he said.

She thought to herself that, if people like this were Chief Inspectors, no wonder the crime rate was through the roof. Aloud, she said, "And what did you mean by that remark?"

"Just think it over, Doctor," he said. "Suppose you invented something—a disease, a chemical, who knows what?—that could *in theory* wipe out everybody's memory on a massive scale and make them obedient sheep. Now, the brain's a pretty complicated place, and you can only do so much on animals, so you start guessing. You hit the wrong

centers the first few times out. Then you get lucky—
you hit a nice reaction that does exactly what you
wanted it to, maybe more. Pick small towns, the easier to observe effects, rate of spread, and the like. I
think they hit it early on. Here."

She was appalled. It was a nightmarish vision
beyond her comprehension.

"No one would do such a thing," she protested.
"What you are suggesting is monstrous. Do you
have any proof of this wild idea?"

He shrugged. "Only logic, Doctor, for now. Logic
and a few other things." He looked around. "That's
about all I can say about it for now, but we'll be seeing each other again, in, ah, quieter surroundings."

Not if I can help it, she told herself. The man gave
her the creeps. "Just what department are you Chief
Inspector of?" she asked, starting to turn away and
attend to her business.

"Counterespionage," he replied matter-of-factly,
and walked off, humming a bit to himself.

"It's mighty public to be going on with that shit,"
Joe Bede said. "Hell, there'll be scare stories all over
the evening papers tonight."

She stared after the strange little man. "I think he
already knows that much," she muttered. "I think
he said that because he really likes scaring people to
death."

But as she tended to her own duties, made up organization charts, dispatched teams to the hospitals,
recommended NDCC Dietrick lab geams, and all
the other ten million things she had to do, she
couldn't get those two visions from her mind.

The blank zombies being processed, and the
strange little man with the ability to construct a
nightmare so casually.

FOUR

The air was fresh and clear; the night sky over the eastern California mountains was ablaze with stars, and the night chill quieted the insects so that only the sound of gently rolling wind through the mountains could be heard.

Five men sat atop a ledge looking down into a culvert well off the main road. A small cabin was there, looking toylike and so natural that it was almost invisible but for a glow coming from a window. In reality it was a fairly good-sized cabin of tough hardwood, a mountain retreat that predated the National Forest in which it sat and which could be rented for up to two weeks by arrangement with the Forest Service. A thin trail of white smoke issuing forth from the small pipe chimney was the only sign, other than the flickering lantern glow in the window, that the place was inhabited at all.

One of the men shifted slightly. "Sure glad this is on federal land," he said casually. "No hassle over jurisdiction."

One of the others nodded and checked a shotgun. "Give 'em about five more minutes," he told the others offhandedly. "They been going to sleep pretty early lately. Better if they're in bed."

The first man, a large fellow dressed in typical hiker fashion, picked up a walkie-talkie.

"Mountain Man to Tourister," he said softly.

"Tourister bye," came the response.

"Five minutes," he informed the unseen others on the opposite side of the culvert. "Check with the blockers for position." He looked at his watch, touching a little stud so it lit up the time. "I have 2250 hours. Shall we say at 2300 exactly?"

"Good enough," said the other team leader. "I'm getting pneumonia sitting here anyway."

"Line of duty," the other cracked. "A week in the hospital on Uncle." He turned serious again. "Okay, count off if you're in position. Tourister."

"One," said the other team leader.

"Blocker?"

"Two." A different voice.

"Salamander?"

"Go—I mean, three," came a third voice.

"Bulldozer?"

"Four." A dry, deep voice that sounded more bored than tense.

"It is now 2254," said Mountain Man. "Check and sync. On my signal, go, 2300."

They waited. The others in the Mountain Man team shifted into position, checking out sniperscopes, tear gas launchers, and the like. The cabin seemed blissfully unaware of all this activity, which suited them just fine.

They waited, peering anxiously at the target. Nobody spoke as the time crept onward to their zero hour.

Mountain Man stared at his watch, waiting for the numerals to change. Suddenly, they did, and tension reached the breaking point.

"Okay, hit 'em with One!" he snapped into the walkie-talkie.

Suddenly a mild, almost unnoticeable rumble far off increased in intensity, the sound of an engine echoing through the mountains as if a horde of giant super-trucks were coming their way.

Tremendous floodlights came on, centered on the cabin, turning night into day for fifty meters in all directions.

A small device atop a rifle in a Mountain Man team member's hands suddenly issued a loud, echoing report, and a large object was hurled down into the culvert, landing near the cabin.

Mountain Man lifted the walkie-talkie. The device near the cabin was a miniaturized receiver-amplifier.

"You in the cabin," his voice came back to them from below, hollow, gigantic, almost supernatural in tone. "This is the Federal Bureau of Investigation. You are surrounded. You have thirty seconds to throw out your weapons or we will gas the cabin. There is no escape, and gas may well set the cabin on fire. Throw out your weapons and file out of the cabin—now!"

The light in the cabin window went out, although it was almost impossible to tell it because of the brightness of the strobe lights.

From the window came the sudden sounds of automatic weapons fire, spraying the area around the receiver with a withering fire.

"Looks like a Thompson for sure," one of the agents said. "Want to burn them?"

Mountain Man shook his head. "Naw, let's do a little demo work first. Those logs are too thick to hurt anybody." He turned to a different channel on the walkie-talkie.

"Salamander? Give 'em a steady stream. Don't

aim for the window or door, but pour it on. Thirty seconds. Then Blocker, give a Two directly in the window. Okay? Go!"

The rise to their right erupted in smoke and noise. The cabin was struck by an enormous, deadly hail of bullets at the rate of thirty per second, and wood flew in chips as it continued.

At the thirty second mark a sound like a mortar being launched went off not once but three times, *whomp! whomp! whomp!*

Computer-guided shells flew directly into the window one after the other and exploded with a flash of light.

"One's coming out from under the cabin at the back!" came a cry over the walkie-talkie. "Must have a trap-door exit!"

"I'm on 'em," Salamander assured the other, and fired.

No attempt was made to hit the figure, but a wall of bullets drove the person back under the cabin.

Tremendous clouds of smoke, along with a lot of yelling and screaming, showed that the shells had all gone off. The gas, a special product, made those who breathed it dizzy, off-balance, and so sick that they would do nothing but start retching, while the gas itself burned inside their lungs like fiery pepper and made their eyes almost useless.

The front door opened suddenly and a figure ran out, shooting a submachine gun in a random pattern. The person was in a lot more control than he or she had a right to be.

Mountain Man sighed. "Okay, Salamander, burn the bastard," he said into the radio.

Immediately there was a line of fire that sliced through the runner's legs, felling the fugitive in mid-stride.

It was a woman, they saw. She lay there, bleeding, in the full glare of the spotlights, and still she was firing, raising the submachine gun this time, aiming for the lights.

Salamander fired again, and she twitched violently and was still, even in death gripping the submachine gun which continued to fire its load, now harmlessly into the hillside, until its clip was exhausted.

"*Whew*," Blocker said over the radio. "Man! They're *nuts!*"

Mountain Man nodded, more to himself than to anyone else. He switched back to the receiver channel, and it was still operating. The cabin, they all saw, was almost engulfed in smoke, not only the yellow-white smoke of the gas, but with a darker color, thicker and grittier, mixed in. The scent of burning wood came to them.

"You in there!" his voice bellowed. "There's no escape! You can't even take any of us with you! Come on out! Come out or we'll just wait for you to fry."

Now other figures emerged, two from the front door, three more from under the house, all running in different directions and spraying fire with semi-automatic weapons at the lights and hilltops.

Salamander and Blocker didn't wait for the order. Small fixed machine guns with tiny minicomputers attached locked on to each target in turn and practically cut the runners' legs off with intensive fire.

"Bulldozer! Four and plenty quick!" screamed Mountain Man into the radio.

More engine sounds, and now streams of chemical propelled at great force rained down on the cabin. The ground around the cabin became a quagmire of chemicals and foam, engulfing the wounded fugitives as well.

Two of the people on the ground seemed to realize this, and tried crawling through the foam toward the darkness beyond the spotlights.

With a roar a large truck-like vehicle on tank treads went over the side of the culvert. A device like a cannon on a huge turret turned under the guidance of an operator and a stream of water washed the area for many meters in front of the cabin, dissolving the foam.

Most of the fugitives were still moaning and writhing, no harm to anyone. Tiny figures quickly moved down into the culvert to get to them and retrieve their deadly weapons.

One had crawled almost all the way out of the lighted area under cover of the foam, but as he saw the leading edge of the darkness he also saw two feet in military-type boots, looked up, and stared into the face of a young man in military-style camouflage fatigues, looking at him sternly and holding a .44 magnum aimed at his head.

"James Foley, you are under arrest," the man with the pistol said needlessly. "You have the right to remain silent, and the right to an attorney before any questioning. If you cannot afford an attorney one will be appointed without charge. Do you understand that?"

"You go to hell, you fascist son of a bitch!" the wounded man spat, and then collapsed, eyes open and starting to glaze. Salamander cautiously approached him, gave him a soft kick, then turned him over with his foot.

The man, still bleeding from no less than a dozen wounds, was quite dead.

Now Bulldozer's special team went in. They were dressed in self-contained pressure suits, complete with air supply, and looked much like invaders from outer space. They approached the cabin warily, with shotguns at the ready. After probing gingerly, the lead man entered the cabin.

"God! What a mess!" came his voice over the radio. "Cabin's clean, though. Holy shit! You ought to see the arsenal here! If they'd stacked it near the window this thing woulda gone off so big they'd have felt it in Sacramento!"

"And what the hell are *these?*" another, higher and thinner voice asked. "Oxygen? Scuba gear?"

Medics gave knockout shots to the survivors, and they were quickly placed on stretchers and carried up the hillside to waiting ambulances.

"Don't touch them!" Mountain Man cautioned.

"One of 'em's been turned on," said the suited man who'd discovered the tanks. "Nothin' comin' out, though. Hah! One of the gas shells exploded too near it. Busted the valve."

This worried the team leader. "Think anything escaped?"

"Naw, I doubt it," came the reply. "But only because of blind luck. I'd say whatever's in this was supposed to do us in or something."

"Well, let them lay," cautioned the leader. "Treat 'em like they were fused bombs. We'll let the tech boys handle it."

Inspector Harry Carillo, alias Mountain Man, walked down to the dead man near Salamander. Unlike the others, he wore the regulation coat and tie, and his nicely polished shoes and business suit were quickly splattered with mud. He didn't seem to notice.

He went over to the body and looked at the dead man's face. "Well, it *was* Foley," he said more to himself than to the younger man. "I'll be damned. I'da made good book he was still in Cuba."

The man in fatigues shrugged. "He sure would've been better off there," he said dryly.

Within two hours of the attack the cabin had been thoroughly searched and photographed from every angle, and the large amounts of explosives and ammunition had been carted away. A little before four in the morning a helicopter arrived with vacuum chambers for the mysterious cylinders, which were treated with a good deal of respect and handled only by pressure-suited technicians.

Inspector Carillo looked over the tagged and numbered set of more commonplace things removed from the cabin and set up on makeshift tables outside until they could be individually processed. He noticed a map, burned around the edges, and fished it out, opening it carefully.

It was a Pacific States highway map from a Utah truck stop. Two towns on the map had been circled in black crayon, and he stared hard to see which ones they were. The first was Evans, Oregon, in print so small it was nearly obscured by the crayon itself. The other made him stop short.

Boland, California.

Suddenly the tension was back full. Those blue cylinders, he thought suddenly. Foley—and Boland.

He grabbed for the radio.

"Mountain Man to Street Sweeper," he called anxiously.

"Go, Harry," came a woman's crisp voice.

"Those blue cylinders. Don't take them to the west lab. I want you to ship them to NDCC labs, Fort Dietrick, Maryland, special courier. And get me a patch on the mobile to District HQ."

The woman sounded puzzled, but said, "All right. What's this about?"

"Just do *it!*" he snapped, and made his way quickly back up top.

By the time he reached the communications van they had the patch in. He grabbed the phone.

"Mark! I want you to put me through to Chief Inspector Edelman in Washington right away," he said crisply. "Yeah, I know it's past seven there, so try his office first, then his home. This is important! And Mark—I want a full medical team and decontam unit here as quickly as possible. I want everyone in on this operation isolated as if they had the Black Plague. Notify the local field office of NDCC to handle the medical."

There was lots of confusion and consternation on the other end.

"Just do it!" he snapped. "And ring me when you have Edelman. Put it on the satellite scrambler!"

He put down the phone, and realized he was shaking violently.

Boland, California, he thought. My god! And Foley, too.

James Foley, alias Rupert, specialist in international terror, the man who'd once blown up six school busses in the Middle East, who'd poisoned a New York state water system, and those were only for starters.

Just the kind of fellow to blind an entire town for the hell of it, he thought. Just exactly the kind . . .

The telephone in the mobile van gave an electronic buzz, and Carillo picked it up.

"Harry?" came a familiar voice from long ago. "What the hell is all this about?"

"You know about Operation Wilderness," the inspector began. "I'm still on the scene."

"Yeah, just got the report in on the telex. Nice job it looks like. So?"

"Jake, one of 'em's James Foley, and there's a map with Boland, California, circled on it."

Edelman was suddenly excited. "So that's it! God! You don't know how long I've been waiting for this! This is the break, Harry! The link! Did you find out how they did it?"

Carillo sighed. "Well, in the cabin, along with the expected stuff, were six blue gas cylinders, look like scuba tanks with a fire extinguisher cap stuck on. I had them sent to NDCC at Dietrick. And—Jake?"

"Yeah?"

"One of 'em was turned on, Jake. We don't know if any of it escaped."

There was silence on the other end for a moment. Then Edelman said, "You've taken all the precautions?"

"Done," said the field man. "We're all going into quarantine. As soon as the lab stuff, which is also going under seal, is sorted out we'll burn the cabin to the ground."

Edelman was silent again, uncertain of just what to say. He knew the other man was scared, and he understood it. He'd be having the screaming fits himself if their situations were reversed. Finally he said, "Well, look. We'll work on those things here as soon as we get them. In the meantime, we need blood samples, everything. I hope you haven't got any problems, Harry—and I mean that sincerely—

but if you have, you'll be the first people we know of within the three-day limit. If the active agent's there, we've got a good crack at isolating it and getting it. It can mean a cure, Harry—or even a preventative!"

Harry Carillo nodded silently, but he had a numbed, detached feeling inside him. Three days. The terror starting now. Three long days . . .

"All right, Jake," he managed. "Remember— we're depending on your side."

"Good luck, Harry—and good job," Edelman said softly, and terminated the conversation.

Harry Carillo sat there for a long time with the dead phone in his hands, feeling the first effects of the disease called terror.

FIVE

"C'm'on, you little bastard, come to papa," Mark Spiegelman said insistently. "Come on, you can do it, yes you can."

The object of the conversation was well away from him, inside a special sealed chamber, and within a gel on a small platform within that chamber. The serologist was watching a CRT screen over 130 centimeters across diagonally, with perfect resolution, the computer-generated picture of what was happening in the gel at that time as seen by the hypersensitive electron microscope.

The creature on the screen was not very thrilling to look at; it was three-quarters of a micron in width and just a little over one micron in length, surrounded by cilia. It was close to a small protein globule, and it almost seemed to be stalking it. The globule, in turn, was obviously attracted to the tiny bacterium, and the two seemed to be in some sort of slow-motion ballet.

Suddenly they touched, and the bacterium absorbed the protein globule.

Dr. Mark Spiegelman smiled in satisfaction, mumbled something about the course of true love, and continued to watch.

Tiny enzymes within the bacterium moved with

unusual swiftness, surrounding the antigen and doing *something* to it.

Spiegelman's mouth dropped.

In the course of the next three minutes, the globule was completely broken down, so much so that it was impossible to tell that it had ever been there.

"Well I'll be damned," the serologist said. He turned to check that the videotape recorder was still running, although hesitant to take his eyes off the creature on the screen.

He grabbed a dictation recorder, punched the record button, and said, "Samples from the Operation Wilderness subjects should be examined for any rapidly reproducing strains of what might appear to be *Escherichia coli* in the bloodstream, stomach, or intestinal tract, characterized by the formation of antigens in pulses, a large number appearing then disappearing, in constant progression."

He switched off, plugged the dictation module back into the panel, punched *transmit,* and settled back.

There were two bacteria on the screen now. He looked at his watch, then turned in his swivel chair to a computer console and asked for a time on the reproductive cycle.

Six minutes forty-six seconds to *complete* division.

Seven minutes, give or take, he thought wonderingly. About four times faster than the fast-breeding bacteria.

Roughly eight doublings in geometric progression per hour.

He pulled out his pocket calculator, put in a "2." Okay, that was seven minutes. At fourteen minutes there'd be four, at twenty-one minutes sixteen, at twenty-eight minutes 256, at thirty-five minutes 65,536. He swore. This was getting hairy and he wasn't even close to the end. At forty-two minutes you had—god!—4,294,967,296! At forty-nine minutes his calculator overloaded and refused to compute any further.

And if the thing defended itself as he'd seen, there'd be little loss. Some, of course, but not very much.

Inside of a day your bloodstream should be crawling with the things, too thick to miss.

He returned to the computer terminal, requesting a comparison of the Wilderness Organism with the microbiology reports from the autopsies and blood samples of prior victims.

None.

Were there abnormal numbers of *Escherichia coli* in the bodies of the victims? he asked the computer, thinking that they might have been passed over as the common variety often, in fact invariably, found there.

No unusual counts of that or any other bacillus.

He frowned. Why? There was the villain, all right, sitting there fat, dumb and happy on the giant CRT screen, in living color just like home television. He didn't know a lot about it yet, but he knew for certain that that creature had caused at least the blindness at Boland, and maybe the other ailments as well. Why it acted where it did, and how it did its little tricks there, was still a mystery, but nothing a lot more hard lab work wouldn't solve.

But it mutiplied faster than any known bacteria or anything else. Okay, he accepted that. But that should make it a thousand times more conspicuous.

Why wasn't the damned thing in the bodies of the previous victims?

He typed in more instructions to the computer. They would step up the magnification to impossible limits and do a molecule-by-molecule analysis of the damned thing.

President of the United States Jefferson Lee Wainwright looked appropriately grim.

It had been said of him that he was the absolutely perfect presidential candidate; had someone the means and methods of production to create the perfect robotic politician, the result would have been Wainwright. The strong, rugged, Olympian look, the perfectly coiffured light brown hair, the warm, sympathetic blue eyes and patented smile, the sonorous voice—all perfect. His rise to power had been meteoric; Governor of Texas at thirty, senator at thirty-five, President at forty. A liberal on domestic issues, a staunch conservative on foreign policy, he had something for everyone except the radical fringes of the political spectrum.

"My fellow Americans," he began, radiating charisma, "I speak to you tonight on a matter of grave national emergency. The people of the United States are under attack from a foreign agency."

He paused for effect, letting the words sink in.

"Everyone is aware of the mysterious and tragic diseases which have struck a number of towns across the United States," he continued. "From the beginning, all agencies of government were placed on a priority basis to discover the cause of these baffling ailments. *All* agencies. This morning, at approximately 7:00 A.M. Eastern Time, the break came. The

Federal Bureau of Investigation conducted a raid on a cabin in the Sierra Nevada Mountains of California where several wanted terrorists of international repute were reported to be. Those terrorists, which included some of the wickedest and most insidious minds possible in the human race, were indeed there. All were either killed or captured. They resisted with such fanaticism, though, that it is possible none will survive the results of their resistance."

Again the pause, the slight shift.

"Inside their cabin," he went on, "were found mysterious containers and some papers indicating their familiarity with at least one of the towns stricken by the mysterious disease. The contents of these containers, now under analysis by the National Disease Control Center of the Department of Health and Welfare, contain bacteria—a germ, if you will—that all of our scientists are convinced is responsible. The conclusions are obvious. Someone, some foreign power, is using germ warfare against us."

He sat back, aware of the stir, even the panic that he'd just caused. But his timing was perfect.

"Now, *there is no cause for panic*. So far they have limited their vicious attacks, and we received a lucky break in the raid. We're on to them now. Your morning newspapers will be printing photographs of the known terrorists connected to the ones in the raid this morning; your local newspeople will be on immediately following this broadcast to give you methods and procedures, and to show you what to look for. All law enforcement personnel are receiving even more intensive training. More, *it is a bacteria,* like the germs that cause most human ailments. Shortly we will have the information we need to produce some sort of serum, or antitoxin, for your protection, and this will be distributed freely to every human being in the United States. H&W Secretary Meekins is even now mapping out the tremendous job of making certain you are protected and quickly."

He paused yet again, then flashed his confident look for assurance.

"In addition, I have this evening created a Special Presidential Task Force to coordinate the battle against these agents of terror. We will strike at them. We will catch the terrorists and give them what they deserve. We will have a means of combating their dirty germs. And we will find the source of this terror and neutralize it. *We will win.*"

A last pause, and then he turned and looked out beyond the camera. "I'll take your questions now."

There was instant pandemonium as the members of the press clamored for attention. "Mr. Ackroyd," the President said, and the others quieted for a moment.

"Mr. President," came a voice familiar to millions, "are you planning any additional measures to make sure these agents don't strike again?"

He nodded. "I will ask the Congress tomorrow morning to declare a state of national emergency," he told them. "We must have extraordinary enforcement measures, you understand. But I feel certain that the public and Congress will understand and allow some additional latitude in their own interests."

It went on and on. Somebody in Conference Room A at Fort Dietrick, near Frederick, Maryland, got up and switched him off.

"Why do I feel like you just committed sacrilege?"

quipped an elderly woman, Georgianne Meekins, Secretary of Health and Welfare.

General John Wood Davis, who had turned the TV off, grinned wickedly. As Chariman of the Joint Chiefs of Staff he didn't worry much about how others saw him.

He resumed his seat and looked around. "Who's missing?" he asked.

At that moment a door opened and a small figure walked in. The military guards closed the door softly behind him.

Dr. Sandra O'Connell looked up in surprise. He was well-dressed this time, clean-shaven and distinguished, but he still had that foul cigar and he was still ugly as sin.

Jake Edelman smiled, nodded to her, and took a chair.

Davis nodded in satisfaction and began.

"As you all know, this task force has a nearly impossible task before it," he began. "We are under attack, yes—but by whom? The Russians? The Chinese? Who?" He looked at a distinguished-appearing gray-haired man two seats down, and everyone else followed his gaze.

"The CIA has pulled out all the stops on this one, but nothing," the Director of Central Intelligence told them. "Russians? No, I don't think so. True, some of the radicals in the Wilderness Raid came from Cuba, but they were definitely not trained and equipped there, and our people inside the Cuban government are positive that the Cubans know no more about this than we do. They've been falling all over themselves reassuring us on that point. There's nothing to contradict them so far. It's true the Russians and Chinese have germ warfare programs—

don't we all, really, despite the treaties?—but we have them pretty well covered. Nothing like this, no tests, no top people unaccounted for or on super projects. And the way their governments are reacting makes us feel that they are either as scared as we are or are putting on the best act in history."

General Davis frowned. "But the blue cylinders—they are of Bulgarian manufacture, are they not?"

The DCI nodded. "Yes, they are. They are used for the storage of freon and other specialized industrial chemicals. But it's a dead end there. All of these cylinders were part of a foreign aid deal with Chad, and were filled with agricultural chemicals when they left. The shipment was bound for Lagos, Nigeria, and it got as far as the harbor. There it vanished."

Davis' raised eyebrows asked the question.

"Lagos harbor's been notorious for thirty years for piracy," the DCI explained. "It's never been properly enlarged, and ships sometimes sit stacked up for days or even weeks waiting their turns to unload. Sometimes men come in small boats, overpower the crew—or use bribes or threats—and steal various things off the ships. In this case, they stole the blue cylinders."

"How many?" Jake Edelman's dry nasal voice cut in.

The CIA man looked uneasy. "Nine hundred sixty," he said.

That stirred all of them.

"And how many do you figure have been used so far?" Sandra O'Connell asked, not caring who answered.

"There were a dozen of them in the cabin," Edelman told them. "Five were empty, so we can infer that Boland took five. The other target was not yet hit, I don't think—we've had the watch on them longer than three days. So figure five and a spare per town hit. What have they hit? Five, six towns? Figure over nine hundred left at least, assuming they all have the germs in them."

That upset them, even the unflappable General Davis. He looked at Sandra O'Connell. "Doctor, what about your end?"

She considered what to say. "Dr. Spiegelman and his team have been working non-stop on this. We don't know all the answers yet, particularly not how it works and why it isn't in the body, blood, or tissues by the time its effects appear. All I can tell you is what we *do* know."

"Go on," Davis urged.

"First of all, it's not a natural organism. It's related to a common bacteria, yes, an organism inside all of our intestinal tracts at least right now. It's a parasite but it causes little damage, and may even aid in the digestion of some foods. Because it was common, familiar, easily isolated, and easy to grow in cultures, it was one of the primary organisms used in early recombinant DNA research."

Several of them looked surprised. "I thought all that was discontinued after the Cambridge and Limitov disasters," someone said.

She nodded. "True. It's dynamite with an unstable fuse. Anything done in that department runs the danger of creating an artificial mutant strain that could cause a horrible plague. Both here and in the Soviet Union such things occurred more than a decade ago, and that ended any real research into the subject except in computer models."

"But the technology exists," Edelman said. "It

could be done by anyone who knew how."

"That's true," she admitted. "But nobody would do it without tremendous safeguards. Even a fanatical group wouldn't run the risk of self-contamination. Bacteria do not recognize rank or social position. You'd need a lab setup that cost tens of millions of dollars at the very least, and a scientific team capable of handling the risks as well."

"So you're saying," Davis put in, "that no place short of a government or perhaps a major university lab could do it?"

She nodded agreement. "Yes, and even the university lab would be government supported. They're the only ones with the money."

"Just what's involved in this recombinant DNA thing?" Jake Edelman wanted to know. "I'm no biologist." He felt a little better when he saw a number of other heads nod almost imperceptibly. *They* didn't know, either—they just didn't have the guts to admit that they didn't.

She sighed. "I'll do the best I can. A short course in molecular biology is a tough order, though. Let's start by saying that we're all made up of trillions of living cells. All organisms are made up of one or more of these cells. And, in a given organism, like a human being, all the cells are from the division of a single cell. You started off the product of one sperm with half a set of genes that penetrated an egg with the other half, creating a single, primal cell. That single cell duplicated in your mother's womb over and over again. As it did, the cells changed.

"As far back as the 1940s," she continued, "it was found that the culprit was an odd double-spiraled compound called deoxyribonucleic acid, or DNA for short. The stuff is made up of four chemicals,

and these are strung together in long chains inside
each cell, the chains—the order of the chemicals—
telling the specific cell its place, order, and function
in the developing organism. It becomes a hair cell,
or a tooth cell, or a nail or part of the lung. Back in
1961 Dr. Marshall Nirenberg of the National Institutes of Health, of which NDCC and this center
are components, showed how it worked. You string
together a series of DNA molecules, use a dash of
protein as a period, and drop the thing into a soup
of RNA, a compound related to DNA, and amino
acids, the building blocks of all life. The DNA gives
the orders, the RNA takes them, goes to work on
the amino acids, and builds a protein molecule to
specifications. All of the instructions necessary to
build and maintain you were in the DNA of that
original cell created by the union of sperm and egg."

He nodded. "I understand that. I read about the
cloning experiments at Harvard. But what's this recombinant stuff?"

Sandra O'Connell sighed. "Well, once we knew
how to read the code, the next step was to write it.
Original experiments used *Escherichia coli,* a one-
celled animal. DNA from one was chopped up as
was DNA from another. The chopped DNA was
placed in an amino acid solution, and the DNA
chains from different bacteria combined and built
new organisms with differing characteristics. Pretty
soon scientists isolated DNA molecules with specific
instructions and were able to insert those in place of
the originals."

"A build-it-yourself bacteria," Edelman said dryly. "A living erector set."

She chuckled. "I guess you can say that. But the
lab conditions had to be rigidly controlled. The or-

ganism takes well to man, and the lab strain, being
artifically grown in sterile conditions, was particularly susceptible to mutation—to having its DNA
changed by outside forces, like cosmic rays and other radiation always present. There was always the
danger of producing a carcinogenic organism—a
germ, in other words, that would be a new and deadly disease."

"And that happened in two separate sets of experiments," General Davis put in. "Just a few little bacteria, ever so tiny, got through imperfections in the
labs both here and in the USSR. Maybe it happened
a lot of other times, but these two were lulus, and
they happened within a year of each other—the result of, I guess, too much research on the stuff when
no initial disasters happened. Somebody got care-
less, and nineteen thousand died in Cambridge and
Boston, and almost as many in Limitov. That scared
hell out of the people and leaders of all the governments. There was a quick conference, the Treaty of
Basel was signed, and that was it. No more active
recombinant DNA experiments without the consent
of all the signatories."

"But somebody's done it anyway," Jake Edelman
pointed out.

Sandra O'Connell nodded. "Yes, somebody has.
And I would guess that it would have to be in a lab
totally isolated and perhaps deeply buried. Served
by a closed staff that contained no leaks, not to the
scientific community, not to anyone."

"Such an installation would have to be a major
one, staffed by major people," the intelligence director pointed out. "I don't see how something on that
scale could be set up without leaks. We might not
know *what* they were doing, but we'd know they
were doing *something,* and be able to infer what it

was by the installation and personnel, particularly matching what we now know about this stuff to the intelligence involved. So far—nothing."

Jake Edelman shifted uneasily. "Now, Bart, that'd be true if it were, say, Russia or China or one of their satellites, maybe even France or one of the other powers. But suppose it was, say, the Central African Empire or maybe Paraguay? If Bhutan had the Bomb but didn't test it, would you really know it until they did?"

The CIA man shrugged. "I don't know, Jake. But if it were a third world country not on our questionable list, why pick on us? Besides, they'd still have to have their own nationals highly trained in molecular biology, which means here or in one of the major powers. We've already run those through. A few minor question marks, yes, but nobody unaccounted for that I would invest millions in."

"Which brings us back to Go," General Davis pointed out. "Now, what do we do about it?"

"Well, here's what we *do* know," Edelman responded. "First, someone, unknown, is manufacturing a disease and, using international terrorists, anarchists, and overage radicals looking for a cause, is testing it out on small towns in the United States. Its incubation period is three days, after which it damages or burns out some area of the brain, then totally vanishes without a trace. In all probability there are over nine hundred additional cannisters of the stuff ready and waiting for us."

"And it's a stable organism," Sandra pointed out. "If, as seems to be the case, those radicals you got yesterday hit Boland, *they didn't go blind!* That means that they were immunized. An antitoxin for the bacteria exists."

That gave them hope. "So what can we do about

it all?" Davis asked. The question was rhetorical; procedures already were being formulated. "We assume the CIA is doing all it can. The Coast Guard and Border Patrol is at maximum, with the full cooperation of Canada and Mexico. NDCC and NIH are on the problem."

"Let's be truthful and realistic," Honner, the President's man, put in. "First, there is no way in hell to seal the borders of the United States. We leak like a sieve and there's no way we can close all those leaks for a few people here and a few more there. Even the Iron Curtain leaks like mad, and we have nothing approaching *it*. And for every known possible agent of whoever's doing this there are three dozen we don't know about. Inspector Edelman, just how many of the Operation Wilderness terrorists were known to the Bureau?"

"Three," came the glum response.

Honner nodded. "See what I mean? Three out of —what? Eight? And as for the disease itself—well, suppose we *do* find a cure or an immunizing agent? They have only to vary the next batch slightly and we're back to square one again. That's fine as long as we're in small towns, but suppose it's New York or Washington or Los Angeles next? It's obviously highly contagious." He didn't need to go on. It was already in their minds.

"So what do you propose to do about it?" General Davis asked him.

Honner shifted uneasily. "The only defense is preventive medicine within our means," he said.

Their eyebrows rose. "Which means?" Davis prompted.

"Contingency Plan AOX7647-3," Honner said flatly.

The rest of them looked puzzled, but Davis appeared shocked. "What the hell? How do you even *know* about . . ." He let it trail off.

Honner shrugged. "The President is Commander in Chief. That sort of thing, just its existence, has been rumored for years. We decided to find out, and we did. Presidents can do that sort of thing, you know."

"I'm confused," Sandra O'Connell put in. "What the hell is this contingency plan, anyway?"

Davis thought it over, then shook his head. "I don't think we ought to," he told Honner. "That's a little too drastic even for—"

"For what?" Honner exploded, cutting him off. "We are under attack and we have to defend ourselves! It may be the only way!"

"Congress will never buy it," Davis objected.

"Oh, yes they will," Honner said. "The people will demand it when this goes on and on and we're obviously powerless to protect them. They will *demand* it!"

"You may as well spill it," Jake Edelman told them. "If you can't trust the people in this room, who *can* you trust? Besides, it looks like Honner and his boss—who's also *our* boss—already has it in the works."

General Davis sighed. "You tell them, Honner," he said, defeated.

"Contingency Plan AOX7647-3," the presidential aide explained, "is the latest incarnation of a series of plans that's been drawn up regularly since the Second World War, at least. It is a plan to declare martial law throughout the entire country."

Most of them gasped. Jake Edelman just nodded. "I thought as much. I can't see you getting away with it, though. It's unconstitutional as hell. The Supreme Court at the very least will throw it out."

Honner shook his head. "During World War II the Supreme Court allowed the internment of all Japanese-Americans, even American-born, and the confiscation of all their property. As far back as Lincoln, this very state of Maryland was placed under military occupation even though it didn't secede. There were wholesale mass arrests without trial, curfews under which violators would be shot, and so forth. For every man Lincoln pardoned a hundred were jailed for up to five years without charge, trial, or anything else. And the people backed him up! It was the *only* way. The President and the National Security Council hardly want mass jailings, let alone murders, but we do feel that such a military administration for the limited term of the emergency would be accepted, even welcomed by the people, who are already close to panic. And, unlike Lincoln or the camps, this would not be done without Congress accepting it. What they do can be undone."

Jake Edelman shook his head sadly. "It's not that easy to undo," he replied. "It's a cure worse than the disease."

Honner looked a little exasperated at the FBI man. "Can you suggest a better way? Our entire country can be overrun, our military crippled, by these people before we even know who they are. You *know* it's the only way."

Edelman nodded sadly. "I know that, in a blind crisis, people will trade their freedom for security every time," he admitted. "That's why the Germans accepted Hitler and the Italians turned to Mussolini."

Honner jumped to his feet, enraged. "Are you

saying President Wainwright is another Hitler?" he shouted, enraged.

"Of course not," the FBI man said tiredly. "He just ain't no Abe Lincoln, either."

Dr. Mark Spiegelman came back with his hundredth cup of coffee and sat again in front of the CRT screen. He glanced at it idly, then turned, did a double-take, and stared again.

The colony of Wilderness Organisms had changed. The great mass on the slide plate wasn't growing any more.

It was dissolving. The bacteria were slowly breaking apart.

Quickly he was at the computer console, typing away, coffee forgotten. "Of course! Of course! Why didn't I see it before?" he muttered to himself.

The view changed, shifted, as the computer sampled, looking for what Spiegelman told it to find.

And it found it, almost at the limits of its magnification range.

It was a pattern, like an irregular honeycomb, an alien, odd shape that was growing, rapidly now, attacking the very core of the bacteria cells.

"Sure!" he breathed. "Super-bacteria, super-bacteriophage!"

SIX

Dr. Sandra O'Connell made her way through the double security maze to the experimental lab section of Fort Dietrick. The routine military security was almost equivalent to that of an atomic missile launch site—television monitors all over, locked and sealed doors three or more centimeters thick with pressurized compartments, each with its own air supply. Guards and electronic safeguards, too; sets of keys that could be used only from the *inside,* with ID photos, fingerprints, and retinal patterns checked every step.

The special new security was just as severe. Complete change to sterile clothing, shower which included chemicals designed to kill any forms of micro-organisms, and much more.

The place hadn't always been a part of the National Institutes of Health. At one time the U.S. Army had been here alone, playing deadly games of chemical and biological warfare, trying to create organisms such as the one someone else had now created. For years its nearly perfect medical security system had been superficially in effect. Only since the Wilderness Organism had arrived had the military returned.

Still, it was here that mysterious organisms were brought, it was here where cancers were probed with the best staff and best equipment to find the keys to switching them off, it was here where microbiology was practiced to the limits of technology and international treaty.

Through the last checkpoint, Sandra followed the sterile wall of pale yellow to the double doors marked *Serology Control Center* and went in.

Mark Spiegelman turned in his swivel chair and brightened as he saw who it was. He had been alone in here for thirty-four straight hours, after only a few hours sleep before, and he looked like hell. Somewhere in far-off Arlington, Virginia, he had a wife and two kids he hoped understood.

"You look awful," she said. "You can't go on driving yourself like this. You start making mistakes. There's eleven other people working on this down here—I'm going to call Ed Turner and tell him he's on in here."

He started to protest, but she was frankly saying what he wanted to hear, and her taking it out of his hands removed the guilt.

"You're the boss," he said tiredly.

"Before you go, tell me what you got," she insisted. "Ed will have your data upstairs, but I don't want to have to go through everything again with him."

He sighed, leaned back, and dared to relax. "Well, first of all, it's one of the finest little nasty pieces of engineering I've ever seen. An incredible organism—or set of organisms," he added.

Her eyebrows shot up. "Set of organisms?"

He nodded. "Yep. Two of them. That's what threw me. One does the dirty work and the other murders the bum."

She was excited. "You know how it vanishes!"

He nodded again. "Yeah, a neat trick, too. Anybody can design a bug. The basis of this little bastard, at least its long-ago ancestry, was almost certainly *Escherichia coli,* the bacteria used in the earliest recombinant DNA experiments—including Cambridge and Limitov." He turned, punched up a picture on the CRT. "There it is—or was."

She stared at the thing, a pretty common-looking organism considering its effect. "Doesn't really look like *E coli,* though," she said.

"Oh, it isn't—not any more," he told her. "It's something new, unique. Damned well designed and built. Lots of little tricks. Denise Murray will probably be able to tell you what it does in the system— my guess is it's a borer. Gets inhaled into the lungs, bores into the capillaries there and thence into the blood stream. You probably could get it a million ways. Inside of twelve hours there's enough of them in there to make a colony visible without a microscope. What it does in its swim through the brain I couldn't guess, but somehow it must recognize a particular place and secrete some nasty little enzymes that produce that catalyst I was talking about a couple days ago."

She frowned. "But if it's a standard-sized bacteria, why didn't we find antibodies in the victims?"

"Oh, it does a neat trick, it does," he said. "You know as well as anybody that an antibody is a reaction to a foreign agent, not really a disease-killer. That little baby on the screen has a number of antigens and they do, in fact, stimulate the production of a globulin protein in the human system. There are nine antigens in the bacteria, and nine different antibodies. They *should* react with each other to do nasty things to each other. Only they don't.

When the antibody approaches the Wilderness Organism, it's absorbed into the bacterium—which then does a neat trick not in the biology catalogs. It slightly changes the composition of its own complementary antigen—and pretty damned quickly, too, as if it sampled the threat, then decided on a counter-move. It's not all that tough, though. There are three basic changes it can make, so it's usually one step ahead of the body's ability to manufacture the proper antibodies. It's just getting into full steam on antibody one when WO, here, adds a dash of this or that from a small amino acid reserve and changes the antigen composition. You remember your basic biology."

She nodded. "An antibody is the exact complement of an antigen. It can't react to any other. It's helpless."

"Exactly!" he said. "So our little WO-soldier here can escape the enemy by changing its uniform. But, additionally, it does something even nastier—*it eats antibodies.*"

She shook her head in disbelief. "All of them? Digested?"

"More or less," he said. "It has the ability to break down the antibody into its component amino acids and store them. What's an antibody but a protein globule anyway? And the engineer behind this had the advantage of knowing exactly what three antibodies he'd be facing. So the antibodies invade, the WO-soldier changes its spots, then attacks and breaks down the antibodies. Anything it can't use it expels as waste."

She considered this. "But such a parasitic organism with those defenses would be impossible to stop. It'd finally grow into colonies so large it would

cause strokes, block flows all over, kill the host—
and very quickly if it reproduces as fast as you say."

"True, but look at this." He punched up a different picture.

"It's a virus of some kind," she said, waiting for
more information.

"Not just *a* virus, a second engineered organism,"
he responded. "It, my dear, is inside every lousy little WO-soldier. Our parasite's got a parasite—a bacteriophage. Jillions of them in the world of the mi-
crobe, but not like this one. It just rides along, fat,
dumb, and happy, eating some excess from the bacteria but nothing harmful, and growing at precisely
the same rate as the bacterium—for the first twenty-
six hours. Then it goes wild, starts growing like mad,
eating our poor kamakaze WO-soldier from the inside out. Its appetite is enormous and insatiable. Its
little clock is perfectly timed; no matter if the WO-
soldier is an original or a latest generation a few
minutes old, twenty-six hours after the first pene-
tration of the host they start getting eaten alive. It's
fast—damned fast. By the thirty-sixth hour there
isn't a trace of the invading army. All broken down
into a mess, and passed out in the usual manner.
Without anything left to eat—and bacteriophages
are absolutely matched to one type of bacteria and
no others whatsoever—the colonies break apart,
crumbling like so many old cookies, and are themselves treated as waste by the body. By our seventy-
two-hour trigger mark, there wouldn't be a trace of
either organism in the body we could discover. Some
leftovers, maybe, but never could they be found or
shown to be unusual unless we were looking specifically for them."

She was silent. Finally she asked, "Mark? Is it

within our current technology to build something like this?"

He shrugged. "I guess so. The bacteriophage would be the toughest. Give me Fort Dietrick, about twenty or thirty million dollars, and a staff of a dozen really good medical technicians, and I think I could do it in half a year or so."

Sandra shivered slightly, even in the controlled atmosphere of the labs. "Now I see why they had all those conventions against this sort of thing. Edelman—that funny little ugly FBI man—said upstairs that it was an erector set for scientists."

"At least that," Mark said grimly. "And somebody's really made a nasty toy here. Or toys. There's one other thing."

She looked up at him. "What?"

"The empty cylinders contained, of course, some of the Boland strain. Apparently it's kept in a nice mixture of freon and other gases which make it totally dormant until exposed to air. Some of the stuff would be left, naturally."

"Naturally," she agreed. "So?"

"It's different, Sandy. It had the same ancestors, but that's all. It's not the same bug at all."

She stared at him. "So much for the universal vaccine, then," she said flatly.

He smiled. "What can be engineered can be destroyed," he assured her. "At least we got the start. Now, as for me, I think a good eight hours and I'll lick it. You get some sleep, too. You're as dead as I am."

She smiled weakly. "Okay, we'll both go. You going home?"

"No, I'll go beddy-bye upstairs in the clinic. You?"

She sighed. "I'm going to try and make it. I need clothes, a shower, and sleep. They know where to find me if they need me. I'm only the paper-pusher here."

"No you're not," he said kindly. "You're the glue."

Her sleep was deep and dreamless, the best sleep, the kind her body and mind craved. In her own apartment, in her own bed, a comforting sleep that, deep down, she knew might be her only chance for many days.

As it always did, the telephone's constant ringing brought her out of it. She sought to ignore it, even as it drew her consciousness to the surface.

She awoke as if drugged, and reached for the phone. As she did her eyes fell on the little electric clock next to it.

It said 4:12 P.M.

My god! she thought. *I've slept almost thirteen hours!*

She picked up the insistent phone. "O'Connell," she managed, her mouth full of mush.

"Sandy? This is Mark," came a familiar voice. "I figured you'd still be out. Good girl. Now get over to the labs here as soon as you can."

She tried to shake the sleep from her. "What's happening?"

"I—I can't tell you right now," he said hesitantly. "Something nasty. Something I stumbled on by accident. Just—well, get over here quick as you can, okay? I'll be in my cubbyhole."

She was puzzled, but said, "All right, Mark," and hung up.

*   *   *

It's funny how when you oversleep you feel like you've never slept at all, she thought for the tenth time since starting out. The trip was a quick one, under an hour if you had the traffic with you, and she pulled into a space assigned to NIH bigwigs and hurried inside. Mark's tone on the phone worried her. Something nasty, he'd said. Something I stumbled on by accident.

Of course most business couldn't be done by phone anyway—security and all that. But his tone— he'd been upset, terribly upset, and fear tinged in his voice.

What would cause fear in the medical Rock of Gibraltar?

There were the usual procedures to go through. Nine guards, twenty-six TV cameras—maybe more, they never told you everything—four airlocks and the whole sterilization mess.

Finally in her medical whites she walked again down that familiar yellow-painted corridor to those double doors and pushed them open.

Nobody was there. The computer was on, the whole lab was activated, there was even a sample on the electron microscope. A pad lay on the floor as if hastily dropped, and she picked it up. It held a lengthy serological series in Mark's handwriting. He had been trying to find the key, the organisms from which the two Wilderness Organisms had been bred.

She was curious, but not concerned. *He went out for more coffee, probably,* she told herself. She settled down to wait for him, passing the time until his return by going over his notes. They were in a typical doctor's scrawl, and highly disorganized, and outside her specialty at that, but she roughly followed what he was doing.

Having isolated from the protein "punctuation mark" the first signal in the DNA message of the Wilderness Organism, he and the computer were trying to duplicate it using computer models.

Dr. Denise Ferman, a petite little black woman who was a crack expert at toxicology, stuck her head in the door.

"Oh, hi, Sandy!" she said. "Where's Mark?"

"In the canteen, most likely," Sandra replied.

Ferman shook her head. "No, I just came from there. He must be up top—I'm pretty sure he's not in A-complex."

That worried Sandra. She reached over, pressed an intercom stud and three numbers on its face.

"Security," said a voice in her ear.

"This is Dr. O'Connell," she said. "Is Dr. Mark Spiegelman in A-complex or did he come out?"

"Let me check," said the voice. There were a few seconds of dead air, then the voice returned. "Dr. Spiegelman logged into A-complex at 12:15, cleared security and decontam at 12:45, and has not yet emerged."

"All right, thank you," she said, hanging up. "He's got to be here someplace," she said to Denise Ferman. "Security says he is."

The toxicologist looked puzzled. "Let's go see," she suggested.

There were eight one-person control centers in A-complex, four multi-person labs, and a small automated canteen. They checked them all.

Nobody had seen or heard Spiegelman in hours.

"This is impossible," Ferman insisted. "You *can't* disappear out of a place like this. He *has* to have gone up, no matter *what* security says."

She didn't know why, but she was suddenly feeling nervous and a little scared. "I'm going back up," she told the scientist. "You let me know if he somehow turns up here."

Ferman nodded, and Sandra O'Connell began the long procedure back out. Something smelled—and smelled bad. First that strange phone call, then this.

At each step in the chain she questioned the human attendants. None had seen Dr. Spiegelman leave, and his initial passes were still there. Once out, she called down to Denise Ferman once more.

"Still nothing," the toxicologist told her. "He isn't here."

She went to security and made a scene. They, too, assured her that it was impossible for him *not* to be down there, but when they checked with the others they agreed to go down and take a look. A huge black sergeant and four very efficient-looking squad members went down, through the same procedure, checks, and watches that made it impossible for anyone to just vanish.

The security team was very efficient without being intrusive. They searched the obvious places, then the less than obvious, then the impossible places as well.

Over an hour after they went in, the intercom at the security central desk crackled. "We found him," came the sergeant's voice.

She could hardly restrain herself. "Oh, thank god! Where was he?"

The sergeant hesitated. "Inside a vacuum chamber in Con 3. Somebody knocked him out, dragged him in there, and pumped all the air out."

SEVEN

The great airliner rose slowly and majestically like a giant silver bird, looking too impossibly huge and bulky ever to become airborne. But its nose went up, and suddenly, painfully, it started to climb.

Suzy laughed and rubbed her hands. It would pass almost directly over their position in the woods just beyond the end of the runway. With George and Alicia holding the mortar steady, Suzy held the shell just over the mouth of the round, squat mortar until the plane was almost on top of them, then dropped it in the hole and fell back.

There was a whump, a swirl of smoke, and something shot upward, catching the great plane amidships. There was a tremendous explosion, and the huge silver bird started to collapse, almost to fall apart in a ball of flame.

He swore he could hear the screams of the dying passengers, 386 ordinary men, women, and children burning, falling to their deaths. He was only superficially aware of Suzy and the others dancing and cheering as the plane came down. He was up there, screaming with the dying innocents, no longer sure as to why they were dying.

Someone was grabbing him, poking him.

"Come on, Joe! Wake up!" a deep, throaty voice urged.

He awoke with a cry stifled in mid-utterance as he realized where he was and that it had been a dream once again.

Doug Courtland looked at him in concern. "You oughta see a shrink or somethin' about this, man," he told the other. "My lord! This is the third time this month!"

He sighed and wiped the perspiration from his face. "I'll be okay, Doug, thanks," he assured the other. "Just a nightmare. Nothing more."

Courtland looked uncertain, but finally nodded, shrugged, and walked back to his own bed.

He sat up, holding his head in his hands, trying to stop the shaking, to get a grip on himself.

A nightmare, yes. Just a dream. A bad dream.

Only once, almost ten years ago, it'd been real.

There was a Hell, he told himself, and he was in it. He got up, went into the bathroom, closed the door and switched on the light. He steadied himself on the sink and looked into the mirror.

It was a strong face on a strong body; a Caucasian complexion but strong Negroid features and a bush of thick, wiry hair now tinged prematurely with gray. The face was lined, etched in with experiences he could not forget; his brown eyes looked old, empty, hollow.

When would it let him alone, this past that haunted him? What did it want? What sort of penance would sponge away the guilt?

Look what's happened to you, Sam Cornish, he thought bitterly. *Ten years older than your age of thirty-four and growing older at twice the clip every night. A hundred years in Hell already served—how many more to go?*

How young and bright and starry-eyed Sam Cornish was when he was alive, he thought. Black power and the Revolution and all that. *Black power!* He snorted in derision. Too white for the Blacks, too black for the whites, but just right for the Revolution. Read Marx and Mao and protest march and all that shit.

But to most of his contemporaries that was passé, lip service. Hedonism replaced the Revolution before he'd gotten there. Blow pot, disco dance, go all night in bed with Suzy, blue jeans and bennies . . .

Suzy. There she was again. The Revolution would sweep away decadence. Come the Revolution and all would be perfect. Society was rotten, capitalism was poison, they'd drugged the world into submission. They had to be awakened.

He'd believed it, all of it. He'd drunk it in like an alcoholic in a liquor store.

Seven or eight committed "patriots," a tight little cell. Hit a bank here, a bank there for money. It was easy. Just pass a note. Pick small banks, never be ambitious. George with his chemicals. Steal some weapons here, some explosives there. Even that damned mortar from a National Guard unit in summer camp. Easy. Fun.

Some notes to the papers, a fancy name, the Synergistic Commune Action Brigade, some bombs in harmless places. Everybody so sure of the Revolution nobody even stopped for a moment to ask what the Revolution was, who would run it, and other things like that. It was "us" against "them," kiddies playing revolutionaries against the fascists.

Until that plane. Three hundred eighty-six dead innocent people, and the SCAB celebrated a great victory.

Somehow, deep down, he'd kidded himself.

Somehow he'd rationalized, told himself that the Revolution was *real,* the Revolution would come, that what he was doing was building a better world.

Three hundred eighty-six dead people. And they danced and laughed in their joy.

Three hundred eighty-six dead people.

Building a better world for who? And what sort of world?

There'd been 387 casualties in that plane crash, the extra one being Sam Cornish.

He'd run and run and still it pursued him. Here, at Sky Forest, he'd stopped physically, and in the strong-man work of the commune and its unquestioning ways he'd worked it off, put it away from him, become Joe Conway, tapped maple trees in these beautiful Vermont mountains, cut cordwood, built buildings and dug post holes for fences, and he'd dropped out.

Except now, except in the night, when the ghost of Sam Cornish still haunted him. Dope didn't work, pills didn't work, nothing worked.

He was checking out the site they'd picked for a new stable for the horses, farther away from the main buildings, deciding how much wood would be needed, how construction would have to proceed, when the man came out of the trees toward him. He turned and looked at the stranger curiously; unknowns were rare up here, and this fellow seemed particularly out of place in suit and tie and tailored overcoat.

He waited, wondering, for the newcomer to reach him.

The man stopped a little away from where he

stood and looked him over. "Hello, Mr. Cornish," he said in a soft southern accent that was as out of place here as the man himself.

Sam Cornish froze, ice shooting through him. He'd been here so many years that he no longer feared capture or exposure, never even thought of it any more—and here it was.

"Joe Conway's the name," he responded nervously.

The man smiled. "Don't worry, Mr. Cornish. I'm not here to arrest you. We could have done that years ago."

Something twisted within him; he wasn't certain whether to attack or run, so he stood where he was. "What do you mean by that?" he asked.

"Mr. Cornish, we deal in the public safety. We try and remove threats to it. If they cease to be threats, well, there's a lot of other folks still menacing the public who need attention. Some of your old buddies, for example, got to Cuba. They sat there on their fannies in shacks cutting sugar cane and singing revolutionary songs in Spanish. Well and good. Let them stay in their own self-imposed prison. It's cheaper. You came here. We traced you here inside of a few months, and let you be first because we hoped that some of your lovable friends would join you. After a while it was pretty clear that you had had second thoughts about the revolution, and were in your own version of a Cuban sugar cane field. We picked up Granger, as you probably know. He told us you tried to stop the plane attack, and left when they carried it out. So we left you here. Cheaper and convenient. Of course, we keep an eye on you and hundreds of others like you just in case, or in case some of your more dangerous friends decide to renew old friendships, but that's all."

His emotions were in turmoil, jumbled and confused. Somehow what the man said made sense, but
it was, in its own way, more depressing than being a
hounded fugitive.

"So why tell me this now?" he asked. "Or are you
finally getting around to the leftovers?"

The other man shrugged. "I told you I wasn't here
to arrest you. I want to make a proposition to you.
If you say no, well, then, that's that. Business as usual. Stick to this commune and this lifestyle and
you'll never see us again."

This was more confusing than before. "What sort
of a proposition?" he asked suspiciously, not trust-
ing anything the man was saying.

"You're pretty cut off here," the man noted. "Do
you know about the Wilderness Organism?"

He nodded slowly. "We get the papers. Lots of
talk about it, naturally. There are a lot of small
towns in Vermont."

"And you've heard that the thing is a laboratory-
created disease? That someone is planting it?"

"I heard," he said, not sure where this was leading.

"Suppose I said that we just shot Jim Foley trying
to plant the disease?" the man continued.

Cornish's mouth dropped. "Foley!" Suddenly his
mind raced. "Any other—"

"No, no Suzanne Martine yet," the man replied,
guessing his question. "Wouldn't be surprised,
though."

He relaxed a bit, strangely relieved but unable to
figure out why.

"Mr. Cornish, I'd like you to come down to the
village with me," the man told him. "I want to show

you a couple of movies, that's all. At the end I'll
explain all this, and you can say no, no thanks, and
walk out of there and back here. No hassles, no conditions, no blackmail. Will you do it for me? Just to
humor me?"

The old suspicions were back. "You're not just
looking for an easy arrest, are you?"

The man sighed. "Mr. Cornish, I wouldn't have
to trick you and you know it. Come on. I promise
nothing else will happen."

He gave in, his curiosity overcoming his massive
doubts. "Why not?" he said, resigned.

They used the back of the sheriff's office, which
was cleared. An FBI badge and a call from the governor did wonders.

The films were a horror story. Hundreds and hundreds of ordinary people, men, women, children, all
in some way horribly stricken. The blind, the feebleminded, the palsied and the paralyzed, and those
haunted faces of those who'd lost their pasts.

And then the big show, a tape of Operation Wilderness itself.

"It was dumb luck we caught them," the agent,
who never had given his name, told him. "Sheriff of
a ski town not far from the cabin was an ex-Bureau
man who'd been on your case. Foley came into town
for supplies, and he made him, even after all these
years, even with the beard and dyed hair. He'd
worked sixteen solid weeks on the plane sabotage
case, and our artists had portrayed you all in every
way we could think of to disguise you. The pictures
were just burned into his brain. So he followed
Foley back to the cabin, got a make on two others

through the Bureau telex, caught sight of a sub-machine gun, and we set it up."

He watched the whole operation from start to finish, saw the bodies, the dead face of Foley. He'd have recognized him anywhere, like the man said. There was a sense of satisfaction in seeing that lifeless form; Foley had dreamed up the airplane job, Foley had planned it.

And now the blue cylinders, and some tape-to-film of the Wilderness Organism itself.

"There's no question that the perpetrators are former radicals, fugitives from dozens of places over the past few years. They've been stagnating, waiting for a cause, a charge to action again, and this is providing it," the FBI man explained.

Sam Cornish felt violently ill. All those faces, all those innocent people. The agent seemed to understand.

"You can't run away from that plane crash, Mr. Cornish," he said as gently as he could. "And they're doing it again. You've tried to run and it's no good, it's inside you."

"What's the bottom line on all this?" Cornish asked brusquely. "Get to the point."

"They're your old people, Mr. Cornish," the agent explained. "They know you and you know them. They're recruiting. The word's out. You probably heard it yourself."

Yes he had, he thought. Not what for, just that they wanted old pros for a new and massive operation.

"We want your help in making sure there are no more crippled and hollow innocents," the man continued. "We can't seal the borders. We can try, but any good pro can get in and out. We'll catch some now, of course, now that we know what we're dealing with, and who. But not all. Not most. Their toll is already in the thousands, all innocent men, women, and children. Not even soldiers or cops or bigshot capitalist leaders. Just random mass-mutilation. We need you, Mr. Cornish. We need you to help us save those people."

He was sick, disgusted, and not a little scared. "What would you have me do?"

"Put the word out you want to get active again. Let them recruit you. Get in with them, join them. Find out who's behind this if you can, and what the object is. Find out where this terror will strike next. Get the information to us if you can. We want you to save lives, Mr. Cornish. Nothing less."

He shook his head. "I—I can't," he protested. "Damn it! I just *can't!*"

The agent looked at him squarely, a grim expression on his face. "There are still over nine hundred cylinders unused. Nine hundred."

He thought of the faces he'd seen, the small children and babies cheated, cheated of life not merely by senseless violence but—

By Jim Foley.

"They'll never accept me," he protested. "I ran out on them. Left them, deserted them. I wouldn't even help in the plane thing. I just couldn't do it."

The agent smiled. "We'll take care of some of that. Don't worry so much. Remember only one thing—remember that, in a worst-case situation, it'll be you there with a blue cylinder, or helping others with them. It'll be the plane thing all over again."

He nodded glumly. "I been thinking of that. I guess it's what I'm scaredest of." He stared at the FBI man with haunted eyes. "I could have stopped them, you know. I could have stopped them but I didn't."

The other man returned the nod. "That's why we picked you," he said softly.

EIGHT

"In thirty-one years in law enforcement," Jacob Edelman muttered, "I have never once had to solve a murder."

Sandra O'Connell looked at him in wonder. She still hadn't gotten over Spiegelman's death, but she was as much angry as sad. She wanted whoever had done this caught. "Isn't that what policemen do?" she asked.

He smiled a crooked smile under his enormous nose. "Policemen, yes. But the FBI is not a police force, not in the sense of your local police or something like Scotland Yard. Our powers, and the crimes we investigate, are strictly limited by law to those local powers could not handle. Murder isn't usually one of them, except in a case like this."

"Connected to espionage, you mean," she guessed.

He shook his head. "No, that just complicates it. Crime on a government reservation, it's called. Mostly to do with stuff on military posts and Indian reservations. But this one's my baby all the same—and what a way to begin at my age. The ultimate locked room."

She frowned and looked puzzled. This strange little man was impossible to understand. "Locked room?"

He nodded. "It's clear you don't read murder mysteries. I do. A lot of 'em. Takes my mind off the job." He shifted, punched a dictation-style cassette in a small player built into the security desk. "Like this one. There's no way anyone could have gotten into A-complex. No way to get out, either." He punched *play*.

There was a ringing sound from the speaker which seemed to last a very long time, then a click and she heard her own voice say, "O'Connell."

"Sandy? This is Mark," Spiegelman's voice responded. "I figured you'd still be out. Good girl. Now get over to the labs here as soon as you can."

"What's happening?"

"I—I can't tell you right now. Something nasty. Something I stumbled on by accident. Just—well, get over here quick as you can, okay? I'll be in my cubbyhole."

"All right, Mark."

Click. Click.

Edelman looked at her sheepishly. "You think with the Wilderness Organism we weren't going to tap the phones? Don't worry, it's legal. National security warrant, government phones and all that." He sat back in the chair, lost in thought. Suddenly he shot forward in his chair with a suddenness that startled her.

"Question one: why couldn't he tell you over the phone?"

She thought about it. "I don't know, really—unless it was something to do with the Wilderness Organism. He wouldn't compromise it. I suppose he knew the phones would be tapped. I suppose I did, too, except it just didn't occur to me."

He nodded approvingly. "So we assume he knew

the phones were tapped. The question then becomes, what was he afraid to have listened to? If he started to compromise anything we'd have broken the connection and knocked quickly on your door. He could only call a few people on that phone, anyway. So, either what he had to say was in the really classified range, or he didn't want to say anything *because he didn't know who might be listening.*"

She considered it. It seemed absurd. "But that would mean a—a spy or something, right there in A-complex! That's ridiculous. There isn't anyone there without the highest of security clearances, and they've worked for NIH and NDCC for years. All top professionals!"

Jake Edelman sighed. "Many years ago, in England, a fellow named Kim Philby became the head of the British version of the CIA. Good family, all the right schools and connections, top clearance. Except that he was a Russian—not merely an agent, but a Russian! And he was caught only by accident."

"You're not seriously suggesting . . ." she began, but couldn't bring herself to say it.

Edelman keyed the digital memory on the recorder. Again Spiegelman's voice came out of thin air.

"I—I can't tell you right now. Something nasty. Something I stumbled on by accident."

"Something nasty," Edelman repeated. "Something he stumbled onto by accident. Except for some sleep up here, he's been a prisoner down there since the Wilderness Organism came in. He seemed normal when he went back down, and he didn't call you until after four in the afternoon, right?"

She nodded. "Four-twelve exactly. I remember it

because I noticed the clock and thought how much I'd overslept."

Edelman was thinking again. "He confided in you. You were more than his boss, right? A good friend?"

She nodded numbly, and tears started to well back up into her eyes. "A very good friend," she managed, voice breaking. She took a handkerchief out of her bag and wiped her eyes. He waited for her to get herself back together.

"Okay, there were fourteen people down there. Just fourteen. One of them killed him, and did it between about 4:15 and 5:00 P.M. Almost certainly shortly after his call to you. Possibly they heard the tap, but I doubt it. Maybe he went to the canteen and looked upset. Somebody picked up on it and followed him. Maybe somebody was outside and heard the conversation. We don't know. What we *do* know is that he needed to talk to you. There were fourteen colleagues down there he knew well and a security force at the call of a fingertip, yet he doesn't call in the marines, he doesn't go to the others, he calls you. It's his first impulse. I think we can assume that whatever he discovered he discovered between four o'clock and his call. First the discovery, then the call. Give him maybe an extra fifteen minutes to decide." He looked at her. "I need you to go over the tapes of everything he was doing for the hour before his death. And particularly what he might have gone back to immediately *after* his call."

She shook her head. "It's not my specialty," she protested. "Some of the other team members are far more qualified."

He smiled mirthlessly. "But one of 'em's the one

who did it. No, they're out. Look, you're a doctor, aren't you?"

"Yes, but—"

"Well, I'm an investigator. I don't specialize in murder. As I said, this is my first—and I hope my last—murder case. But I'm doing my best because, with the help of special Bureau teams, I'm closest to the case. Can't you do the same?"

She considered it. "I'll try. I might need some help on the hard parts, though."

He looked at her. "What kind of a doctor were—are—you, anyway?" he asked, genuinely curious.

She smiled wanly. "A psychiatrist."

Jake Edelman looked up at the ceiling with a sort of resigned yet questioning expression. It faded as that dull look crept back. She now understood that it meant his mind was working hard.

He came out of it suddenly again, turned, and asked, "He did most of his work alone, didn't he?"

"With a massive computer, part of the whole NIH setup," she replied. "You don't need more than one man for this—although Ed Turner was the alternate serologist who did some of the work, and they served as a check on each other."

Edelman scratched his massive nose. "Doc, what would you do if, somehow, you discovered that one of your close friends and colleagues was a Russian spy? You're all alone in a lab, you and the computer. What would you do?"

She considered it. "Call security, I guess," she said. "Unless it was somebody so close I just couldn't believe it."

"He believed it all right," the little man said. "Something nasty, he said. Pretty definite. But how would he find it out, alone in the lab there? Nobody

was gumming up the works; a spy could just read all
the data from a computer terminal. Nothing in or
out, though, so he better have a phenomenal memory." He paused. "You see? Nothing to catch a spy in
the act, is there? So let's say he didn't. And let's say
it wasn't a person at all, at least not one down there.
Where else could he have stumbled onto something
nasty?"

She thought about it. "The computer," she suggested, a slight chill going through her.

Edelman nodded. "The computer. Something in
the computer, something he stumbled on by accident. What? Evidence of spying? Tampering? What?
I'd say the odds were a thousand to one he didn't
suspect anybody in A-complex. If he did he'd have
called security or at least gotten the hell out of there.
And there we also have just how the killer knew he
was on to something." He put his hand up and
rested his chin in it on the desk. "Sure! Anybody in
A-complex could get the transmissions he was getting. Common line. Somebody suspected he was on
to something, watched his work, and when he discovered something he shouldn't they killed him."
He leaned back suddenly and struck his left hand
with his right fist. "It fits!"

Sandra O'Connell was fascinated in spite of
herself. And impressed. Behind that ugly face was an
amazing if highly neurotic mind.

"The work between three-thirty and the cutoff,
Doctor," he told her. "That's the key. Somehow
we've got to find out his 'something nasty.' It's
there. I know it. I can *feel* it." The expression was
serious but the eyes glowed with excitement. "You
find it for me."

*   *   *

As she sat, not deep in A-complex but at a special-
ly constructed terminal inside NDCC, reviewing the
complex symbols and biochemical models, sometimes with the help of others from serologists to top
biochemists, going over and over those complex and
cryptic mathematical models that must mean something, something dark and sinister, the world was
changing outside her guarded doors.

Three more towns were hit, in Louisiana, Michi-
gan, and New Mexico. One town went stark staring
psychotic. Another completely lost the sense of
touch. In a third all of the male citizens simply
seemed to drop dead, while the women were singu-
larly unaffected.

The country panicked. Congress, which panics
only when the voters panic, magnified the call.
There were demands that something be done, some
sort of protection. There were riots in places. Towns
barricaded themselves and shot at strangers. One
jokester painted some tanks blue and left them in
another town's trash bin. A mob, discovering the
hoax, tore the man limb from limb.

People started packing, deciding to move from
their little, safe towns into the untouched cities. Everyone was upset at this, since it was tending to
crowd the already overcrowded metropolises, and
this would make it all the easier to wipe out a major
city.

City folk, too, feared their own small-town kin.
Relatives were barred, hotels closed down, lest the
newcomers be coming with the Wilderness Organism inside them.

President Wainwright bowed to the demands to
act. He revealed an Army plan to secure the U.S.,
but warned that it meant the total surrender of civil
liberties until the answer could be found.

The people demanded it. Congress grasped at it
like a drowning man. General Davis didn't like it,
but there it was, just as Honner had promised. The
people demanded the loss of their freedoms.

There was resistance, of course, but not too much
after it started. People who refused to go along were
sometimes lynched by their increasingly paranoid
neighbors.

Large numbers of troops on foreign soil were recalled, despite the protests of some conservatives
that this might be just what the whole thing was
about, weakening America abroad so that the Russians and Chinese could move from their
generations-long stalemate.

But the Russians and the Chinese wouldn't move,
and didn't. They were much too nervous themselves,
not so much about the Wilderness Organism as
about the fear that a totally panicked and paranoid
America would seek someone logical to blame.

Fleets put to sea, and missile bases were raised to
full war alert.

And still the string of mathematics made no more
than ordinary procedural sense. Going back to the
start of the work on DNA molecule matching, it still
proceeded in a perfectly sound, normal, scientific
manner. Nothing out of the ordinary.

She tried again and again and again as the United
States went slowly mad from sheer frustration at the
lack of an enemy to hit back.

NINE

He'd put out the word, of course, but he never expected anything to come of it. That's what made the whole thing, the final agreement to help ferret out the perpetrators of the Wilderness Organism, so easy.

If these people were really the old-line radicals, the last person they'd trust on something like this would be Sam Cornish, the man who'd refused to take part in the airplane blowup, the man who'd run out on his "brothers and sisters" and hid out in a Vermont commune for years, plagued by terrible dreams.

It was a compromise his conscience could accept. Say "yes" and do what they wanted, knowing nothing would happen.

About four days after the FBI man had approached him, he received a message at the commune. It came to his cover name, by mailgram, and was very simple.

If you are seriously interested in alternate employment, we will be interviewing applicants from your region in Boston on April 4. It gave an address in that city not really so far away, a time, and was signed *The Woodbine Laboratories, Ltd.*

He just stood there staring at the thing for several minutes. He knew what it was, who it had to be from, what it had to be about.

Well, here it is, Sam, he said to himself not once but over and over again. He was sweating although it wasn't a warm day, and shaking slightly.

He walked out in his beloved woods and stared at the mountains for the rest of the afternoon. He wanted to think it out, but he couldn't seem to think at all. He felt drained, empty somehow, a dreamless sleepwalker.

He'd have to go, he knew. Deep down, he'd given his word—and the pictures of those stricken innocents in the towns would join those screamers in the airplane if he did not try. He knew it, knew also that the damned all-knowing smugly self-confident Federal Bureau of Investigation had known as well, known even before he would admit it to himself.

He was sick, upset, shaking, and felt more alone yet more of a pawn to others' desires than ever in his whole life. He didn't like it, didn't like it at all.

But he would go, damn their eyes.

Curiously, that last night at the commune he didn't dream at all.

Boston had changed radically since the Cambridge Disaster had swept the metropolitan area as the Black Plague had swept London centuries earlier, striking down more than eighty percent of the area's population. It was no longer a huge port, business and commercial center—people were still reluctant to return, despite the vaccines—but it retained its old character, its odd mixture of old and new buildings, and some commerce was returning, for it was still the most convenient harbor for the New England region.

And many people, those who never thought of the Death any more, actually preferred it as it was—a rustic city center of about 50,000 people, uncrowded, uncluttered, many of the old neighborhoods burned to the ground during the panic now replaced with trees and grass, giving it almost a garden air in the April sunlight.

He had a little time, and briefly toured some of the historic structures from the nation's founding that had survived everything thrown at them. It was almost as if he were trying to kindle inside himself some sort of feeling that would make the coming ordeal a matter of belief rather than blackmail.

He could sympathize with those early revolutionaries. Sam Adams, the fiery rabble-rouser who'd moved mobs to stone the British. His nasty yet principled cousin, John, who took time out from figuring how to overthrow the British to defend the soldiers accused of shooting citizens in the Boston Massacre—and won.

Somehow those two men meant something, he thought. Sam—he stirred the crowds to mob violence in that very Boston Massacre, yet Sam wasn't there to get shot, nor had he ever had any clear idea of what the revolution was about. Sam, his cousin once remarked, just loved overthrowing governments.

Who were Sam Adams' inheritors? Robespierre, the aristocratic lawyer who executed tens of thousands in the French Revolution including his own best friends, yet could not rule or control the revolution he wrought. Another man better suited to overthrowing than governing.

Karl Marx, the studious scholar and social scientist, who labored for a proletariat against the intelligentsia when he himself was one of the latter, and who left his wife and eleven children in the slums of London to talk of the coming revolution with international intelligentsia at the British Museum. Friedrich Engels, a millionaire who always lived like one and never even helped out his friend Marx with the rent. Lenin, the upper middle class student who'd never done a day's real labor in his life. Mao the librarian, and Stalin the former monk.

What a collection. Was *any* great popular revolutionary a member of the masses, the proletariat for whom he claimed to labor? Could any of them swing an axe and build a stable in the Vermont forests?

And yet they all got to where they were through the blood of those masses. Sam Adams wasn't at the Boston Massacre he precipitated, but the blood of honest working people was. Crispus Attucks fell, shot dead, a mulatto sailor between ships, the first of them.

Is this, really, what revolutionaries are like? Sam Cornish wondered. Didn't Joseph Conrad write derisively that the revolutionaries who want to smash their way to universal happiness will simply add to the sum total of human misery?

But, he told himself, *if all this is true, then everything else is a lie.* Man's dreams were but a ghastly Midas Touch, turning everything they reached to instant putrefaction.

"We hold these truths to be self-evident, that all men are created equal," Jefferson, the aristocratic slave owner wrote.

Why did the beautiful spring day seem so dark and ugly now? Why did the bright green grasses springing from early rains and warmer, longer days seem suddenly like evil things, grasping and clawing their way to the surface? Why did the charming old buildings now seem so shabby and sinister?

He walked across the ancient Boston Common, pausing in the center of it to see the great, black sculptural arches of the artist Sean Spacher, with the eerie gargoyle-like creatures at the base and the eternal flame framed by the ugly yet majestic curving beams.

He paused to read the plaque.

Erected by the People of the United States as a continuing memorial to man's folly, as a remembrance for those lost who were so dear and as a commitment that they shall be the last to die in such a manner.

Almost a million people, dead of a simple bacteria created just across the Charles River by eager scientists when one tiny little bacterium escaped somehow to the outside world.

. . . A commitment that they shall be the last to die in such a manner.

California . . . North Dakota . . . Maine . . . Nebraska . . . Maryland . . .

Carried there not by a mistake, but by Sam Adams' grandchildren, none of whom had ever worked, and none of whom that he could ever remember had a clear idea of what the revolution was all about.

Whatever happened to Sam Adams after the Americans won that revolution, anyway? Or Thomas Paine? Or Patrick Henry?

That's right. Paine left here and went to France to do it all again.

He glanced at his watch and quickened his pace. This wasn't the time to be thinking such thoughts—or was it?

The building, a middle-aged office building with some character to its architecture, looked innocent enough. He walked in and checked the directory. A good deal of the building was vacant, that was obvious. Not a real business center around here.

Woodbine Laboratories was easy to spot. It was one of only eleven tenants.

He took the elevator to the ninth floor and stepped out. It was an oddly empty and deserted place, yet it had the smell of new paint. Most of the doors were closed and dark; but there was one with a light on that said *Woodbine Laboratories Ltd.* on the door, and he hesitated a second, considering knocking, then reached for the handle.

Inside was a small, comfortable office with a large switchboard staffed by four middle-aged women. It was the last thing he expected. He looked around, trying to spot any other offices or branching corridors, but this seemed to be it. And none of them were paying the slightest attention to him.

He stood there a moment, feeling lost and foolish, then *harrumphed* a few times. Finally one of the women finished a conversation, wrote something down on a pad, and looked up at him with a smile.

"Yes?" she inquired pleasantly.

"I—ah, I'm a job applicant. I got a telegram to come here at 3:00 P.M.sharp."

She looked puzzled. "That can't be right. We sure don't need anybody here and there's nobody higher-up around, ever. We're just the mail drop."

He was certain she wasn't talking about revolutionaries. "Mail drop?"

She nodded. "Sure. We take orders for mail-order beauty creams, hand lotions, and the like. You know. You must have seen the TV ads. 'Call this number now to have your Magic Creme rushed C.O.D. to your door.' "

He was feeling a little numb and thoroughly confused. "That's what Woodbine Laboratories makes? Beauty creams?" was all he could say.

She nodded again. "Far as I know. Of course, I've never seen them. They're actually out in California. We just call in the orders at the end of each shift."

He turned. "I must have the wrong place," he muttered, and touched the knob to leave.

"Wait a minute!" the woman said. "Hey! Mary! You know anything about somebody interviewing for jobs today?"

He sighed and turned. A matronly-looking woman turned from her switchboard and eyed him, nodding slightly to herself, a slight smile on her face.

"Mr. Cornish?" she asked pleasantly.

He felt suddenly tight again. "Yes," he responded.

"The hiring isn't done here." She scribbled something on her order pad, tore it off, and he walked over and took it from her. "Go over there and I think you'll find who you really want."

He stared at her, and for a second he thought he should know her, but the feeling vanished. He smiled back at her, thanked her, and left.

They were damned clever, though, he had to admit to himself as he rode back to street level and walked outside. A hell of a way to see if it's the right man without any problems. A hell of an information front! God! You could even pass code messages in the phoned-in orders through your own toll-free number! Who could tell?

The new address wasn't in Boston at all, but in West Newton. He debated for a moment how to get there, then hailed a cab. There were a lot of cabs and few private vehicles in Boston these days.

The cabbie was a surly sort who didn't talk much and looked like a balding fugitive from a bad jungle movie. They sped quickly out of the city.

Finally they pulled up at an apartment house on the outskirts of West Newton. Sam looked at the scribbled memo. "This isn't the address," he told the driver.

"Yes it is, Mr. Cornish," the cabbie replied in an accent that sounded slightly Spanish.

He had to laugh. All the angles. "Tell me, what would have happened if a real cabbie had beaten you to me?" he asked.

The man shrugged. "I am a real cabbie, for the record," he replied. "In any case, you'd have gone to the other address and someone would have directed you here."

He laughed again and started to get out. Suddenly he heard the man yell. "Hey, man! I said I was a real cabbie!" He pointed to the meter.

Sam paid him, wondering what would have happened if he hadn't, and walked into the apartment.

It was an old, smelly, musty place built a good thirty years before and not well maintained since housing got cheap in the Boston area. It was very quiet, too. Not a sound behind any of the doors, and no names on the doors or mailboxes. He wondered where he should go.

A door opened down the hall and a woman's head leaned out. "Down here!" she called pleasantly. He shrugged and walked to her.

There were two other people inside, a man and a woman in addition to the woman at the door. All looked to be in their thirties or forties.

And, again, they all looked somehow familiar.

"Sit down, Sam," the woman who'd called him said, and gestured to a chair. He sat, and she took a seat on a sofa opposite him, the other two sitting on either side of her.

"You don't remember me, do you, Sam?" said the woman.

He shook his head. "You look vaguely familiar, I have to admit, but . . ."

She smiled wistfully. "We've all grown older, Sam. You, too. Your body sure as hell is in good shape, but your face! Man! Like all the others! Reminds me that we're all getting old."

He relaxed, remembering her now. Take off twenty pounds around those hips and smooth out that pitted face, put a reddish-brown pageboy wig on her thin and frazzled black hair, and you had her.

"Hello, Maureen," he said.

She brightened. "So you *do* remember! Wow!" Suddenly her manner and tone softened. "I guess we're all getting old."

He remembered her, all right. One of the original old college crowd. The sex groupie type, he recalled. Slept around bisexually with all and sundry. She wasn't so attractive any more.

He managed a chuckle. "But not too old, right? Back in harness after all this time."

She was suddenly all businesslike. "Why do you want to get back, Sam?"

He thought about it. He'd thought about it all day, the answer to that question.

"I was dead, Maureen. I just had a breakdown, couldn't take it any more. I needed out, a rest. But walking out—well, it kind of killed me. Once up there in the commune I just couldn't bring myself to leave. I guess it was like a return to the womb, few responsibilities, no cares. I'd been living tense, expecting to be dead at any moment, for years. Then I was safe, secure—I don't know how to explain it."

"But why come out now, Sam?" she pressed. "Why leave the cocoon at all?"

He sighed. "I was a zombie. Oh, I didn't admit it to myself, no, but I was. Up there I was safe, insulated—but without purpose. I just *existed,* Maureen. I reached that point a couple of years ago, but I had no place else to go. All of you were underground or in jail or dead, and I was still wanted by the feds. I kinda put myself in prison up there—I couldn't get out when I wanted to."

Maureen turned to the others one at a time, then asked the man, "Well? What do you think?"

The man shrugged. "Why not? I don't think he'll gum up anything, and at least we know he's safe."

Maureen turned to the other woman, who just shrugged and nodded. She then looked straight at Sam. "Okay, I guess that's it. Welcome to the club."

He smiled and started to say something, but suddenly he felt a series of tiny pricks in his arm. He whirled around, surprised, and saw two other men, both huge and muscular, grinning at him. One had a needle-gun in his hand.

He started to say something, started to protest, panic rising within him, but the whole world was suddenly spinning and he blacked out.

TEN

"You look beat," Jake Edelman said sympathetically.

Sandra O'Connell smiled appreciatively. "I *am* a little tired. I've been going over that stuff for days now—and nothing. There's just nothing there!"

Jake Edelman lit a cigar, inhaled, and blew out a stream of blue-gray smoke so dense it almost choked her. He looked thoughtful.

"I really wish you wouldn't do that," she protested.

He shrugged. "Sorry about that. My office, my social conventions. No place left to enjoy things any more. No this, no that, everything's banned. The whole damned world is bad for you and mad at you at one and the same time." He reached over to the window, flipped a control, and a fan started dragging the smoke behind him. "Better?" he asked.

She nodded. "Thanks. But I've come to report bad news. There simply is nothing in Mark's last work to show that he stumbled onto anything odd or unusual. It's just good science, so good that I've had to consult with a few dozen other people just to follow it. The man was a genius. Not just in his field. In any branch of medical lab work." Her expression grew sad. "What a terrible loss it was."

Edelman nodded sympathetically. "I know. I

broke it to his wife and kids. Toughest damned thing I ever did. Back with the Navy I once lost two young boys in a carrier accident and had to do the same thing, but this was worse. Murdered in the most secure place I know of outside of Fort Knox, in a particularly nasty way, by person or persons yet unknown."

She looked at him, trying to figure him out. "*You* saw Sarah? Why? Surely there were dozens—"

He cut her off, holding up a large, vein-etched hand and reaching over for some pictures. He handed them to her.

A pleasant-looking if fat little woman. Other pictures—one a small boy on a horse, another a little girl playing with a dog. In back of them were adult pictures.

"They got their mother's nose, thank the good Lord," he said, and took the pictures back and replaced them in their proper position on the desk. "The boy's now a man—a dentist in Cleveland, three kids of his own. The girl's a pretty damned good lawyer, just got married herself to a rabbi in Philadelphia." He paused for a moment. "I been in law enforcement since the Navy. Most of it's boring stuff, routine work, but there's always that chance. More with me. I live with it fine—hardly ever think about it. But I think about *them* all the time—they all had to live with that fear all their lives. Nadine— that's my wife—got ulcers while I was working the New York labor front. Every day she never knew when she kissed me good-bye if somebody'd drive up that afternoon and say that somebody got me. Not much chance, but it was always there." He looked back at her, straight into her eyes. "That answer your question?"

She smiled and nodded.

"So what's a pretty doctor girl like you doing in a place like this?" he continued, shifting subjects. "Unmarried, too. Not even living with anybody. That's not natural."

It seemed like an accusation. "I just never had the time," she said. "Long ago I had to make a choice, and up until a few days ago I was convinced I'd made the right one. But it wouldn't be fair to drag anybody else into a life like mine."

He shrugged. "Then you should make time. It isn't too late. You know what one of your co-workers said about you?" He shifted some papers, brought up a typed form. "He said you were trying hard to prove something you proved ten years ago. I wonder what he meant by that?" The tone was such that it left no doubt he had no questions at all as to its meaning.

The question disturbed her, as well as giving her a chance to change subjects. "That form—you've been interviewing people about me?"

He grinned sheepishly. "Sure. You and everybody else down there before the body was found. Woman, I know more about all you people than you know yourselves!"

"And you still don't know who killed Mark," she said in a flat tone of voice.

He softened. "No, I don't. Well, I have some ideas, but I don't want to air them yet. This is going to be one hell of a hot potato. One of the worst in history. I have to be absolutely certain."

She was interested. "What have you found out? What is all this about?" she pressed.

He chuckled and held up both hands as if to fend her off.

"Take it easy!" he protested. "I said nothing certain yet." His tone grew more serious. "But when the time comes, you'll know, I promise you."

That didn't satisfy her, but she had the feeling it was all she was going to get.

"You look as tired as I do," she said.

He nodded. "I worry a lot. My ulcers have ulcers. I worry about how a bunch of overage radicals suddenly get ahold of an engineering marvel and decide to try it on small towns. I worry about how so many strangers can lug big blue cannisters through small towns without being noticed. What can their cover be? Exterminators?" He paused a moment, then continued. "I worry about lots of good men, women, and children getting crippled for life. I worry about how a damned fine scientist can get murdered under the best security we can muster." Again he paused, then said, much more softly, "I worry about my country going quickly from a free one to a military dictatorship—so very quickly! I wonder how it'll get out from under."

She looked at him curiously. "That's an odd remark. You know why it's happening. It's only a temporary thing. Nobody can hold this country under control forever. Such things can't happen here."

He smiled humorlessly. "Such faith! Well, God Bless America, it *can* happen here and it *is* happening here. Just look out that window and see it happen."

She involuntarily glanced over at the large window to the left and behind his desk.

Pennsylvania Avenue looked almost deserted; there was a soldier on practically every street corner, and one or two were talking to civilians. An Army truck was going up the street, except for some busses the only vehicle there.

"But—" she started, but couldn't think of anything to say.

Jake Edelman nodded grimly. "So you put the Army, all the troops, reservists, guardsmen, all of 'em, everyplace. Federalize all the cops, make 'em a zillion times more powerful and important. Clamp down censorship on radio, TV, everything. Slap taps randomly on everybody's phones, but cut off long distance service. Ban the sale of gas and oil. Nobody moves except to work and back on makeshift bus routes." Again the characteristic pause. "We're arresting tens of thousands of people. Anybody who ever said a kind word about anything the government don't like. They're already building big camps for 'em out west."

Her jaw dropped. "I didn't—"

"And you wouldn't," he cut her off. "When they control the news nobody knows what's going on."

"I'd think this would make your job and life a lot easier," she pointed out. "After all, isn't crime 'way down?"

He nodded. "Oh, yeah. It's practically nil, until the Army boys invent a new one. Safe to walk the streets of Washington at midnight—who'da ever thought *that* was possible? Unless an over-eager soldier just shoots you for violating curfew," he added. "Look, when I joined this Bureau it was in the middle of a big scandal. The FBI was violating everybody's rights. Nasty old FBI. But they were wrong."

She shook her head. "What do you mean?"

"A bureau's not a creature. It's just stone and paperwork. Like all man's creations, it's as good or as bad as the *people* who run it and make it up. If they're bad, you can make all the rules in the world and nothin's accomplished. If they're good, you needn't fear them at all. Hell, there was a time when marijuana was illegal in this country. There was a time when *alcohol* was illegal. All it did was increase the consumption rate a thousand percent on both products. A law's only as good as the people who enforce it. That's what's so insidious about that, out there—the potential, anyway. In the wrong hands this won't go away—but the people actually begged for it, just like Honner said they would. And Congress *did* go along. And the courts are letting it happen. It's a horror. What kind of people will tell my grandchildren what to think?"

"You're being too melodramatic," she said. "As you say, it's the people. As that Mr. Honner said, what Congress can do it can undo."

"If it gets the chance," Edelman said ominously. "Once you got this thing in effect, you can rig Congress and the courts at the point of a gun."

She started to protest. "But the government isn't going to—"

"You been around this town and you can say that?" he shot back. "I been here since before you were born. This is a company town, and the product is power. The workers are the bureaucrats who keep everything going by following orders. They like power, too. Hell, they're having a ball with all this power. They don't think of people as people. When you got to talk in trillions on a budget, what's a dollar? When you got to figure a 900-page law that affects all the people, who thinks about the people it pushes around until election time?"

"You're a fine one to talk," she pointed out. "You're one of them."

He frowned. "No, never. Never one of *them*. I just understand them, that's all."

"With your attitudes I'm surprised you're still around," she said. "I'd think you were very unpopular about now."

Jake Edelman shrugged. "So I'm one man still doing his job. They don't even think about me, as long as the paperwork's right and I don't somehow make this speech over TV or even the Bureau intercom. But I worry all the same."

She didn't like the tenor of the conversation. He seemed to sense this, and changed the subject again.

"So what was Dr. Speigelman working on?" he asked.

"The Wilderness Organism, of course," she told him. "He'd worked out a good deal about it and its behavior which tallied with the findings of the other lab personnel. In a sense, he'd finished his job."

Edelman's bushy gray eyebrows rose. "So? And yet he still worked? On what?"

"I told you he was a genius," she reminded him. "Once he determined the basic nature of the Wilderness Organism—or organisms, really—he set out, it seems, to try and duplicate them, to find out how they were constructed."

Edelman was interested. "You mean he was doing this recombinant stuff? I thought that was a no-no."

She nodded. "Oh, yes, in real life. What he was doing was running computer models, where you take the basic chemicals and start trying all sorts of combinations and see if you can make something that matches your live sample."

"And did he?" Edelman was more than interested now.

"Oh, in a way," she said. "He had a start anyway. A really amazing start considering the number of random possibilities to build that organism, but, as

I said, he was a genius."

"Give it one more try, will you?" he urged. "The clue—the motive—has got to be there. It's what I need. I need it desperately and I need it yesterday. You don't know how bad I need it."

She didn't understand, and she was tired, but she said, "All right, I'll try. Another work day. That's about it, though. I've called in Joe Bede—a really fine biologist, and the first on the scene in that Maryland tragedy—to see if I'm missing something elementary. But if this doesn't work, that's it. I can't do it forever."

"That's all right," he said softly. "Do it that once. There are others working on it, of course. I just figured that, while you might not be the best microbiologist in the world, you knew how Mark Spiegelman thought better than anybody else. I want to know what would panic him and not a dozen other scientists. Go to it, Doc. Give me what I need."

Again she said, "I'll try."

Dr. Joseph Edward Bede shook his head for the hundredth time. "I just can't see it, Sandy," he told her. "A really good run of model work, yes, but nothing that would cause me to run screaming." He looked up at her, and she was staring off into space. "What's the matter? Too many tabular columns and bar graphs?"

Her expression didn't change.

"No, it's not that. Something the FBI man, Edelman, said. About me knowing how Mark thought."

Joe Bede chuckled, but his voice was gentle, consoling. "You were always in love with him, Sandy. We all knew it. I think *he* knew it. He was always Jupiter up on Olympus to you. The perfect man."

Suddenly she was agitated, but not by Bede's revelation that what she had always believed was her innermost secret was out.

"Maybe that's it," she murmured, more to herself than to Bede.

The other doctor was interested. "What? Got something?"

"What you just said, about me always thinking of Mark as Jupiter. Perfect. A genius who could do no wrong." Suddenly she whirled around and looked straight at him, slightly excited.

"Joe, maybe I've put Mark on *too* high a pedestal."

Now he *was* puzzled. "What the *hell* are you talking about?"

"Listen!" she continued, growing more intense. "Joe, how many chemicals go into making up a DNA molecule?"

He thought a second. "Four. Adenine, thymine, guanine, and cytosine," he told her. "Why? You know that. You been looking at the four of them for days now."

"Okay. Now if you're going to build the Wilderness Organism, you first construct your DNA molecules so they transmit the right instructions, okay?"

He nodded. "Sure. You get one of twenty protein molecules made by RNA. The amount and combination of these determine the cellular makeup."

"Joe," she asked slowly, "what are the odds of getting several hundred correct genetic orders in a period of three hours' research?"

He thought for a moment. "Pretty slim," he admitted, "although not outside the realm of chance with a good mind and a good computer."

She shook her head. "No, no. I mean getting the code right to build the specific organism under study. Think of the variables! It's days, weeks of work at least! *But Mark got almost the entire bacterium built in model in a little under three hours!*"

He considered this. "But we all knew he was a genius."

"Joe! That's what's caused my block!" She was almost yelling. "I was so damned in worship of him I admired how easily he did it. Joe! I don't think he *did* do it!"

"Sure he did," Bede said, still puzzled. "There it is."

"Joe!" she persisted. "Suppose he just got the first few steps right inside the overall problem? Suppose, Joe, that the computer took his admittedly genius-level start *and completed the rest of the model for him?*"

Bede was incredulous. "No way, Sandy. That's impossible."

She sighed, seemed to collapse, and started feeling a little scared. She felt, in fact, just what Mark Spiegelman had radiated over the phone in that last, fatal coversation.

"Not if the Wilderness Organism was already in the computer, Joe," she breathed.

Joe Bede laughed nervously. "Oh, come off it, Sandy. In order for that to be so, either somebody else would already have had to have broken the WO code makeup . . ."

". . .Or designed it on our own damned computer," she finished.

He shook his head in disbelief. "That's not possible, and you know it," he objected. "Why, that'd mean that somebody inside our own staff was behind all this."

She was shaking now, very scared indeed. "Yeah, Joe. And Mark was killed inside the Dietrick secured labs. Imagine! A lot of trial and error, then a few combinations hit, then several—and suddenly the machine completes the model for him! My God!"

Joe Bede was looking a little nervous himself now. "Hell, Sandy, if what you say is true we'd better damned well get the hell out of here and over to your FBI friend. If they killed Mark . . ."

He didn't have to spell it out.

She grabbed the phone and dialed Jake Edelman's number. There was a click and a whirr and then a mechanical voice that said, "The-number-that-you-have-dialed-is-not-in-service-to-this-telephone. Please-hang-up."

She slammed it down like it was an angry snake.

"What's the matter?" Bede asked nervously.

"The phone." She gasped. "I—I called Edelman on it this afternoon. To get a chance to see him. Now it won't connect me."

He shrugged uncomfortably. "Probably just more of this martial law nonsense."

"Let's go, Joe," she urged, getting up. "Let's go over to the FBI Building ourselves."

He sighed. "Okay, Sandy. Hell, I won't look scared if you don't."

They grabbed their coats and walked out the door. The sentries were still there, and they nodded politely.

Sandra O'Connell suddenly felt extremely paranoid, as if unseen eyes were watching everything they said or did, as if unseen enemies were waiting to pounce at any moment.

The elevator came at last, and they got in. She pushed "G" and the doors closed and the car started up, taking an incredibly slow path by her imagination's reckoning.

It opened and they walked out. Immediately four men converged on them. She felt panic.

One flashed a badge. "Secret Service, Doctors," he informed them in a crisp, businesslike manner. "We'd like you to come with us for a few minutes."

They were puzzled, but complied. It was reassuring, at least, to be in the hands of the law, she thought.

A small office door down the corridor was opened by one of the men, the other three of whom flanked them, and they entered.

"Now, will somebody kindly explain to me what this is all about?" she demanded angrily.

"This," said one of the men, wetting down a rag from which issued the strong odor of chloroform.

ELEVEN

He was in a hazy fog, vaguely aware of what was going on but unable either to do much about it or to care very much. The drug was a minor hypnotic rather popular with the young; you floated, you felt wonderful, everything looked beautiful, and you didn't think but were willing to be led around or do anything you were told. In the popular culture two people took it, whispered wonderful things about love or sex or something in a nice, quiet room, then acted out their fantasies until, in a couple of hours, they went to sleep and woke up feeling great.

Like most such substances, its popularity sprang from the fact that the average person's life is simply too damned boring. And, it was true, the stuff didn't hurt you at all—but it had one nasty little effect, being a hypnotic. You were totally open to suggestion and unfiltered outside stimuli; in wrong or, worse, sadistic hands, you were strictly at the mercy of whoever was around.

It was a handy little drug for an underground force.

So he'd cheerfully gone with the nice people, with vague, blurry memories of a long car ride to a small private airfield, and from there into a plane with numerous other people. Then he was asleep.

In between the periodic dosages administered in

cups of juice or even water, there were occasional flashes but not much else. A seaplane landing, a ship pickup on the ocean, a voyage of who knew how long, a landing on some deserted shore, more flights, funny-looking people with strange languages and accents—but all of it ran together and none of it made much sense.

Sam Cornish awoke. It was a gentle awakening as if from a deep and restful sleep; he yawned, stretched, and felt really good.

He was strapped in a plane seat and was in the air somewhere. It was a very old crate; there was a lot of vibration and the interior hadn't been maintained in quite some time.

Looking around he saw a number of other men and women in the other seats, most sleeping deeply but a few awake and looking around or just staring.

For the first time he realized that all of the windows in the aircraft had been painted jet black. He looked over at the person in the seat next to him, a black man with a few streaks of gray in his kinky hair who was still sleeping, then turned to the window. He was still wearing the clothes he'd worn in the apartment back in West Newton. They, and he, smelled pretty gamy. He fumbled in his pockets, but there was nothing there. Wallet, penknife, everything had been taken.

He had fairly long nails, though, and found after a few tries that he could scratch off a little paint with his index fingernail. It was slow and frustrating, but he didn't have anything else to do, anyway.

Finally he produced a tiny line of glass under the paint, and he leaned over and tried to see if anything was visible outside.

Either it was night out there or else they'd painted

the outside, too. All was still blackness.

He sighed and settled back. There was nothing to do but wait.

After a while more and more of the passengers came awake. Finally the man next to him stirred, blinked, and sat up, looking around at the plane and then at Sam. His expression was more thoughtful than puzzled.

"Very efficient," he mumbled at last. "Much better than the old days." His voice was deep and rich, and there was the slight trace of a West Indian accent in it.

"I think we could all use showers, though," Sam said, trying to open a dialog.

The other man nodded, then smiled wistfully, as if remembering. "Even so, back in the old days we used to have to go under for weeks." He chuckled. "I often wondered why the pigs never caught us by our stench alone."

"Who were you with?" Sam asked.

"The Black October Brigades," the man said. "You?"

He shrugged. "A number of different groups. Synergistic Commune Action Brigade was the last one."

The other nodded again. "I remember that. Jim Foley and I were in Cuba for a while together a few years back. Whatever happened to him, anyway? I got a little fed up cutting sugar cane and came back, but he stuck it out. Never thought somebody like him would stay—drives you nuts."

"He didn't," Sam Cornish said then checked himself. No names had been released on that California raid; he wasn't supposed to know about Foley. A slight tinge of fear rose inside him and he suddenly realized how easily he could betray himself, and how fatal that would be. His mind raced.

"I got word from some mutual friends that he was back in action again," he managed. "I don't know much else, but I *did* hear he was back in action."

That seemed to satisfy the other and he let it drop, looking around. "Several familiar faces here," he noted, "and a few who might just be familiar. I think a lot of plastic surgery has been done."

"And a lot of years have passed," Sam pointed out. "Less hair, dental work, and a decade can do a lot. I know it did for me."

The dark man sighed. "Don't I know it. This hair is grayer than it looks, and these wrinkles and vein pop-ups are constant reminders. What happened to us, I wonder? We believed so damned much in all of it. It's not much better now than it was then, but here we are, here we *all* are, out of it and domesticated."

Sam knew what he meant better than the other understood himself. Here, on this plane, were a bunch of overage radicals, ages from the mid-thirties to almost fifty. From their college days and into their mid-twenties they'd been committed, fanatical firebrands, but, slowly, and not usually from a clear cause as his had been, they'd retreated from the front lines. The job was left to the newer, younger radicals whom they didn't even understand, couldn't even talk to.

"I think it's a lot of things," he said. "In my case I was just plain tired. After all, I'm human, like you, like everyone. You can only hit, run, live forever fearing the knock on the door, in a constant state of tension, for so long. It gets to you the older you get."

The other man shrugged. "I don't know about that. I suspect it was as much our small numbers and lack of unity. We kept our groups very small to minimize betrayal, and that worked well enough, but we never got together, never got a common program, and, worse, were so far underground we couldn't recruit our own replacements." He grew less reflective, more serious. "I think that's what this is all about."

Sam Cornish's eyebrows rose. "Huh?"

"Look around you," the man said, gesturing with his right arm. "A lot of folks from the old days. Suppose some of these younger cult-groups and the remaining members of the old guard could be brought together under a single unified structure, a common program, with proper money and support?" His eyes gleamed. "Why, man, we could take over *anything!*"

Sam shrugged. "Who knows? I think we'll find out in a little bit, though. My ears just popped and I think the plane's banking for an approach."

It was true. Almost as he finished saying those words they heard the *thump, thump,* of the landing gear being lowered and locked, and within a minute or so more they were on the ground, there was the rush of engines reversing, and the plane slowed to a crawl and began to taxi.

It was a short ride on the bumpy ground until the plane stopped with a jerk and a groan. Most of the people were awake now, many talking in hushed whispers, but all eyes were looking forward to the pilot's cabin and the door just before it.

Now the cabin door opened and a bearded young Latin-looking man in olive drab fatigues emerged and opened the door. The engines shut down, and when the door opened a blast of tremendously hot, dry air rushed in. The temperature in the cabin rose tremendously.

A stair or ramp of some kind was quickly attached and there were footsteps running up to the plane. A thin, small woman in fatigues entered, shook hands with the crewman, exchanged a few words they couldn't make out, then walked back to the main passenger cabin, stopping at the galley.

Cornish wasn't the only one who noticed four V-shaped chevrons in dark red on her left sleeve. She was tanned darkly, but could have been any nationality with European antecedents. Sam guessed she was no more than twenty-five.

Her voice was deep, rich, and loud, and had the ring of confident authority. "Welcome to Camp Liberty," she announced. She sounded like she was from Kansas or another of the midwestern states—neutral, a little nasal, and totally American. "I am Sergeant Twenty-Four. As far as you are concerned, that will be the only name you'll ever hear. All of you will receive code names and/or numbers here. Stick to them and do not use any other. You will be training with, and trained by, literally hundreds of freedom fighters from around the world. Naturally, when we go into action, a few of us may wind up in enemy hands. If so, you will be placed under conditions where you might tell all you know. Because of this, you will know what you need to know and nothing else. That way no one can betray another."

The man next to Cornish chuckled. "You see?" he murmured. "Organization. Yes, sir, real pros."

"Camp Liberty is a military camp and is run as such," the woman went on. "You are all now in the Liberation Army. In the times ahead, we will train you, equip you, and weed out those who can and

will carry out the armed struggle and those who can
or will not do so."

Sam felt slightly ill, not entirely from the building
heat and effects of little to eat and drug suppression.
There was very little doubt in his mind as to what
would happen to those these people found could not
or would not aid in the struggle. Everyone there was
a non-person, someone easily and efficiently
eliminated.

"You have many long and hard days and nights
ahead of you," the sergeant warned. "However, you
are among friends, people from across the globe
committed to eliminating the fascist corporate states
who still dominate the world. In the past you
worked alone or in small groups, and you know what
that got. Publicity, and little else. Now, this time, we
are in a different position. Revolution not only
within our lifetime, but within the year."

She went on and on with it, but Sam was tuning
her out rather quickly. A fanatic like those in the
past; her face shone with vision and purpose, and
the rhetoric was the same.

It was getting damned hot, and sweat was pouring
out of most of them. He was uncomfortable and he
itched. He admired the way this overdressed young
revolutionary seemed oblivious to all that, and, indeed, oblivious to the discomfort and boredom of
her passengers, all of whom had also heard this or
said this long before, when this woman was a
pigtailed elementary schooler.

"I wish she'd run down," he whispered to his seat
companion out of the side of his mouth.

"I think this is the start of it," the other said in the
same hushed tone and manner. "She wants to see
who the troublemakers are at the very beginning,

who can't take this and who can."

Sam sank back in his seat and wiped the perspiration from his brow. They'd even taken his handkerchief.

The other man was right, though. The more she droned on, the clearer it became to everyone that they were in a contest, the sergeant in those heavy fatigues versus those in regular clothes in the plane. Suddenly he noticed the plane crew in the background. The fellow who'd opened the door was standing there with a clipboard, eyes looking around at the passengers. Every once in a while he'd jot something down.

The other two of the crew, both of the same type and background as the man with the clipboard, stayed for a little bit, then walked out and down the ramp.

Sam began to be amused by it as time wore on. The woman started slurring her words slightly, and seemed uncomfortable and a little dizzy. She kept recovering, but these flashes were coming more and more frequently now, and her uniform was drenched. Finally she admitted defeat and wound it up.

"You will now exit the plane from the front. When you get to the door, Navigator Nine Sixteen will hand you a card with your own identity for the duration of this exercise. Memorize it, learn to use it exclusively for your own sake later on."

They disembarked. When Sam passed the navigator he was handed a little white index card on which was printed *2025*. *Easy enough number,* he thought, and went out.

It was even worse under the sun, but it was dry as hell and with a slight wind. The greedy dry air sucked up much of his perspiration.

They were in a desert, that was for sure. Whitish sand was everywhere in great dunes and depressions, with no features and no signs of living things.

The sand was hard-packed right here, though, and felt solid as a rock. Somebody had put down a paved runway and a little bit away was Camp Liberty.

It looked like something out of an old desert movie combined with a cheap war picture. Lots of large tents all over, interspersed here and there with old-type quonset huts, buildings of tin that looked like the upper half of buried tubes.

There were lots of people about, all wearing either the military fatigues and boots of the sergeant and flight crew or olive tee-shirts and shorts. Some wore armbands of one sort or another, and all wore incongruous-looking hard khaki-colored Jungle Jim hats. Men and women were about equal in number.

They headed first for a large tent nearest the plane, directed by a few uniformed people. They didn't enter, though. Instead they were broken up into groups of ten, equally male and female, and made to stand there a bit more. The sorting was by number.

There were eight groups, he counted. Eighty old revolutionaries on that plane.

Now a big man and a husky woman in uniform emerged from the tent. They went to the first group, and the man, in a Slavic-sounding accent, said, "You will follow us, please."

As soon as the first group was away, the second was met by another man-woman team, and then it was his turn.

An Oriental-looking man and a tiny black woman were his group's caretakers, and both had soft but definite accents as well.

"You will follow us," the woman commanded in

an accent that was somewhat African-English with traces of French. They followed, all feeling like they would drop any second.

Several hundred meters later they reached another large tent.

"As I call your number," the Oriental man said, "you will enter, disrobe completely, then enter the shower and rinse completely. When you emerge, you will give your number to the person there and they will give you a box with your number on it. Go out the back, dry off with the towels there as necessary, unpack the box and put on the top set of garments in the box. We will be there to take you farther."

There was a big bin inside into which they shed clothes, then walked to a set of a dozen or so showers fed by large tanks plainly in view. They were not on; water was to be conserved here. You went in, turned one on, and bathed in the cool liquid using a little bit of gummy-looking soap, rinsed, turned off the shower, and walked out the back.

There was some grumbling from a couple of the people at being pushed around, but all realized that they were there by choice, and they had no other option.

Sam took the box marked *2025* and walked back outside, still nude. He felt slightly embarrassed and uncomfortable standing nude like that, although he was in exceptional condition and almost nobody paid him any mind. Old conditioning dies hard, he thought in self-reproach.

The top clothing proved to be one of the hard hats with his number stencilled on it, the tee-shirt and shorts, some short matching socks that seemed to cling, and a pair of low military-style boots. To his surprise, they all fit perfectly.

Finished, they lined up in front of their boxes.

"I am Sergeant Eight Eighty-One," the Oriental man told them. "This is Sergeant Seven Sixty-Four. We are your training instructors. We will be living with you for the duration of your stay here, and we will chart your progress and go with you to classes and drills. Please feel free at any time not in class or drill to ask us any questions you like or to register complaints, make comments, et cetera, et cetera."

A woman about thirty-five, small, plain, with short-cropped reddish-brown hair, spoke up. "Sergeant, will we get to eat and rest?"

The Oriental nodded almost imperceptibly. "Yes, yes. First we will go to our living quarters, your new home, and store your boxes. Then we will eat, then sleep. Tomorrow you will awaken before dawn to start. Most of our physical program will be done very early, very late, or at night. Mid-day, as you can imagine, is rather too hot for this, and that time you will spend inside at classes. Any other questions?"

One thin, tall, lanky man raised his hand and was recognized with a nod.

"Where are we, and how long will we be here?" he asked.

"You are in Africa . As to exactly where, that you will never know. You will be here as long as it takes. If you all progress at the correct rate, a few weeks at best. Remember, though, that you are older than many of our recruits, and unused to our ways. Also, you are, on the whole, in less than the best shape. This program is designed to help you survive when you go back into action. Once back into action, you will be in small groups, on your own, as you used to be, the difference being that you will be part of a larger and well-coordinated infrastructure. Together, we will accomplish the impossible, and we will do it quickly and effectively. Together, we will accomplish the collapse of the fascist corporate state of the United States of America, and when it tumbles the world will quake so much from its fall that those of us who survive will truly see the revolution for which we've prayed so long."

The food was typical field kitchen stuff. What it was and how it had gotten into that condition were total mysteries. They were starved, though, and it tasted just fine.

Sam had a bad night of it. His own inner fears combined with his personal demons. He did not cry out—some subliminal self-preservation brake kept that from happening—but he saw it all once again: the plane, the launcher, Suzanne Martine's ecstasy as the great airliner exploded . . .

He awoke several times in his hammock, staring. By the time the two sergeants came to get them up at 4:30 A.M. he guessed he'd slept less than three hours.

Breakfast wasn't great, either—powdered eggs, some tough sort of meat, and a vitamin-fortified juice that tasted like rotten tomatoes. It filled, though, and then they went to work.

In the gloom and through sunrise they did basic calisthentics right out of gym class, running, jumping jacks, pushups and situps, the whole routine, until their bodies ached from it. Sam alone had no real problems; he was in superb physical condition and found the exercises refreshing and effortless. The two sergeants were duly impressed.

Another shower, some coordination drills to instill teamwork, and then it was time for class.

The indoctrination lecturer was a matronly woman of late middle years with a Russian accent, although she made it clear that they were not working for the U.S.S.R.

"Camp Liberty was not established by any of the major powers," she told them. "Instead, it is a project of a number of radical revolutionary third-world nations working in concert, financed in part by the patriotic work of brigades around the capitalist world and by some excess revenue from some of those states better endowed with natural resources. We look upon the U.S.S.R. and the People's Republic of China as stalled regimes, continually reactionary once the elite assumed power. They are better than the U.S.A, of course, but only in degree, and we shall attend to them in due course. However, it is the U.S.A. that has only a sixteenth of the world's population yet consumes a fourth of its resources. It is the principal cancer holding back the attainment of basic human rights to food, shelter, and protection throughout the less fortunate nations of the world. Remove it, and you excise eighty percent of the cancer.

"However," she continued, "we wish to remove it without placing the entire world in the center of a war it has avoided for decades. Atomic rain benefits no one, for there would be no one left. As a result, this project was established by progressive theorists. To the capitalists of America, the enemy remains totally mysterious. They cannot attack or threaten or pressure or cajole when they do not know whom to do it to. In the meantime they are being shown up as impotent fools, and already America is taking its first steps toward becoming a fascist state in day-to-day practice. We will let it continue, while the people chafe under true dictatorship for the first time.

Then, suddenly, we—you here, and the others who have passed through this camp—will strike, massively, despite all of their militaristic repression. Out of the rage at their heavy-booted impotence will come the popular revolution many thought impossible."

During the questions, one thirty-ish man with a southern accent stood.

"I'm an American, born and reared," he told her, the implication that she was not obvious in his tone. "I firmly believe that the American just doesn't think in those terms. That's why I quit the Movement. All we were doin' by our little bombin's was to entrench the government in power. It's the lack of pressure, good and uneventful times, that make Americans forget about their nationalism. How can this work now?"

She didn't seem upset at the question. "First of all, Americans have never before experienced true repression. The poor may be starving to death, but they are free to gripe all the way to the grave, which is what keeps things as they are. We have induced a situation where, now, for the first time, they are finding out what it means to be dictated to, to have the Army and a single group run them. Since it is in power to serve the corporations and bankers, it is those institutions who will be protected and prosper; the individual will simply get stepped on, constantly. This will fuel revolutionary fires. And as for there not being a revolutionary spirit there—well, the U.S.A. was founded in popular, bloody revolution although it was perverted in the hands of the merchant and slave-owner aristocracy who seized control. And as late as the 1930s, under the Depression, granges and collectives in South Dakota took up the red banner and had to be suppressed by federal troops. The seed is there, it needs only to be fertilized and nurtured to grow."

There was more. This was only the introductory phase and it only spelled out the theories. Sam realized that he could only place two people in the camp, old revolutionary hands he knew more from the newspapers than experience. He didn't know who these people were, where he was, what countries were involved, or anything.

Some spy, he thought glumly.

The next class, in another tent, was on modern counterinsurgency techniques. They sat again in folding chairs and waited for another lecturer to come in.

Finally, she did. A small woman, exotic and dark-complected who moved with the grace of a cat to the front, where she turned and looked them over.

Sam Cornish could only stare at her, a knot forming in his stomach and a tingling coming over his body. His mind raced and couldn't settle; he was numb, overcome.

After a decade, Suzanne Martine was as beautiful as ever.

TWELVE

A tall, good-looking man in a business suit entered the room and looked at the unconscious forms of Sandra O'Connell and Joe Bede. He turned to the other men who'd done the deed; the chloroform smell was still in the air.

"Give 'em each a hypo to keep them out," he said. "Harry, go get a laundry cart. Phil, call Baker Control and get a laundry truck of ours over here. Then get back here."

The others nodded and went to their tasks. He turned to the remaining ones in the room. "Edelman's people are watching the building, so we have to move fast," he warned them.

Harry came back with a large laundry cart, complete with laundry. They removed a lot of it, all medical whites and other standard uniforms used internally by the R&D and lab departments. Joe Bede, who was large, they put in first, then the smaller and lighter Sandra O'Connell. Neither stirred, although they had some problem getting them both in so that they didn't harm each other. Both would be bruised and battered by this, but finally the leader was satisfied that they wouldn't die on him. Some of the laundry was piled loosely on top, allowing breathing space, with a single loose crumpled cloth hiding the faces.

Within five minutes the one called Phil reentered the room with a small and mousy-looking white-clad man. The two men got behind the cart and started pushing. It was heavy going, uneven and unbalanced, and they were straining. It looked extremely suspicious to be laundry.

The sentries at several checkpoints noticed the problems, but at each point the high-level IDs of the men and their passes got them through unquestioned. Soldiers are trained to obey higher authority; once the authority of the men was established, it was none of their affair what was in the cart.

Finally they got the cart into the truck and it started off into mid-day Washington traffic. After an extraordinarily long and complex route through the streets and clearances at dozens of military checkpoints, they were satisfied that they had not been tailed or spotted and relaxed. The state of emergency helped them; the normally congested streets were nearly empty of vehicles, and a tail would have been pretty obvious.

Now the driver made for the Capital Beltway, also nearly deserted and with military checkpoints at each entrance and exit ramp. They cleared the first, got on, and went around until they reached Andrews Air Force Base and cleared two more checkpoints. They drove onto the base, down to the airfield itself, and to a small hangar off to one side. There the two were unloaded, and the little laundry truck rumbled off to its pickup points. As it actually was the Andrews area truck, it followed its routine with no trouble. Later the driver would report some mechanical problems that had delayed him, and there would be a motor pool sergeant with appropriate paperwork to back him up.

Two small planes were inside the hangar, and a crew of efficient technicians placed Sandra O'Connell's still unconscious form in the back of one, tying hands and feet and gagging her just in case, and the equally limp form of Joe Bede in the other.

Two military-garbed men got into each plane, and, one by one, they rolled out and took off. One man made certain the passenger stayed unconscious, the other flew the plane.

As they disappeared into the afternoon sky, one of the men came over to the leader, now visibly relaxed and smoking a cigarette.

"I don't get it," he said to the smoker. "Hell, why not just wipe 'em and be done with it?"

The other man smiled. "They're both useful people. Better to ice them than wipe them if you can. You can always wipe 'em if the icing doesn't take."

The small plane circled and landed at a private field in upstate New York. An ambulance was waiting for it, and they made the transfer at the far end of the field. Few words were exchanged; the plane was off again in moments, ready to make seven scheduled stops on minor errands so that no one would ever know that anything was out of the ordinary.

The ambulance carrying Dr. Sandra O'Connell travelled back roads for close to an hour. During that time a technician monitored her, making certain that she remained out. Finally it pulled up to a gate, where the driver said a few words to a guard, and then entered and drove up to what appeared to be a cross between a hospital and a rest home.

Sandra was wheeled in, taken to a special room, undressed and then redressed in a hospital gown, then placed in a bed with sensors attached to her skin monitored by a technician outside. As soon as she started to come out of the drug-induced state of unconsciousness, they would know it. When the first signs showed, he punched a button.

A man dressed as a doctor and another wearing nursing insignia responded almost immediately and went in to her. The doctor checked her over. She shifted, mumbled, and groaned. Not completely out of it, but emerging.

"The usual dosage?" the nurse asked.

The doctor nodded. "Standard. Remember, this stuff's dynamite. I want her on the B schedule, twenty ccs every thirty-six hours, like clockwork. No slips."

The nurse nodded and prepared the syringe. "You worry too much," he told the doctor.

"I don't like using the stuff," the doctor said. "Just a little too much and you kill them. A little under and they come out too quickly. I wish we had a better way."

The nurse put down the syringe and picked up a little chart, glancing at his watch. "Sixteen twenty?" he asked.

The doctor nodded. The nurse picked up the syringe again, waited until his digital watch clicked over, then plunged the needle in. Sandra O'Connell started, seemed to come awake, then sank back down as if asleep once again. The doctor checked her nervously, waiting a few minutes for full effect.

"What're you gonna use on her, Doc?" the nurse whispered as they waited.

"Regression. I don't know enough about her to

do much else. It's as good as any."

He made some more checks, then seemed satisfied. The unconscious woman was breathing deeply
and regularly, and did not respond when he
thumped her in a few places and even partially
opened an eye. The pupils were heavily dilated. He
seemed satisfied, and pulled up a chair close to the
head of her bed.

"Just relax," he told her soothingly. "You are in
a deep, deep sleep but you can hear me, you can hear
only the sound of my voice, hear and understand me
and even talk to me although you will remain in that
deep, ever deepening sleep."

He kept it up as a trained hypnotist would for several go-rounds, then seemed satisfied.

The drug, a derivative of several compounds used
both legally and illegally, had been developed as a
truth serum, a chemical hypnotic of the strongest
sort. It hadn't worked; there was a kind of euphoric
effect that sometimes produced the same sort of
falsehoods as scopolamine and the other so-called
"truth" drugs. But it *was* found that anyone under
its influence was tremendously susceptible to
hypnotic-type suggestion, not merely while under
but for almost two days after.

Behavioral scientists and the CIA both found it
useful.

"How old are you, Sandra?" the doctor asked her.

"Forty," she said. He sniffed. A lie already.

"All right, but now you feel yourself drifting, drifting in time and space. You are not forty any more
or in your forties at all. You are thirty years old
now, but you are still drifting back. Now you are
twenty-five. Now you are twenty. Now you are fifteen." He paused.

"How old are you, Sandra?" he asked again.

"Fifteen," she answered. Her voice seemed slightly different tonally.

"I see. And you go to school?"

"Um. Hum."

"Where do you go to school?"

"Sacred Heart of Mary High School for Girls," she said.

"All right," he said. "But now you are drifting again. You are not fifteen. Now you're fourteen . . . thirteen . . . twelve . . . eleven . . . ten . . . nine . . . eight . . . seven . . . six . . . five . . . four. Now you are four years old."

Her face and positioning changed as he said this. She seemed to curl up, her face showed an almost childlike gleam, and, slowly, she brought her thumb up and put it in her mouth.

"A good subject," the nurse whispered. "The bright ones usually are the best."

The doctor nodded and turned back to Sandra O'Connell.

"Now, how old are you, Sandy?"

The thumb came out, and she drooled slightly. She tucked the thumb in and weakly held up four fingers. "This many," she lisped, and back the thumb went.

He nodded. "Now, listen to me, Sandy. You are four years old, and no matter what happens don't you forget it or think otherwise. You will see yourself as four years old, you will act as if you are four, you will believe you are four, and you will react to other people as if you were four. You are away from home, in a hospital, but that's okay. You're not scared, and you're not really sick. You like it here. It's fun. Now, when I say 'four' again you will go into a normal sleep and sleep really nicely, and when you wake up you'll feel real good and you'll be a four-year-old little girl and if you ask nice the man who will be here will give you a lollipop. Okay?"

Her head nodded yes but the thumb stayed in.

"Four," he said, and sighed and got up. He and the nurse walked outside to the hall and shut the door.

"You sure this'll be okay?" the nurse asked, worried. "I mean, why four?"

"Literacy and vocabulary," he replied. "She's a doctor. Lots of stimulation around here. Three's too parent-dependent, five's a little too old. It's only for a while. Maybe after I study her records a bit and come up with a profile I can get a better and more useful set. Right now this'll have to do." He turned to leave and the nurse turned to go back into Sandra's room. Then the doctor stopped, turned, and called, "Oh, Jerry?"

"Yeah, Doc?"

"Next cycle integrate her with the rest of the Baby Brigade so she can play with them." He frowned as if trying to remember something. Then he had it. He reached into his pocket, pulled out a large lollipop, and threw it to the nurse who caught it and pocketed it.

She awoke several hours later and looked around. It was a strange room, and for a few minutes she was scared; then she remembered she was in the hospital for something, and hospitals were fun places. When she grew up she wanted to be a doctor.

There was a grown-up dressed all in white sitting by the door reading something. "Hi!" she called out, removing her thumb from her mouth to do so, then putting it back.

The man put down his book, got up, came over to her and smiled. "Hi, yourself, big girl!" he responded warmly.

"You have a lol'pop?" she asked playfully.

He grinned. "It just so happens I do," he replied, and took it out.

She had some trouble until she finally figured out that she couldn't fit both her thumb and the lollipop into her mouth at the same time. She settled for the latter and lay back, contentment on her face.

Hospitals were such *fun!*

THIRTEEN

Jake Edelman was furious.

"How the hell could you let this happen?" he demanded of a young man and woman standing before his desk. "It was your responsibility! I *warned* you something like this could happen!"

The man shifted nervously. "Look, I mean, we had all the entrances and exits covered, and the guards as well. Hell, we had no reason to believe they'd pull this today—and those guys had proper IDs and everything. Passed everybody by."

Edelman picked up a sheaf of reports on his desk and gestured with them.

"All right, let's see what we *do* know. We know they found out something, possibly who or why Dr. Spiegelman was killed. We also know that, as soon as they found it out, somebody else knew as well and sprung the trap. Somebody with real top connections in government."

"I don't see how that's possible," the woman said. "I mean, that would mean somebody big in with these terrorists."

Edelman shook his head. "Now you're catching on. That's been obvious from the start of all this. How else could Spiegelman have been murdered?"

The line of thought was uncomfortable for the two agents. "I just can't believe somebody like that

135

could be in such a position without us knowing about it," the female said.

Jake Edelman gave her a grim smile. "Years ago in Italy they had a terrorist organization that kidnapped big shots and sometimes killed them—despite bodyguards, varied schedules, everything. They were so damned cocky they often used the same trash can for ransom drops time after time. How? Were the Italian police *that* bad? No, it's because everybody has a fear line or index, and upper level people have husbands, wives, kids, too. Find the one weak link in the bigwigs and you got a man on the inside. In that case they actually had a bunch, including a cabinet minister who wasn't being buffaloed but was part of the brains of the outfit, figuring to run the place in a revolution. No, being high up has very little to do with it." He paused for a second, collecting his thoughts. "So now we have to ask ourselves why these things happened and what we can do about it."

"You said yourself it was because they found out something," the man pointed out.

"Yeah, sure, but what? I ran the tapes of their conversation." He noticed the expressions of the others. "The place was bugged, of course. After Spiegelman you think I'm that much of an ass? Our opposition knew it, too, or suspected it—which is why they weren't collared until they were out into the halls. Well, enough of that. Their conversation indicates that the NDCC computers had a number of variations of the Wilderness Organism already in their memory banks. Once Spiegelman figured out the nature of the beast, he asked the right questions and, instead of a lot of possibilities coming up, the computer gave him precisely what he asked for. Obvious conclusion: somebody in NDCC had used the computers to create the Wilderness Organism."

"You mean it was created right here?" The woman agent gasped. "Oh, my god!"

He nodded. "Sure. The easiest place to work treason is within the civil service. One in eight people work for the government, you know. True, they couldn't get to the military computers, but a can opener's a weapon in the wrong hands. Someone who really knew his or her stuff got the NDCC bio computers to whip up a nicely complicated Wilderness Organism, complete with variant recipes. This was then passed to our terrorists, who found a lab capable of whipping the buggers up. Much easier to make them than to design them. Now, the question is how this person knew that Spiegelman got those results so quickly—and the answer tells us a lot about where our bigwig is."

The young man's eyebrows rose. "Sure! A biggie in NDCC, of course! They could plug into the computer, maybe program it to flag them when and if Spiegelman or, later on, O'Connell and Bede stumbled onto anything."

Edelman nodded. "True enough, but let's take it further. First, why wasn't the information erased from the computer? Why was it left there to incriminate somebody? And, second, who in NDCC has the authority to have CIA or whoever it was on hand, order them unquestioningly to snatch these two and get them out under our noses in an operation tight enough that these people wouldn't leak it to our own contacts?"

They saw what he meant. "I used to do some computer work," the woman said. "With the newer types with fully integrated logic you might be too intrusive if you tried to erase certain types of basic work. That is, anybody going into that area would immediately see that things had been tampered with. Easier to take the very good chance that nobody will ask the right question."

Edelman nodded again. "That makes sense. An alternate explanation is that it was left there to be found, but it was found much too soon. But, we'll let that pass for now. How about the second question? Who at NDCC has the authority to call in the cloak-and-dagger boys?"

The young man shook his head. "Nobody, really, unless it was done with GSA security staff, and I'd seriously doubt that. It would have to be one of the Pentagon boys at the very least, and they wouldn't necessarily have monitoring capabilities for the computer."

The senior agent took out a cigar and lit it, letting out a huge cloud of blue-gray smoke. "Okay, then. I agree military's in on this, but I doubt if that's the direct link. Too obvious. We need the go-between. What agency would be able to coordinate the NDCC stuff with some of the Pentagon boys?"

They saw it and they didn't like it.

"The White House," the woman said, amazed.

Edelman looked satisfied. "Okay, then. That's our boy. Now it's time for *our* computers to go to work. We want a rundown of the top-level White House staff—we already did security checks on all of them. We need a key scientist at NDCC who owes his or her position to somebody in the *current* administration, and likewise somebody in the top brass, probably military intelligence, we can link to this same person in the White House." His expression turned suddenly grim. "I hope you realize that we're battling against time here. With the state of emergency on and getting more and more pervasive, this top-level agent we want will become more and more impregnable with each passing day. If we don't find out who the son of a bitch is pretty quickly, when we *do* finger him we might wind up disappearing ourselves."

That was the most unsettling thought of all.

"Now we have the next question. Why not just bump O'Connell and Bede off?" Edelman continued. "Ideas?"

"Maybe because they didn't have to, or they needed them for something," the woman suggested. "After all, with Spiegelman they had no choice."

Their boss nodded agreement. "Okay, so they have some kind of plans for the two of them, or some need, that called for taking the risk of icing them. So, if you were using the government to subvert itself, where would the government stash two such hot properties?"

"Mental hospitals," the young man answered. "Military or VA, probably. Anyplace else and you run the risk of somebody from NDCC or with NDCC experience bumping into them. Besides, we all agree it was a military-style snatch despite their IDs."

"Okay, then, get on it," Edelman told them. "But —remember. Since we're dealing with a diabolically clever traitor at the White House level, that person's going to be watching us like a hawk. Tread softly and assume you've got the enemy looking over your shoulder. Use our special teams of reliables and stay out of the general Bureau hierarchy as much as possible. Somebody around here probably owes this SOB a favor, too." He growled slightly, looking down at the sheaf of papers. "I want this bastard. I want this person bad."

According to the military guard's records before him, the chief agent with the laundry cart had been an FBI agent named Jacob Edelman.

FOURTEEN

Sam Cornish could hardly believe his eyes when he saw Suzanne Martine up there, lecturing. But then, of course, a corner of his mind told him, if she were still alive this was where she'd be, and if this place was in fact the center of the mysterious virus attacks on the United States she would quite naturally, almost as a law of nature, be in the center of it.

She had changed, of course; she was older, face more firmly set and somehow tougher, too. She was still very small and thin; her voice was still incongruously deep, brassy, commanding when it wanted to be.

He sat through the whole thing without really hearing a word she was saying. He wished he knew if she knew he was here. The thought both excited and scared him; they had once been lovers, but Suzy knew him better than anyone, and was the greatest threat to him on this base.

And now it had ended, and they'd marched out, and through the next few hours and, in fact, the next few days there was no sign that she had noticed.

Still, to be here, in the middle of nowhere, and suddenly find her again, to know that she was around, that any chance might bring them together, was ever on his mind. He couldn't help dwelling on what would happen if they did meet, and was chided several times by the sergeants and some of his own comrades for daydreaming.

Life in the camp pretty much resembled all those movies he'd seen on Army basic training. A lot of lectures, many political in nature, and a lot of physical training—running, jumping, doing obstacle courses and the like. Some of the old-timers were having a really rough time of it, and several simply gave up along the way, refusing to get out of their hammocks in the morning. No one said anything to them about it, but when the group returned at the end of the day they and their effects were gone.

There was something wrong with the base, too, although it took him a while to figure it out. Occasionally there'd be jet contrails overhead, and billowing trails to mark their progress—far more than there should have been, with no one apparently minding or nervous about any detection. More, people seemed to come and go very frequently, particularly some of the upper level people. Jeep tracks went off into the desert, and occasionally helicopters of short-range type with nondescript markings would land or take off. He couldn't help wondering where in this waste they could be going.

At the end of the second week things got more serious but the pressure eased up. The extremely tough and demanding regimen, he realized, was to weed out the weaklings. Now the winnowing was done; those who remained were deemed qualified and fit, and classes went from being basically polemic to the practical.

Tactician One Thirty was a case in point. A black man with a heavy English-African accent, he finally got them down to specifics.

"The plan, you see, is really simple," he told them. "We will organize you into small teams. Each of these teams will have a major city as its target. Under the new rules of overtly fascist America, you will have to move undetected to a rendezvous point, there to get both your target and your weapons. On one glorious day we will strike—simply, silently, but not without a great deal of personal danger and risk. Three days after that, the major cities of America will crumble from an enemy long since through and gone, and fully protected in any event. Our ultimatums will be everywhere; the alternative to the bulk of the American people will be revolution or death. They will chart their own revolution, of course; we shall simply be there to provide the leadership when it comes."

"But what about the Soviets?" somebody asked. "Or the Chinese?"

The tactician smiled. "Right now both of those countries are straining to demonstrate that they have nothing whatsoever to do with the attacks. At all times the leadership of the United States, whether in present hands or ours, will have control of the nuclear arsenal. The Chinese are not postured for a first-strike iniative on the United States in any event. The Soviets have finally managed to get two generations by without war. We feel they will welcome the revolution as an alternative to nuclear confrontation. At first they will see us as friends and allies. We will welcome them as such, and send home with them little delayed-action presents, again not attributable to us. We feel that if we can accomplish internal revolution in America, it will be that much easier in the U.S.S.R."

Cornish saw what he meant, although he sincerely doubted the end result. No matter what the risk of nuclear confrontation, though, there was the specter of horrible plagues marching, first on the great cities

of the United States, then across densely-populated
Europe and the Western Soviet Union. The leaders
of Camp Liberty were fanatics, that was for certain.
The kind of people so committed to the idea of total
revolution that they would never even dare permit
the hard questions to be asked.

And willing to massacre half the human race in
the name of the Cause, a cause they could only
vaguely define.

The man on the plane had been wrong; it was *not*
like the old days. It was the same blind, mindless
devotion to undefined revolutionary principles, yes,
but where ten could only dream themselves a threat
to power, this network of who-knew-how-many-
thousands could cause the massive death and chaos
that revolutionaries of the old days only dreamed
about.

And, in further lectures, they unfolded their long-
range plans. Massive liquidations of the middle and
upper classes; a return of the citizens of the world to
a controlled subsistence economy, a world of happy
peasants with none above.

Somehow, he thought, it all sounded like a return
to the New Stone Age.

Ten days after he first saw Suzanne Martine on
that podium she came to him. He was just lying
there in his hammock, looking over a manual on a
new Czech sniper rifle they were going to be issued,
when she walked in.

"Hi, Sam," she said softly.

The book fell slowly. "Hello, Suzy," he managed.

She smiled and looked him over approvingly.
"You haven't changed all that much. A little older,
a little more hair on the face and a little less on the
body, but that's about all."

He didn't know what to say, so he echoed her.

"You haven't changed a bit. How long have you known I was here?"

"I saw you the first lecture," she told him. "I couldn't believe it was you at first, so I checked and checked and kept sneaking peeks to see if it really was. Then, as soon as the indoctrination was over, I got here as quickly as I could." She stared at him again unbelievingly. "What the hell are you doing here, Sam?" she asked.

So many emotions jumped up and down in him that he didn't know what to say or do. There she was, standing there, and he wanted her again, even after all this time, even though he'd walked out on her before. Wanted her, and feared her, too.

Suddenly he had it. "Penance," he said dryly.

She chuckled, then suddenly grew serious once again. "Why did you walk out, Sam? Where'd you go and what did you do? And why?" She sat down on the canvas floor of the tent, looking up at him.

Honesty, to a point, was the best policy, he decided. "I had a crisis of faith," he said slowly. "I really *believed* in us, in our group, in our ultimate motives. I never once minded ripping off a bank or an insurance company or like that. We were fighting for those people who never had any money to put into a bank or buy insurance. Hell, I wouldn't have minded if we'd knocked off Congress. But—we knocked off 386 innocent, ordinary folks and Congress and the President and Wall Street just went on and laughed at us. It was like, well, going out to assassinate the President and winding up snatching purses from little old ladies on Social Security. It blew my mind, and I had to get myself back together again. I had a —a breakdown, I guess. Like the kid who finds out there's no Santa Claus right on Christmas Eve. I couldn't handle it."

He could see in her face that she was trying to understand but couldn't, quite.

"You knew what terrorism was all about," she said, not accusingly but questioningly. "To achieve the greatest goals for the greatest number of people, some have to perish. The innocents were martyrs to the Cause; they died so that their children and neighbors and their children could have better lives. That's the principle of terrorism. That's how a very small group becomes a force huge enough to topple governments."

He nodded. "I know, I know. But, Christ! There were sixty-four kids on that plane! Children! It blew me away."

"And yet you're here," she noted.

He nodded again. "Yes, I'm here. I'm here for a lot of reasons, Suzy. I'm here because I've spent ten years rotting in a commune in New England not thinking or accomplishing anything. I'm here, too, I guess, because there's a goal in sight. What did we accomplish by knocking over the stuff we did? Federal fugitives, exile, death, that's all. No rocking the corporate boat, nothing. *This* time we can accomplish something. *This* time it's make-or-break. We'll see the results or we'll die. That's something I can get a handle on, work for. I never lost my dreams, Suzy, only my feeling of doing something worthwhile."

She seemed to accept that, although he still was certain she hadn't understood the logic. It was a good story, a convincing story to explain his presence here—one he and a number of experts had worked long and hard on.

One that was very close to the truth.

For the first time, lying there, looking at Suzy and seeing the organization of Camp Liberty and the enormity of their plan, he began to wonder whether or not he didn't really want to be reconverted. He yearned for the comradeship, felt thrilled by being an instrument of history.

And he wanted her. Just sitting here, after all these years, with Suzy this close, he was totally turned on.

She seemed to sense it; she softened. "Come on, Sam. You're not due for anything else today. Come with me over to my quarters. Get some air conditioning and some decent food."

He went with her, although air conditioning and food were not really on his mind at all.

She lived in one of the quonset hut structures. This one had small but comfortable individual rooms, air conditioning, and storage space.

"How did you wind up here?" he asked her.

She flopped on the too-narrow bed and sighed. "After the big bang, they caught Knapp and shot Crowder to death. You walked out and vanished, and the rest of the group panicked. We split, saying we'd get together at such-and-so, but we never did. I took the pipeline to Havana first, then to Iraq, finally to Thailand—mostly training guerrillas, recruiting and organizing women's brigades, things like that. When this came up and the word went out, well, hell, of course I volunteered." She paused, and her voice lowered. "But I missed you, Sam."

She was undressing slowly now, and he followed suit. He wanted her, wanted her badly; it was the only thing in his mind.

And hers.

And yet, when the preliminaries were finished, he couldn't do it. He wanted to, but something just went out of him. He couldn't follow through, make himself stay in that aroused state.

It'd been like that for years. He'd always told himself that it was because of Suzy. Now he found that, even with her once again, he was emotionally short. It upset him, disturbed him.

He wasn't impotent; he knew that, deep inside. All those other girls, they had been Suzy-surrogates. He'd acted with them as if they were Suzy, imagining them as Suzy.

It was that barrier that still stood now that she was reality and not fantasy.

He loved her, yet there was a gulf there. They were of two different minds, from two different worlds, alien creatures deep inside. This same kind, loving Suzy had cheerfully killed 386 people she didn't even know and had thought nothing of it, and this same Suzy, who reacted to him as a loving human being, saw all other humans as ciphers, statistics, somehow unreal.

He could not cross that barrier. He had to be one or the other, with Suzy or with humanity, and his subconscious was making that choice.

She was disturbed, but not angry.

"If not now, tomorrow or the next day," she said philosophically. "We'll have plenty of chances, Sam, like old times."

He looked at her strangely. "What do you mean?"

"I arranged for you to be with my team," she told him. "You and me, Sam, again! Back home and back in action! The Liberation Army rides again, back from the dead past to haunt them!" Her enthusiasm was genuine. She shifted, looked at him, doubt and hesitation creeping into her eyes. "Isn't that what *you* want, too, Sam?"

"Yes, Suzy, it is," he told her, and cursed himself inwardly because he was telling the absolute truth.

FIFTEEN

The four-year-old mentality of Sandy O'Connell, fortified by the addition of a teddy bear called Mr. Jinks, fell into the routine very easily. The floor she was on was devoted almost entirely to cases such as hers; people who were hot and needed to be put on ice for a while, and were expediently regressed. The drug-induced hypnosis was useful in many ways; those under it could also be persuaded for fairly long periods to see others differently. All in all, there were fourteen "children," nine males and five females, in the wing. Their average age was forty-four.

This technique allowed a close but relaxed watch on all of their activities. Like most drug-induced things, there were no certainties here, and the human biochemistry differed from individual to individual, making dosages tricky and occasioning a few times when reality began to peer through at inopportune moments. For the most part, though, they saw themselves and each other as children, and they laughed together and cried together and played together. The one drawback to regression was the necessity of keeping their section on the ground floor, since they needed to be outdoors regularly. A playground had been established, and a fence built to prevent wandering, but from the playground could be seen rolling hills and thick green trees, and not too far away a small stream on the other side of which passed a road down which occasional trucks and official cars passed.

There were no ordinary patients at Martha's Lake Veterans Hospital, as the place was called. There had been, once, before the emergency, but not now. Many of the people there were there without a lot of medical hypnosis; they were there because wives, children, others they were close to were hostage to their willing self-commitments. They, on the other hand, had no reason to believe that this venerable government sanitarium did not contain some real patients, and the impression that it did was reinforced by the staff. The old fellow who insisted that he was Secretary of the Army under Millard might well have been—but he might also have thought he was Napoleon last week. And who remembers the name, let alone the looks, of even current, let alone former, Secretaries of the Army?

So, too, it was unsettling to see the childish adults in the yard over there beyond the fence. Whether they were truly retarded or insane, or whether they were made that way, was not for the others to say. If the latter, those poor people were a reminder of what could happen to those who made trouble or got out of line.

But the drug only made you *think* you were four; these regressed adults were still in possession of their reasoning faculties under it all, although filtered through their delusion. That fact was becoming an interesting and unforeseen reality to the warders, who found themselves the victims of devilishly sophisticated childish jokes and games, and also caused still greater problems.

Hospitals *were* fun, Sandy O'Connell thought, but she missed her Mommy and Daddy and her big brother and sister. The longer things went on, the more she thought of them and the more she missed them. They hadn't come to visit her once, and she was beginning to fear that they had abandoned her here, didn't want or love her any more.

It was an oversight for the strained technicians at Martha's Lake; a parental visit could have been easily programmed in. They were simply too busy and too pressed to think of everything.

Finally, Sandy started to stare at the green fields and trees and road beyond the fences. Down that road, maybe, was home, her home and her friends, and her Mommy and Daddy. Maybe they *couldn't* come to see her, maybe the doctors wouldn't let them.

She decided to go to them.

It became one more game, but this time with a purpose. She snuck around, Mr. Jinks in tow, watching how the attendants in their white jackets walked and worked, how closely they watched everybody and how sloppy they sometimes were.

She also found that where the big, tall fence met the brick side of the building, there was a narrow gap. The fence hadn't been put in with a prison in mind; it was part of the original establishment, and the fence post was prevented by its design and mooring from being too close to the building. Even so, there were roughly twenty centimeters between wall and fence. A terribly tight squeeze, but very inviting to the four-year-old child who discovered it.

Like most children's plots, though, this one was only partly thought out and not deeply considered. The idea was simply there, and when the opportunity came along it was available.

That opportunity came when a big fellow named Mike suggested hide-and-seek with the seekers to be the warders. The other "children" thought it a tremendous joke for all of them to hide in and around the ward and make the hospital people find them.

There was only one of the white-coated attendants watching them, half-heartedly, his bored mind on a lot of other things than this.

And now it was on. With a yell from Mike a bunch of them started running for the door where the attendant sat, leaning back on the rear legs of a folding chair. They caught him completely by surprise, deliberately bowling him over as they rushed to their hiding places.

He yelled, picked himself up, and ran through the entryway after them, screaming bloody murder. He ran right past Sandy O'Connell, not very well hidden behind some large metal cabinets stuck in the hall just inside the door. When he swept past and she saw she wasn't discovered, she crept outside, looking for a new and better hiding place. Her eyes went to the fence and that telltale opening she'd discovered but shared with no one except Mr. Jinks. She headed for it, made it, and started trying to squeeze through.

For a while it was tough going; the jagged ends of the fence snared her flimsy hospital gown, which tore when she pulled the material away, and it hurt and scratched when she pressed on. She began to be afraid now, began to be afraid first that the attendant would come and see her and her secret would be lost, afraid, too, that she wasn't going to make it, that she was going to be stuck between the fence and wall forever. She started to cry and tears welled up, but she kept at it, and suddenly, with a ripping sound, she was through and falling on her side, rolling down a grassy meadow.

She stopped at the bottom and lay still for a minute. A lot of little cuts stung, and she was still afraid, looking back up at the fence. There was no one in sight.

Finally she picked herself up and ran off toward the trees. Once there, she picked a big tree near the edge of the glade and looked back, fearfully. She could see the whole playground now, and still there was no one.

Now, suddenly, a couple of white-clad adult figures emerged and stalked around, looking over the sliding board and other kid's apparatus. Satisfied that none of the "children" were hiding there, they took one last glance around and went back inside. Sandy O'Connell pressed back into the recesses of the tree as the men seemed to look her way, but when she peeked out again they were gone.

She turned and walked deeper into the forest, toward the small but fast-flowing stream she could hear, still clutching her teddy bear and suddenly preoccupied with other things a four-year-old would find fascinating on a warm summer day: flittering butterflies, pretty flowers, and a babbling brook.

The brook itself looked inviting, and she managed to get her sneakers off and wade in. The water was real cold, and she got out fast. The sneakers wouldn't slip back on, though, and she didn't know how to untie the laces to get them on, so she left them. The adult Sandra O'Connell would have followed the nearby road; the four-year-old Sandy followed the pretty if cold brook.

*   *   *

The chief of security was furious. "Crofton! Damn it! How could you have let this happen?"

Crofton, the attendant bowled over by his charges, looked sheepish.

"Jeez, boss, I was just sittin' there, lookin' at 'em, you know, when all of a sudden, pow! They all give a big yell and charge right at me! Hell, I didn't know what was goin' on until they hit me full and spilled me! Even so, it was only one of their kid's games, you know, nothin' serious."

The security man stared at Crofton hard. "You have them all back in their rooms now?" he asked softly.

Crofton looked distinctly uncomfortable.

"Well, no, not exactly. A couple got all the way past the ward desk and out into the lobby. They were hell gettin' back, let me tell you. We got all but one now, though. Looks like she managed to lose herself in the shuffle and got into the main hospital, but it's only a matter of time, you know. After all, she's only four in the head, you know."

"Name?"

"O'Connell," the attendant replied. "Nice-lookin' broad, you know? A little older than I like 'em, but—"

"Can the evaluation," snapped the security man impatiently. "You sure she's still in the hospital? No chance of a break-out?"

"You know the exits are all guarded, and there's the main gate, too. She didn't get through there, so she must've got into the other wings."

The security chief was dubious. "Show me where you lost her," he ordered, getting up from behind his desk.

*   *   *

Eight attendants were still searching the "Children's Wing" and many more the rest of the hospital when the chief of security and the hapless Crofton walked down the hall from his office to the exit to the playground.

All his life John Braden, now the security head, had played hunches. He was in a powerful position here, and he meant to keep it. Things had gone sour many times in his thirty-two-year government career, but never irrevocably so. He was good, and he knew it. Mistakes couldn't be avoided in any situation; the trick was in making sure they didn't get you.

The playground seemed innocuous enough. The fence itself was ten feet high, double-braided chain-link, not something you could easily climb. At the top were sharp barbs at the termination of every strand.

His eyes followed the fence all the way around, until it came back nine or more meters away to meet the brick side of the building. From any angle except almost on top of the juncture, it didn't appear there was an opening.

Still, there was something that caught his eye, something that felt wrong. He walked down to where the fence met the building, Crofton following silently.

Braden spotted it almost immediately. Shards of light blue cloth were caught on the edges of the fence, and the ground dug up in the area of the opening.

"Jeez! You mean she got through *there?*" Crofton gasped. "But—that's so *small!* She ain't no big woman, but she's got enough up front to—"

"Nevertheless, that's what she did," his boss said. "Back when I was with the federal prison system we had a guy over eighty-two kilos get out through a vent shaft less than three-quarters of a meter square." He picked at the torn remnants of cloth.

"Let's get going," he told the attendant. "I want to see the outside here. You notify Region Security Command that we've had a break, then get Dr. Ahalsi to run a check on every one of the patients in the kiddie ward. I want to know if this was a planned break or not. I want Region to know if they're dealing with a retard or a fully functioning adult."

Crofton hesitated. "Jeez! Either way, she must be dirty and bruised and half-naked, with no money or nothin'. She sure shouldn't be hard to spot and pick up."

"Get going, Pollyanna, before I commit you to this place!" Braden snapped acidly.

Crofton got going.

Following the water, Sandra O'Connell came to Lake Martha—not a big lake, but a nice, pretty blue one used by a number of people for trout fishing. It being mid-week, though, there was no one around when she got there.

She stood there for a moment just staring at the picture postcard scene, the girl-woman entranced by this new place. After a moment she went down to the lake, testing the water first this time to see if it was warm. It felt cool, but not cold, and she waded in a little, sat down in the water, splashed around, and had a good time although Mr. Jinks got as wet as she did.

Soaked and sloppy, she started walking around the lake, just a meter or two from the shore. Her more adult common sense seemed subconsciously to keep her from walking out into the deep center.

A thousand meters or so brought her to a partially submerged boat-house. The double doors were locked, but by going under the part that was angled just out of the water she found a number of missing boards. It was an old place, neither used nor fixed up in a decade or more.

Feeling suddenly very tired, she crawled into the boathouse from underneath and pulled herself wearily onto a fairly flat dry section smelling of oils and paints. It didn't matter to her; she was sleepy and it was a nice place to stretch out just for a few minutes.

Just a few minutes . . .

"Mitoricine," the psychiatrist told Braden, "is a funny drug. I've never liked our using it, and its effects and aftereffects are extremely unpredictable. Enough constants are there, though, to tell me that I would not like to be on the stuff myself, ever."

Braden nodded. "Tell me, when is her dose going to wear off?"

The medical man looked at a chart and shrugged. "Hard to say. She was due for it today at two, and repeated early doses at a larger rate were administered, so the last shot, to be on the safe side—this stuff can kill you or turn you into a vegetable if you blow it—was a low to medium dose. Assuming vigorous exercise, which will aggravate the drug condition, she should just about pass out within a couple of hours, maybe sooner, maybe later—it varies with the individual. She'll sleep a good long time, the body fighting the remnants of the drug, then wake up uncomfortable and lethargic. It'll take a long time to get her back to normal, and it'll come gradually."

"So you mean she'll still be a retard?" the security man asked eagerly.

The psychiatrist shook his head. "Not in that sense. Reaction time will be down, things will be foggy, like that. She'll be jumbled, confused, have some trouble behaving normally. It's much like an adverse reaction to pentathol, only much longer."

"So she'll still be no problem to catch," Braden said hopefully.

The other man shrugged. "Who knows? All I can tell you is that she might have a hell of a time convincing anybody she was a doctor."

Military men and State Policemen combed the area with bloodhounds. They quickly followed her to the stream, found the abandoned sneakers, and picked up the trail. They were all convinced that they were after a severely retarded woman, and that intensified their search.

Within minutes they made the lake, and were stopped dead. A complete circle of the lake was made with the hounds, but there were no signs of Sandra O'Connell coming out of that lake. More than once they passed the old, broken-down boathouse, but it was obviously padlocked and there were no signs of any sort of forced entry. Once or twice one of the searchers would duck under and shine a light around, but saw nothing.

They decided then to drag the lake, and it took

time for the local fire department's rescue equipment to arrive. It was past six in the evening before they started dragging; the sun went down a little over two hours later, and they were forced to call it off for the night.

They had found two badly decomposed bodies in there, a lot of junk, and an entire automobile the New York State Police had been looking for as a getaway vehicle for over three years.

They didn't find Sandra O'Connell, and patrols that ringed the lake farther out found no sign, either. They concluded that she had to be in the lake when they knocked off for the evening. They felt sorry that they hadn't found her, but weren't in much of a rush any longer.

During this entire period, Sandra O'Connell slept in a drug-induced comatose state inside the boathouse, unmoving and barely breathing.

They were all gone by ten; most had been out in the field for many hours, through suppertime and beyond. They left their equipment and went home. An all-points bulletin was issued for her, however, on the off chance that she had indeed escaped. Phony name, of course. But they weren't finished with her, no, not finished.

Braden needed a body to preserve his own neck.

SIXTEEN

Jake Edelman checked the funny-looking greenish box that was now attached to his phone. It was a little larger than a cigar box. A three-pronged plug connected it to a nearby wall outlet, but the only sign of power was a dully-glowing red LED in the middle of the box's faceplate.

There was a recess in the top of the box containing a number of copper-clad conductors. From his pocket, Edelman removed what appeared to be a small pocket calculator with a series of copper bars on its back that corresponded to those in the recess atop the box. He placed it in the recess and pressed down, only to fume when it wouldn't go in.

Cursing, he glanced at his watch to see that it was approaching midnight. This thing had to be working by then. Finally he admitted defeat and buzzed for his secretary, an older woman named Maxine Bloom who'd been with him over ten years. She smiled that infuriating smile, grasped the calculator, turned it upside down, and put it in the recess. It snapped into place with a satisfying series of clicks.

He glowered at her to cover his embarrassment, sighed, cleared his throat, and nodded to her.

"You might as well be here anyway, Maxine," he said. "I can't take any notes or written records on this and I'll need a good back-up memory."

She nodded and took a chair to one side of his desk. It wouldn't have made any difference if she'd been there or not, he knew. Maxine was the best spy any office ever had. He was just thankful she was on his side.

He looked at her. "You checked the bug detector?" he asked.

She nodded. "Used the hand-held one, too. You know the department's computer missed two of them?" She didn't seem at all surprised. "The only leak's the phone, now—I guarantee it."

He shook his head in satisfaction. "The phone and box were installed and checked by the best," he said. "And then I un-installed it and had Fred do a number on both. It's clean."

"Let's have at it, then," his secretary suggested.

He turned and stared carefully at the calculator. It really wasn't one, of course; the numbers were more on the order of a touch-tone phone faceplate, with an additional two rows of symbols. He held his breath nervously as he punched the laborious thirty-two digit combination of numbers and symbols that would connect him with the party he wanted. One mistake and it would clear. Three mistakes and, on the third clear, it would short out.

Despite his nervousness, he didn't make any mistakes.

He put it on the speakerphone turned to low volume, then set up an additional desk-top debugger nearby that would let out a squeal if there were any last-minute attempts to eavesdrop. The debugger was the best there was; it was programmed to detect just about every known device except a person in the room or leaning against the door. He had other precautions against that old-fashioned kind of stuff. He was certain that if the device didn't go off no one else would hear him except those to whom he was talking.

A decade of counterespionage work was behind that confidence.

It was amazing, the number of clicks and funny phone-like noises the thing went through. First, anything going through his phone would pass through the incredibly sophisticated scrambler circuits in the green box. Unless you knew the entry key, there was simply no way to decipher the oddball digital scramble that came out the other end. Quite a number of government phones all over the country *did* know the key, and at midnight had punched the proper codes into their decoder boxes and waited for the phone to ring. All of those locations were also carefully debugged, and most would listen, not talk.

Additionally, the decoder slightly altered the received signal. In fact, it could make the speaker sound like anybody the programmer determined. A number of isolated military units using similar devices had given gruff-voiced muscular male sergeants high-pitched, sexy, feminine voices to relieve the boredom.

Jake thought this one made him sound like Mickey Mouse.

Finally the clicks and whirs stopped, and, one by one, lines were connected. He watched a little LED readout on the "calculator" tell him the number of connections being made. It was hoping too much that all would get it, but all but three checked in. Those three would later let him know, circuitously, who they were and why.

He locked the talk bar on his voice amplifier down.

"Ladies and gentlemen, thank you for all the time and trouble you have undergone at my instigation and your discomfort. What we are dealing with here, I believe, is something of such magnitude that such measures may, in fact, still be inadequate.

"Know, however, that *all* of you have undergone extensive mind-probes, so your headache is not a lonely one, nor connected to any one department. Those of you who underwent that ordeal should appreciate the fact that people like me, heading up this extraordinary organization, also underwent the same checks. In the process, we found twenty-six people—twenty-six!—who were, quite simply, on the wrong side. Two of these particularly amazed me, as they were people who had been with my department for years. I knew them personally, and would have trusted them with my life. This should be a warning to all of you. Trust no one, absolutely no one, unless you have personally cleared that person through our methods. And that means husbands, wives, children, you name it, as well as the partner who once saved your life." He paused to let the words sink in, grumbling slightly that so stern a warning should be delivered in Mickey's high-pitched tones.

"Now I will tell you what we are dealing with," he continued. He began with a recap of the history of the Wilderness Organism, sparing little. "And so, you see, the fact that the basic blueprints, as it were, for the Wilderness Organism were in the NDCC computer bank means that the disease is of domestic, even government manufacture. The killing of Spiegelman in an absolutely secure place and the kidnapping of O'Connell and Bede from NDCC itself just after they made the same discovery shows just how pervasive all this is."

He paused again for effect, about ready to drop the bomb. "Despite the use of those overage radicals and the tacit cooperation of some rather oddball Third World dictatorships, it is apparent that we are dealing with a plot that is basically domestic and reaches to the highest levels of government. CIA and FBI have striven in vain to find the source of the enemy, the brains behind it. We believe now that we have been looking too far afield, that this is a plot, carefully planned and prepared for years, perhaps decades, from within. There is a massive conspiracy here, and none of us is safe. We are currently under a state of quasi-military dictatorship, and this is hardening. Those within the government behind this plot can use this dictatorship, which is bureaucracy-supported, to do practically anything they wish, including kill me or you if we get in the way. There is only one way to wage a war against a shadow in your own house, and that is to create and deploy an organization as shadowy and tenuous as the enemy's. That's what you are, ladies and gentlemen. Soldiers in a war of shadows. Whichever side shines the bright light on the other first will win. We will use the computer data bank as our weapon, too. We will use the bureaucracy. And where a shadow is found, we will expose it to the glare of sunlight, extinguishing it. In three minutes this conversation will be automatically terminated; after that, you will be called by your own unit heads for instructions. Good luck and God bless you all."

He sighed and tapped the bar, then looked over at Maxine, herself a veteran of the nasty mind-probing techniques used to gather this squad.

He sighed. "Well, there it is, Maxine. A pep talk

to the troops. Somehow I never expected to be a general."

She grinned. "Jake, you make a fine one, even if you do sound like a mouse. You going to brief the Bureau people personally?"

He shook his head negatively. "No, I'll leave that to Bob. Give him forty minutes, then tell him I want to see him in here." He sank in his padded chair, looking suddenly tired, worn out.

"How long has it been since you've had some sleep?" his secretary asked.

"Two, three days, I guess. I tried a few times, but I just can't. The nightmares are too real."

She understood. "Jake, we're both Jewish. Our people have undergone every kind of horror known to history. We've always won in the end, Jake. Remember that."

"But at such a cost!" He sighed. "Six million in the Holocaust, God knows how many in the Israeli wars—and before that, back to the diaspora. You know what we were in the Middle Ages, Maxine? *Balebatishkeit.* Property. Walled in at night, trotted out when convenient, to get around Christianity's anti-usury laws or when they needed a scapegoat for something. For over fifteen hundred years, Maxine. This republic of ours has gone on for what? Two and a quarter centuries, more or less. A blink of the eye in history. And now—we have over two million people in concentration camps in the Southwest and Alaska, Maxine. Two million! And more coming as soon as they can build them. No trials, no questions. How many more are disappearing forever without anybody even knowing it? Gas controls so nobody can drive. Electricity controls, so nobody can ride. ID cards and lots of paperwork to take a plane or bus anyplace. A soldier on every street corner. How can *we* fight *that?* A totally controlled press. You remember Sonny Deiter, with the *Post?*"

She nodded.

"I saw him the other day. He told me that the big leaks on the Wilderness Organism story came from Her Highness Georgianne Meekins, the H&W Queen herself."

Maxine Bloom looked surprised. "You think *she . . .?*" The question trailed off.

He shrugged. "Who knows? Won't get any more from Sonny, either. The government censor at the *Post* canned him when he tried to sneak a story about the camps past to the copy desk. He's probably in one, now. Hell, Maxie, the American public doesn't even *know!* As long as they get their steady diet of soap operas and shoot-'em-ups, mow their lawns if they have any, and read *Schlock Confessions* while listening to funk music they're oblivious."

"Call Nadine," his secretary said. "Tell her you love her and all that. Then talk to Bob. After that, I'm going to get Maury Edwards up here to give you a sleep shot."

"Now wait a minute!" he protested.

She was hearing none of it. "Jake, we'll probably all be dead or in those camps before this is out," she said ominously. "If we aren't, it'll be because of the passion you've shown here. We can't afford to lose you, Jake. It's my neck, too, you know. How's the heart?"

He grimaced. "Okay, I guess. I feel so rotten it's hard to tell."

Maxine Bloom was one of a handful of people who knew that Edelman had had a triple bypass operation less than five years before. He was to have retired after that, but they needed him.

They all needed him now. He realized that, although the thought made him uncomfortable. So many lives, so many husbands, wives, children needed him, depended on him. He held their lives in his hand.

Maxine went out, and a little while later Bob Hartman came in. Thirty-ish, prematurely balding, Jake had rescued him from the obscurity of an inspectorship in Butte, Montana where he'd been sent for nailing a ranking senator with over $138,000 in illegal payoff money. The senator had resigned, of course, and was convicted and sentenced to three years' probation. They replaced him with another crook, and Hartman saw scenic Butte, where he'd considered quitting and taking a nice police job in a small town somewhere when Jake had tagged him. He was forever grateful to Jake, and intensely loyal to the little man.

"How'd it go?" the chief inspector asked his aide.

Hartman loosened his tie and threw his sportsjacket over the back of his chair. "Not bad. We have a pretty good selection of agents around the country, including here."

"No word on O'Connell or Bede as yet?" Edelman asked.

The younger man shook his head from side to side. "Nothing. Hell, they're probably dead. Even if they aren't, it was pretty easy to bury somebody before, and a cinch now. If anything turns up, though, we'll know it instantly."

That satisfied the boss; there was little else he could expect. Edelman changed the subject.

"What about the old rad connection? Anything?"

"None of the sleepers has surfaced, it that's what

you mean. Still, there're rumblings. Something big is up, something not clear but absolutely strong. Best guess is they're going to hit the cities—maybe one, maybe a lot, all at once."

"When?" Jake Edelman leaned forward.

"Nothing clear. Best guess is sometime during the week of September fifteenth."

Edelman involuntarily glanced over at his desk calendar. It was August twenty-fifth now, as he well knew.

Three weeks. Three weeks to win the war of shadows, and he was still too much in the dark.

SEVENTEEN

Twelve people sat in a small tent watching the instructor, six males and six females. For the last two weeks they'd lived together, trained together, practically showered together and washed behind each other's ears. But, aside from Sam and Suzy, none knew the names of the others.

"In two days," the political officer, who seemed to be an Arab told them, "you will leave Camp Liberty. You will travel independently, although if you wish a pair can go together. No more. You will be provided with all of the identification and background you will need to pass routine muster, but you will *not* be able to withstand a detailed check. Basically, you are all in the U.S. Army, all of you will have military IDs, uniforms, and orders. Act military, think military, and use their system to get you where you are going."

Suzy, who'd given up smoking anything but dope while at the camp, was back on the weeds now. They were foul-smelling, a Middle Eastern brand with Arabic writing on the pack. She lit one, then looked up at the instructor. Sam stared at her; he knew that manner, that gleam in her eyes. The old Suzy was back now, back in action, and she was loving every minute of it.

"Okay, so where are we going?" she asked.

The instructor nodded at a projectionist in the rear, the battery-powered lighting went out, and a slide projector came on.

"On August twenty-seventh you will be dropped at various points up to six hundred miles apart up and down the Atlantic Coast, far enough from each other to minimize suspicion of so many independent personnel going to an obscure place. Your orders will state that you are reporting for duty at Catoctin Station, the alternate Pentagon in the Catoctin Mountains just north of Frederick, Maryland, about a hundred kilometers from Washington, D.C., or Baltimore, Maryland. You won't be going there, though. Instead, you'll be heading here."

The slide, which had showed Maryland, then Frederick County, flipped again to show a closeup of the Catoctin area. The instructor walked to the screen and pointed to a spot just to the right and slightly south of Catoctin National Park. It was still parkland, and there seemed to be a lake there.

"At this recreation area," the instructor continued, "you will use the pay phone to call a number we will give you. You will call it, say your Camp Liberty number, and hang up. You won't be noticed—the place is currently off limits for tourists, and is used entirely by military personnel in the area to take days off. Relax and do the same. Someone will contact you there after they've looked you over and determined that you are indeed you. They will bring you to an old farmhouse we have prepared for you, and there you will wait until our people get to you and tell you where your weapons are."

That intrigued another of the team. "Weapons?"

The instructor nodded. "Standard pistols, rifles, and other equipment will await you in the farmhouse, of course. However, you will have to troop through some woodlands to get your share of blue cylinders."

They understood what that meant. They had practiced with mockups.

"You will, sorry, have to carry them back to your base, check them out, and store them. A supply of antidote and a large supply of syringes will be included as well for that particular strain, although, as you now know, the antidote is only effective for three to five days. That is enough, of course, but don't take it too early and feel protected. After you are set up, we will again contact you with your target, date, and equipment you will need to carry out our task. Please rest assured that we will provide material to effectively paint and disguise the cylinders. Anyone walking in the U.S. right now with a blue sprayer of any kind would get hung on the spot by locals. We had to place the caches before the military emergency ever was declared, though, so blue and exposed they will be when you carry them back to base. Remember that!"

"What happens then?" Sam asked.

"Huh?" The instructor was taken aback by the question, and didn't seem to know quite what was on the big man's mind.

"After we accomplish the mission," Cornish said. "Then what?"

"Why, you get the hell out of there and back to base, and then your target gets very sick, that's what," the political officer replied, still puzzled.

"No, no," the big man pressed. "After that. Then what happens to *us?*"

"You'll have to stay underground for quite some time," the instructor said. "After all, when all of the teams strike all over the nation at the same time, there will be all hell breaking loose." *That* was true enough. "After that, we will have other work for you. I have already told you as much as I dare. One or more of you could get picked up, you know."

The briefing ended abruptly at that point, and they walked back to their quarters. Suzy was silent for a little while, then turned to him. "What's the matter? Why did you press him like that?"

He frowned. "I don't like it. There's something wrong here, something smelly. You don't feel it?"

She shook her head. "I think you've just got the willies."

"It's more than that," he insisted. "Well, like, for instance, why did he tell us about the farmhouse? If any of us were picked up, the pigs could sweep every farmhouse in that county and the others on all sides, looking for one with a new group of tenants who roughly fit descriptions they'd have."

"You're crazy," she said. "Ten to one they've had it established for quite a while, with people who look kind of like us. You worry too much." She reached up, kissed him, then swatted him one in the behind. It didn't shake him out of it.

"Maybe you don't worry enough," he said softly, wondering if in fact she ever worried at all.

EIGHTEEN

Sandra O'Connell awoke. It was pitch dark wherever she was, and damp, and terribly smelly. Everything seemed odd; she tried to sit up and found for a while that she could not. Finally, after several tries, she did it, but her head was spinning and her whole body feeling oddly numb, distorted, misshapen.

She tried to think, to remember where she was and how she'd gotten here, wherever it was. Memories were misty, fragmented, disjointed, but she had a sense of identity, she knew who she was. She remembered, as if through the wrong end of a spyglass, walking out into the lobby of NDCC, being approached by the security men, going into an office—and that was that. Nothing more until now. How long ago? Days? Weeks? Worse?

Almost as disturbing was the quality of the memories; nothing would go together right, get connected. There were odd scenes, strange places and faces, and she couldn't connect names or situations to any of them. It was a disembodied collection; she seemed to remember those things as if she'd been a third-party observer there, and her mind sometimes pictured her own image in a place or conversation fragment as if she were seeing through someone else's eyes.

She moved her arm out a little and touched something soft and large. It startled her, and she almost screamed, but managed to get hold of herself. Steeling herself in the darkness, she reached back out again, felt it, then grabbed it and picked it up. It was a real job picking it up, although it was neither heavy nor bulky. Her hand and arm didn't feel right, wouldn't quite do what she wanted and willed them to do.

At first the shape of the thing puzzled her. There was no light to see by although the perception of a slight glow coming through slats somewhere assured her she was not blind. Finally she felt the sewn mouth, the button nose and two plastic eyes.

A teddy bear? she thought, totally confused.

She tried to collect her thoughts. It was easier to concentrate on one thing at a time, although matters were still cloudy, dreamlike and easily lost.

Drugs, she decided. They had drugged her with some sort of hypnotic or hallucinogen, and for quite a long while, too. This was bad; some such drugs had lasting, even permanent side effects and after-effects, and this scared her.

Somehow, though, she knew, she'd been drugged and locked away and had still managed to escape. That was the only explanation for her being here. But if she had escaped, then they were looking for her, and could find her at any moment.

She felt around the shed, finding the two half-broken boards that had been her entryway. Slowly, carefully, she edged over to the opening, and carefully dangled her legs down.

Her feet touched water. It was odd; that tingling numbness was still there, and contact with the water produced a sensation more like wading in gelatin, but the message of *water* came through.

She hesitated for a moment, first to listen for any sounds—there were none she could hear except insects and the lapping of the water—and then because she had no idea how deep the water would be. Finally she decided to chance it; it couldn't be *very* deep or she'd never have gotten inside in a drugged condition. Cautiously she lowered herself down. It was little more than knee-high, which was a relief.

She bent low and emerged from under the boathouse, looking around. It was still dark, but her eyes, accustomed to it from the moment of awakening, saw fairly well the lake and the looming shadows of boats, lights, and equipment. Only one small light was on now, far over to the other side. There seemed to be some movement there, a guard perhaps, but whoever it was had to be pretty far off. The sky was overcast, and the humid air had the feel of thunderstorm about it.

She moved away from the light, back to the shore behind the boathouse, and looked around. Trees all over, it looked like from the darkness and the sounds. She knew she had to get moving fast or else they would catch her, even though she didn't know who "they" were. Then she heard the sound of a distant truck just off to her left. *A road!* she thought excitedly. Not too far, either. She decided to head for it, despite the risk of exposure there. Roads went somewhere, and somewhere was where she needed to go.

She was still uncoordinated; it took a little time for her to get things moving in a semblance of normality, but she made the trees and bushes nearest the direction her ears assured her the road was.

Once concealed in the foliage, she paused, feeling

momentarily safe and hidden, and took stock of herself. It was dark and she was farsighted without her glasses, so visual checks were blurry and tenuous. Still, she found that she was dressed in tattered shreds of what must have been a hospital gown, and nothing else. She was dirty and covered with grease and grime, but, mercifully, someone had cut her hair extremely short, so it was the least of her problems.

She was a little chilly, but it was the result of the high humidity and approaching storm—and yet the overall warmth and humidity cheered her in that they said that it was still summer, and perhaps not a whole lot of time had passed. The thought that she might be in Florida or some other warm climate area crept slightly up to her thoughts, but was pushed back as unacceptable.

The sound of another truck came, somewhere ahead of her, and she started for it. Stumbling, still dizzy and feeling somewhat disembodied, she made the road in about half an hour.

It was a pretty fancy freeway: four lanes in each direction cutting a swath through the wilderness. It would take a lot of traffic to justify a road like this; in normal times it would be crowded day and night. It was empty now.

There was a green exit sign off to her right, and she headed for it, hoping that it would tell her where she was. Keeping close to the bushes and trees in case another truck should come out of the darkness, she came close to the big sign in a few minutes.

And, suddenly, she felt real panic, and started to tremble and feel sick. Despite her farsightedness, she was in good position to read the huge white-on-green letters and they stood out reasonably well in the lightning flashes.

They just didn't make any sense. Her mind simply refused to put the symbols together into words she could recognize, no sounds or images forming as she stared at them.

She spent a few minutes getting hold of herself, telling herself it was another byproduct of the drug that would wear off in time, but that thought only helped a little.

There was a rumbling sound off in the distance, and before she could move a large tractor-trailer truck came over the hill and rumbled toward her, its bright lights cutting like knives through the darkness. She flattened against the ground, and it came toward her as she held her breath. Finally it passed, fairly close to her, its lights briefly illuminating her but obviously not enough to give the driver a clear look at her. It went past without slowing down, a big rig with a tandem trailer, and passed out of sight.

She turned slowly and looked at the sign again. It still made no sense to her, but now she noticed the little blue signs underneath. These were symbols telling what could be found at the exit. The little white words underneath were so many random squiggles, but there was the tent sign that meant *camping*—the lake, of course—and an additional white cross that meant *hospital*.

Hospital, she thought. Of course.

She looked at the squiggles underneath, knowing what they must say, but they just wouldn't say the words to her.

She'd heard of the effect, but its happening to her was terrifying.

Still, there was nothing that could be done about it. It was probably something that would pass, she had to believe that, and clung to it. For now, she had to get moving, and that meant away from that hospital, away from this exit sign.

She was starting to feel hungry, with a particular craving for something sweet, but she knew that meals might be few and far between in the near future.

Now what, though? she mused, a dark feeling of hopelessness coming on. She was as good as naked, hungry, in a wilderness the whereabouts of which she didn't know, and with, undoubtedly, a search on for her.

Escaping was a lot easier in the movies than it was in real life. Still, the alternative, turning herself in and going back to wherever she'd come from, was as good as death to her. That truck had to be going somewhere important; she decided to keep hidden but follow the road.

Several hours later, when the sunrise told her that she was heading west, she was itchy and aching and even more hungry, but at least the storm had not hit and the clouds seemed to be breaking up a bit.

At the next exit there was a military checkpoint. Several trucks were backed up as soldiers examined cargoes, bills of lading, and the truckers' passes and orders before allowing them to proceed. They were not looking for anyone on foot out here, though, and she avoided them easily.

A bit later in the morning she came upon a small pool, panicking some deer who'd stopped for their early morning drink. In the surface of the pool she could see herself for the first time.

The water could be used to wash off some still painful cuts and to get rid of some of the dirt and grime. It made her feel better, but the gown was only a collection of rags held by tenuous threads into a semblance of a garment now, and stained with oil and grease. Her hair had been cut in a boyish style and to within three centimeters in length. Even slightly blurred and distorted by her vision and the pool, she thought her face looked more like a young man's in his mid-twenties than a woman in her early forties. It looked like a different person entirely. The rest of her body, however, betrayed her sex if not her age. She was in very good condition and had a nice shape which the remains of the gown did nothing to hide.

She drank some needed water and headed back into the woods toward the road. After a minute or two she hit a huge patch of moss and lichens growing out from and connecting several fairly large trees. The result formed a mat which felt soft and nice, and she was terribly tired. She stretched out on it to rest for a few minutes, and was soon fast asleep.

She awoke when the sun was across the sky. She felt rested and refreshed, although her back ached from the uneven natural bed. The disembodied and uncoordinated feelings remained, but could be controlled. A result of the sleep, though, had been, in twisting and tossing, the end of the bindings of the gown.

She considered what to do now. Oddly, being alone and naked in the wilderness had an oddly sexual feeling. This feeling of arousal disturbed her, but she couldn't fight it.

Still, naked she was even more restricted, and she turned finally to the remains of the gown. It was a long one, of course, which had caused some of the problems, but there was a fair amount of whole cloth left. Carefully experimenting, trying it several ways, tearing a bit here and there, she managed to make a makeshift wraparound that covered her from bust to a little below the thighs. Binding it together was a pain. She finally managed, by a combination of biting and tearing, to make a couple of small holes and use the remnants of the gown's straps as a sort of tie, done in front so there would be little chance of slippage without her knowing it.

She was so proud of her fast-thinking handiwork that it was all the more frustrating when she couldn't seem to tie bows in the straps. She finally managed to make knots, knots that might have to be broken to be untied, but it made an unholy mess and drew the thing tightly where tied. They were like a little child's attempts at knots, she thought angrily, but after a lot of false tries they seemed to hold and that would be enough for now.

Near dusk she reached some vineyards. The country was picture-postcard style, with rows upon rows of grape vines stretching out in all directions. They were sour and probably not yet ripe, yet she ate them and ate them, spitting out seeds with abandon. They filled a need, and if they made her sick later, well, so what?

She crossed the vineyards by the light of a three-quarters moon, disturbing a couple of dogs that stayed mercifully distant, and skirting around the large farm area that was obviously the headquarters for the vineyards. She still couldn't read the logo on the sign, but it was obvious that this was part of a major winery operation.

Wine country, she thought. The soldiers at the road check had been in familiar uniforms, so she was sure she was still in the United States. If that were so, where would major vineyards be? Northern California or New York State, most likely, she decided. The land didn't look like the Napa Valley, and the trees looked more northern than anything else.

Upstate New York, then, she decided. It made her feel better. New York State—she tried to think. Wasn't the wine country somewhere in the northwest part? That would make the road the New York Throughway, which went to the Great Lakes, to Buffalo, Niagara Falls—and Canada.

Canada.

And she was heading west!

But how far, she wondered. Hundreds of kilometers, or was it over the next hill?

No matter. For the first time she dared to hope.

The next hill didn't reveal Buffalo, but it did reveal a small town nestled in a pretty valley with a small river flowing almost through it. In the moonlight it looked almost storybook in quality, a fairy tale village of a couple of thousand homes. A number of older houses on a series of very large lots were off on a small road by themselves. She was attracted to them by the long clotheslines they all had in their backyards. She hoped that at least one of them would do washing today, and that, somehow, she could sneak down and steal something, even if a sheet and clothespins, to replace her disintegrating makeshift garment.

She picked a spot and settled down to wait. It didn't matter how long, she thought wearily. The grapes had soured her stomach but stayed down; she could always sneak back for more. She would wait until the opportunity presented itself for her to get clear with what she needed.

Down at the far end of the road, where it met the main road from the town to the freeway, she spied a phone booth. She chuckled to herself. With a quarter she could call for help.

Or could she? she suddenly thought. Who would she get? While she waited for them to find someone she could trust, the inevitable security patrol tap would pick her out, and it would be back to the hospital and the drugs again. The operator could be called without money, of course, but it would bring the local cops and the same result.

No, she decided. She was on her own and she would remain so as long as possible. If she were going to place any calls, they would be from Canada or not at all.

For a while she dozed, awakened once when a curious dog came by. The small black and white mutt proved friendly, however, and didn't betray her. She petted him. He licked her face, and, after a while, lost interest and wandered off.

Nobody did their washing the next day, but the house at the end of the row of a dozen or so caught her interest just the same. She watched through the day and saw a young woman leave the house and walk down the hill to a lot where there were a number of school busses parked. The woman got in one, started it up, and rolled off; soon the others were started by men and women walking from different parts of town.

She watched the house for some time. There was no sign of life there, although other houses along the row had people going to and fro, being picked up in clearly marked company cars and minibusses, and from a few there were the sounds of radio and TV and stereos.

But not the house on the end. The woman was gone about two hours, then came back and parked the bus out front of the house, next to a very dusty little foreign car.

The little black-and-white dog was doing what dogs have done for an eternity in her backyard, and the woman spotted the mutt as she drove up. She jumped out and ran back, yelling at the dog to get out of there. The dog got, but it was too late; he'd already left a messy souvenir.

Muttering to herself, the young woman turned and opened the back door of her house. This excited Sandra O'Connell; she'd opened the back door without a key. The house had been left unlocked.

The back door was still open now, and no noises issued from the screen. The placed looked a little big for just one person, but she dared to hope. Reservists would be off on security duty now; it was just possible that, for one reason or another, the woman was alone in that house.

She waited and watched through the hot, muggy afternoon. Twice the woman in the house emerged for one thing or another, but nobody else. Finally, after a long and hard wait, in which the temptation to return to the vineyards or find a brook for a drink was almost overpowering, the woman of the house left again, entered the school bus and, making a three-point turn, started off down the hill again.

She *had* to take the chance, she decided. Had to. There was no choice in the matter. Later, when she could—*if* she could—she would pay this woman back somehow.

Just when she was preparing to make her move,

the back door of the house next door opened and a middle-aged woman emerged, dressed in a skimpy garden-type suit that made her look ridiculous.

Sandra O'Connell watched nervously, knowing that precious minutes were being lost, while the woman pulled open an aluminum-framed lawn recliner, lay down, slapped on some tanning lotion, and relaxed.

It seemed like forever until the old bag fell asleep. There was the sound of gentle snoring, and her mouth was open.

Sandra saw that the woman with the bus hadn't closed the back door; there was only the screen door to contend with, and without waking up the sleeping neighbor.

Cautiously but deliberately Sandra stepped out of the bushes and walked toward the door. The little dog saw her and ran to her, running around her playfully. She was almost to the back door when the dog started after a butterfly, went over into the next yard, and almost ran into the sleeping woman there.

Silently the amateur burglar opened the kitchen door and closed it quietly behind her, and just in time, too. The dog had made one leap too many at the butterfly, started barking, and awakened the matronly sunbather.

Once inside the house Sandra didn't worry about what was happening outside; time was pressing.

The house was smaller than it seemed: a one-story affair with a large kitchen, a dining room, a small living room, and two bedrooms, one of which was made up to look like a tiny den.

The bedroom contained a queen-sized bed and some dressers. A photo next to the bed of a man in uniform confirmed her belief that the woman's husband was, in fact, away.

Sandra couldn't get her own makeshift garment untied, and finally ripped it off. She opened a closet, and came face to face with a full-length mirror which startled her.

She looked a mess, it was true, but still somehow young and attractive, far younger than her years, although the image remained slightly blurry to her.

Finding a perfect fit was something she didn't expect and didn't achieve, either. She rejected a lot of clothing that would fit, though, simply because it required some kind of undergarments, and those definitely would *not* fit.

An old, ragged, washed-out and faded pair of jeans proved a tight fit, but she managed to pull them around her thighs and zip them up, although it took tremendous effort and more precious time. She felt like she had a tightening noose around her waist.

The woman had some shirts but they didn't fit; she found under a pile of old clothing some white tee shirts that were obviously destined for a rag bin. They were the man's shirts, or undershirts, but they had shrunk in the wash. One of them went on all right, but felt wrong in the shoulders and didn't go all the way down to her jeans, exposing her navel. She looked at herself in the mirror. A bad fit, with the very short haircut setting it all off wrong.

She looked like an overage high-schooler on the make.

Well, it would have to do. None of the shoes or sandals fit; she was in a hurry and decided to abandon them. She took a few precious seconds to put everything back in an undisturbed condition, hoping that it would be some time if ever before the theft was noticed. The remains of the gown she picked up and took with her; it would be discarded outside later, perhaps in a convenient garbage can.

Going back to the kitchen, she noticed, on the small dining table, a purse. She couldn't resist. Looking in, she spotted the wallet with several bills inside. She took them and a little change and squeezed the money into a front pocket of her incredibly tight and uncomfortable jeans. She went back to the kitchen, looked in the refrigerator, and grabbed a piece of cake from a half-finished store-bought creation. Now she went back to the back door, looking out.

The matronly woman was awake and petting the dog. A middle-aged man farther down was mowing his lawn.

Panicked, she walked to the front door, opened it carefully, and looked out. Nobody was in sight, although, down the road, she could see a yellow school bus pulling into the lot and she was pretty sure who was driving. She decided to chance it, walked out the front door, closed it firmly, and went out to the street and slowly started walking down. She was still holding the remains of the gown, and when she got near the bottom of the hill, at a little bridge over a brook leading to the river, she walked down, shoved a rock into the cloth, and pushed it down into the wet stream-bottom. A couple of rocks on top finished the job.

And now, for the first time, feeling satisfied with herself, she suddenly realized that what she'd done meant very little. Up on the overpass to her left was a military checkpoint; to her right and ahead was a small town where a stranger, particularly now, dur-

ing the emergency, would stand out like a sore
thumb.

She didn't care immediately. She was hungry, and
there seemed to be a drive-in food stand a couple of
blocks away. She headed toward it, thankful at least
that she could now walk in civilized company. Even
barefoot and in painfully tight old clothing, she no
longer felt like a wild beast, naked in the wilderness.

There were three trucks stopped at the drive-in,
big, long-distance rigs. She considered it. Trucks
and military vehicles were obviously the only things
that moved without a lot of official help these days.

She still felt uncoordinated and distant, but she
had to risk it. She went up to the drive-in, a little
two-person shack, really, and looked at the hand-
lettered menu. Nervousness started to creep in
again; she couldn't keep it down. The jittery feeling
seemed to affect her thinking; it muddied, and she
felt confusion where, minutes before, she'd been
thinking fairly clearly.

She couldn't read the menu. *That* hadn't changed.
But she could see a small grill near the window, and
smell hamburgers cooking. It was irresistible.

She went up to the window. A girl who looked
young enough to be in high school stared at her
curiously and asked, "Yes ma'am?"

Sandra started to say something, suddenly realiz-
ing that these would be the first words uttered since
she woke up in the boathouse, and she stammered.
She wanted to say, "I'll have a hamburger, please,"
but she couldn't seem to get it up. Finally she
pointed to a picture of a hamburger on the side of
the service window and asked, "How much is one of
those?"

The girl gave her something of a pitying look, and

she suddenly realized that she must have looked and sounded like a retarded person.

"Two dollars with a Coke thrown in," the girl told her.

Sandra reached into her pocket and brought out the bills. She was suddenly doubly confused, and the more confused and frustrated she was the more so she became. She took one of the five crumpled bills and handed it with some difficulty to the girl.

She was patient, at least. "You need one more," she said softly.

O'Connell fumbled, got the other bill and handed it to the girl.

"And twenty cents for tax," the girl persisted. Sandra reached in, took some coins out, and put them on the window ledge.

"Take out what you want," she told the girl.

A quarter was removed, the sale was rung up, a nickel was replaced, and, shortly, a hamburger and a Coke arrived.

Embarrassed, upset, and ashamed as well as a little afraid of her conspicuousness, she put the change back in her pocket and took the food and drink over to a picnic table.

She ate the burger greedily and sloppily, and the Coke was gone almost as quickly. She wiped off her mouth with a paper napkin and calmed herself down.

The drug they had given her, she decided, must be a particularly nasty one. Two days after it'd worn off, her brain still wasn't working nearly right, and she was afraid that it might not ever get back to normal.

The problem wasn't really with her thinking, though. It was with making her body do what her mind commanded. A series of little short circuits kept coming up. She knew what a hamburger was, knew the word, but somehow couldn't get it out when she wanted to. She could count, too, except when she had to.

She was still sucking on the ice, sitting there, letting the sun which had already darkened her body warm it more, when one of the truck drivers came over to the table, put down two burgers and a shake, and sat down opposite her.

"Hello, there!" he said pleasantly.

She broke out of her reverie. "Hi," she managed, listening to how childish it sounded floating from her lips, both a little higher and softer than it should have been.

He was a rough but kindly-looking man, perhaps in his mid-forties, with a sleeveless blue shirt and jeans over cowboy boots.

"You look kinda lost," he said.

She smiled crookedly. "I am, kinda," she admitted.

"You're not from around here, then?"

She shook her head, and now her will power forced itself through. The same mind that couldn't think of hamburger when it needed it managed something more difficult, although haltingly, with effort great enough that it reinforced the retarded image.

"I'm from Buf'lo," she volunteered. "I been stuck here, run outta money an' all."

The trucker looked her over, trying to fit her into his current world picture. The woman was older than she looked, he could see it in her face, but he couldn't guess how old. Mid-thirties, maybe. So here was a woman, mid-thirties, dressed like she was twenty and talking like she was a slow twelve. He made a guess.

"You have an identity and movement card?" he asked suspiciously.

That question unnerved her. It was outside of her available memory, this encounter with military checkpoints, monitoring devices, and such things as identity and movement cards. Since the emergency had begun, she'd been drugged and locked up. She'd had a card, of course, but never the occasion to need it.

"N—no," she stammered.

He shook his head slowly. He was pretty sure he had it, now.

"You wanna get back home, honey?" he asked her casually.

She leaped at it. "Y-yes, sure, yeah."

"I'm headin' to Buffalo. There's plenty of room. I'll take you," he volunteered.

She was stunned. This was better luck than she had reason to dream about. Suddenly a thought entered her head. "The soldiers . . ."

He smiled. "Don't worry none about them. I make this run between Syracuse and Buffalo so many times they know me by my first name." When he had finished his burgers, they tossed their trash in the can and went over to his rig.

She'd never been inside a tractor before. There was lots of room, and even a bed behind the seats. There were too many gearshifts and pedals and such to figure out; driving one of these rigs was definitely a lot harder than driving a car.

With much shifting and double-clutching, he backed up, then moved forward and around to the road. It was an interesting and somewhat exciting view; had the man not been so much in command of his cab, she would have been even more nervous, though. They were sitting over the engine, so when the front of the truck cleared a tree by inches it was inches from the windshield as well.

He pulled onto the entrance ramp, climbed laboriously up, and entered the highway.

"Lots easier since they got the cars off," he muttered.

It was bouncy and uncomfortable, but it was a ride to where she needed to go.

Checkpoints were infrequent on the freeway; for the most part it was exits that were monitored, so it was about thirty miles before they had to slow to a stop. They'd talked little, which was all right with her, and he played irritating country music on his radio and sang along.

Now, as he slowed for the checkpoint, he shut off the radio and glanced at her.

"What's your name, honey?" he asked, seemingly unconcerned.

She was going to give a false name, but "Sandy" came out.

He nodded. "Okay, Sandy. Just sit and look bored and let me take it. This is the only one we'll face until we get off in Buffalo, so relax."

He pulled to a stop, set the brakes, and got out of the cab. She could hear him talking to the soldiers, all of whom looked very young and very bored, and once he came back and reached in, grabbed a sheaf of papers on a clipboard, winked at her, and returned to the soldiers.

Finally, after what seemed like forever, he climbed back in, stuck the clipboard back in its holder, and put the truck in gear.

She was amazed. "How—how did you get me past?" she asked him.

He grinned. "Told 'em a tall story. They like tall stories, they're young enough to want to believe. Don't worry. We'll have you home sometime tonight."

About ten miles down the road darkness overtook them; about three miles beyond that he took a turn for a rest area, pulled up in the rear parking area where it was almost completely dark, and turned to her.

"Okay, honey, time to pay the fare," he said jovially.

She was confused, and reached into her pocket, pulling out the remaining bills. "This is all I got," she said apologetically.

He laughed. "Now I see what happened to you," he said. "They took you out for a party with the soldiers, with some other girls, and when it came time to do what they brought you for, you wouldn't —so they stuck you there. Right?"

She was appalled. "Noooo . . ." she protested.

"Oh, yes," the driver said, still not unkindly.

Sandra O'Connell had been raised in the upper middle class, had gone to sheltered parochial school and a good Catholic college. She was not a virgin, but she had lived alone for a long time. Her whole life had been a protection—the right schools, the right neighborhood, the right government hospitals and agencies.

Even at her age, she was naive about the real world.

Now that real world caused panic to race through her. She fumbled for the door, but the driver reached out, grabbed her with powerful arms, pulled her to him, and started kissing her. She kicked and started lashing out with her arms, and that finally made him mad. He slapped her, hard, and while she was reeling from it she felt him undo her jeans. She tried to pull away, but he'd partially undressed her now and, holding her wrists together with a brawny, incredibly powerful hand, he turned her over and bound her hands with some cord and her feet with a spare belt.

And, for some time afterward, he did to her exactly what he pleased in that little bed in the back of the cab.

When he was through, he climbed back into the front seat of the truck, put his own pants back on, then his cowboy boots, and put the truck in gear. Once back out on the road he turned on the country music and started whistling to it. She was still bound in the back.

Sandra O'Connell felt sick, disgusted, furious. She would cheerfully have shot this animal at the wheel if given the chance, but she didn't have the chance. She was as helpless now as she had been during the ordeal.

She lay there, stunned and helpless, as he rolled on. Finally, after a period of time she could not judge, he stopped again, climbed in back, picked her up and brought her to the front seat. He released her bonds, and when she started for him he belted her almost senseless.

She gave up.

"Git your pants on," he ordered. "Time for you to get out."

She had a hard time complying with that, and he helped, somewhat painfully, with the zipper.

Finally he said, "Okay, now we both got what we

wanted. Now git, and don't fall for any more party
gags again." His tone of voice infuriated her even
more. He was giving her a lecture in morality, as if
she'd done something terrible and he'd meted out
punishment for it to cure her of future wrongdoing.

"I'll tell on you!" she warned him.

He shrugged. "Go ahead. See if anybody'll listen.
All you'll do is get arrested for no IDs and passes.
Hell, woman, they don't *care* about people like us
any more. They never did."

He pushed her out of the cab, slammed the door,
and roared off.

She collected her thoughts, looked around for the
first time, and saw that she was not, as he'd said,
quite in Buffalo. He'd let her out at a roadside area
by the river, before he had to exit and go through
another checkpoint.

What made her feel even more helpless was that
the man didn't realize how safe he was. She couldn't
read his licensing or pass information, couldn't read
the name of his trucking company, or even the numbers on his truck. What was worse, even if she knew
his whole history and full address, she could still do
nothing. She had police to avoid and capture to
evade.

So she climbed down the side of the embankment,
bruised and hurting all over, and found a culvert,
and there she sat down and cried like hell.

She dozed fitfully in the culvert, finally giving it
up as an impossibility. She hurt too much, so at last
she made her way around and looked out on the
water. It was very dark, but a large ship was going
by, a Lakes tanker of some kind, and its flag, lit by

stern lights, was not her flag. A Canadian ship, she thought wistfully. That must be Canada over there, she realized with a surge of renewed energy and hope.

There were other, smaller boats about as well, she saw. Small, fast patrol boats that seemed to keep closer to the other side, perhaps a kilometer or less from her perch.

She searched her memory, and recalled that a narrow neck or peninsula of Canada came over almost to Buffalo, splitting Lakes Erie and Ontario. But why the patrol boats?

Suddenly she was brought up short. She remembered idly reading that the centuries-old unfortified border between the two largest North American nations was now effectively patrolled by both sides, and that fences and guards were being erected all along it. The U.S. wanted to take no chances on an infiltration from Canada, whose borders were far less secure and much vaster than those of the U.S., and the Canadians, in turn, didn't want anyone coming over and bringing any funny bacteria. They were hardly sealed off; there was too much economic interdependence for that. But they were a lot tougher than they used to be.

So near and yet so far, she thought. How will I ever get across?

She considered swimming. She'd always been a good swimmer, but the current was fast here and she was still uncertain of how much stamina and control she had in her body.

And yet, the more she thought about it, the more the idea appealed. There were some bridges, of course, but they were sure to be guarded and restricted. The odds of finding a boat and being able to use it were slimmer still; the boats would be carefully watched and examined.

A kilometer, she thought again. Perhaps less. The small patrol boats seemed to come out in a regular pattern every few minutes to roughly the center of the channel, go down it for a bit, meet others coming the other way, and turn. If worst came to worst, she could hail one of the boats and take her chances. If the swim proved too much, there were alternatives like floating for a while and eventually getting back to shore on this side.

It was worth a try, she decided. She was almost ready to jump in when she saw a different-looking, slightly larger white craft cruise by, spotlights trained on the U.S. bank. It wasn't hard to make out the U.S. Coast Guard logo. The Canadians weren't the only ones patrolling the border.

The light was haphazard and missed her easily, but the patrol gave her a moment's pause. There was that danger, too—as well as the danger of being shot at, perhaps, by either side.

There was no choice. It was dark and the boats were far away now. She slid into the water.

It was damned cold, and that gave her some worry at the beginning, but she soon grew accustomed to it. Her wet clothing was in the way, but she was damned if she was going to shuck it and go through this to the end stark naked.

The current proved deceptively slow; dams and canal locks kept it from rushing with the force of Niagara only thirty or so kilometers north, and the old swimming skills came back to her, were there as if she'd never been out of the water. She wasn't a particularly strong or fast swimmer, but she could swim reasonably well and for long periods. Ordinarily she could take this distance in a moderate pace, but some grapes, a piece of cake, and a hamburger and Coke weren't the best stores of energy. She tired quickly, and let herself drift until she got her breath back, then started again.

The patrol boats with their searchlights came again, and again, but they didn't see her. She reached and clung to a center-channel buoy for a while, until she was ready to try the rest of the way. She was in Canadian waters now, and somehow that felt safer.

Inside of ten more minutes, she was within sight of shore. Some automobile lights were moving on a road back from the dark shoreline, an indication in itself that she was in Canada now, nearly safe.

She made the other side, and faced a wooden wall that didn't look at all hard to climb although a bit slippery. She reached the top, only three meters above her, hauled herself out of the channel and lay there on her back, gasping and exhausted but feeling exultant.

She'd made it!

Suddenly a voice said, in a slight Canadian accent not too far from her, "Just lie still there, ma'am, and don't move. I have a rifle trained on you and it has an infrared sniperscope attached."

She lay still as ordered, too tired to care what he said and too washed out to have made a move if she'd wanted to.

She heard the sentry or whatever he was talking on a walkie-talkie, but couldn't hear either end of the conversation.

"What is your name and why have you swum the channel?" the sentry demanded.

"San-San*dra,*" She forced herself to speak.

"Sandra O'Con-nell. I have been drugged and kept in a pris'n. I got away. I need help."

The sentry relayed this through his walkie-talkie.

A couple of minutes passed with no words between them. She just lay there and looked at the patrol boats and city lights across the way and marveled to herself that she'd swum that. Now an ambulance arrived, and she heard people getting out. She turned, and was surprised to see that they wore protective suits of some kind.

They lifted her gently onto a stretcher and wheeled her efficiently to the ambulance, slid her in the back, and closed the doors. No one got in with her, to her surprise, and they were soon under way.

There was a hissing sound, which, she discovered, was oxygen being pumped into the rear chamber which was, incongruously, sealed.

They have me in isolation, she realized with a start.

For a moment she was afraid that she was not in Canada. However, there was a light on inside her mobile cubicle revealing no inside door handles but also showing the oxygen supply system. She couldn't read the red warnings, but there were two sets of them, one under the other, with a maple leaf atop each.

It was Canada, all right.

The ambulance—or prison van?—stopped and backed up now. Someone fumbled with the doors, and they opened to reveal a strange plastic tunnel of some kind.

"Please get up if you can and walk through the tube," a crisp, official voice said. "If you can not walk, say so, and we will arrange to move you."

"I can walk," she said, and got up unsteadily,

staggering a bit. Suddenly she wondered if she really could.

The plastic tunnel went about ten meters, and felt sticky to her bare feet. She entered a doorway then, and recognized a standard-looking hospital corridor.

"Proceed to the chair facing the window to your left," the PA voice said, and she saw what it meant and went there.

It was a comfortable chair that felt very, very good. There was a microphone in front of it, and, she saw double glass in front. On the other side sat an official-looking gray-haired man in a black suit and striped tie. He, too, was equipped with a microphone.

"I am Inspector Charles Douglas of the RCMP," he told her. "You understand that you are being isolated because we have no idea what you might or might not be bringing us, and medical tests will have to be made to clear you."

She nodded.

"I want you to tell your story into the microphone," he instructed. "Spare nothing. Take as long as you want, but hold nothing back. It is being recorded."

She nodded again. "I have been un'er drugs for a long time," she told him. "Bad ones. They have hurt me, done some brain dam'ge, don' know how bad or if it'll wear off in time."

The inspector nodded. "You aren't the first one we've encountered," he told her. "Just go ahead, relax, take all the time you need to collect yourself."

She did. It was tough going, telling the story in halting phrases and malformed words. She spared nothing, though. Not who she was, what she was doing, about being spirited away, about waking up and its problems escaping, even the rape.

Douglas sounded sympathetic but noncommittal. When she finished he just puffed on a pipe for a few minutes, thinking about it. Then he said, "There is a shower just down the hall, a closet with some hospital clothes, and a bed. I suggest you go make use of them and get some sleep while this information goes to Ottawa. If you're hungry, we can send in some food."

"I'm starved," she told him, "but I'm more tired than an'thing." She got up and he did the same. She looked at him seriously through the glass. "Thank you," she said.

He didn't reply.

She was out of the painful clothing in seconds and showered thoroughly, particularly flushing the memories of the trucker out as much as possible.

Another hospital gown, but white this time and much better made, and a typical hospital bed which she sank into gratefully. She remembered little else.

While she slept, the recording and Douglas's report went to Ottawa by RCMP wire. Officials there studied it, considered it, discussed it. Hospital technicians in isolation garb took fingerprints from her sleeping form, and these, too, were transmitted and matched up.

Finally, decisions were made. They called the National Disease Control Center for verification of the existence of a Sandra O'Connell, and notified the FBI through priority channels to get confirmation of her photo and prints.

The FBI check flagged the computer monitors in the Special Section, Jake Edelman's branch. Bob Hartman was called, checked out the print information, determined that, indeed, it *was* Dr. Sandra O'Connell they had in Ontario, and called Jake.

Edelman was excited. It was the first real break in the domestic side of the case. "Hell, if we can get her back she can tell us a lot about where she's been!" he said hopefully. "We can trace the sons of bitches back to here!"

The Buffalo office was called on the special line, reaching a particular agent at home. She was told to go to Diefenbaker Hospital and see Dr. O'Connell, and if possible to take her out of there and get a plane direct to Washington. One was being readied to pick them up by another friendly commander at an airbase in Vermont. RCMP's Special Branch, which was very much in league with Edelman on this, agreed.

The Buffalo agent, a young woman named Mason, cleared the border checks with special IDs and permissions and was met by the RCMP on the other side. They sped to the hospital, about eight kilometers distant, making it in record time.

When they walked into the special isolation section, they were met by a very confused Inspector Douglas.

"What the hell is this?" he demanded.

"This is Mason, FBI," the RCMP cop told him. "She's got the proper papers to pick up a Dr. Sandra O'Connell."

Douglas looked stricken. "But that's impossible! She was picked up ten, fifteen minutes ago!" he said.

Agent Mason was upset. "Who picked her up? On whose authority?"

"An inspector from the FBI," Douglas said. "Absolutely faultless credentials, with the proper Canadian releases as well. An Inspector Braden, I think his name was. Yes, Inspector John Braden."

NINETEEN

They knocked the team out being moving them from Camp Liberty, of course. Although a few of the top people obviously knew its location, none of the teams going into action could be trusted with the information. If even one were caught by the authorities, it would be impossible to conceal any information from them.

Most of the team chose to make the run individually, but Sam and Suzy wanted to go together. Their old relationship had deepened in the weeks at the camp, and with the possibility of death ahead, they were both unwilling to separate until they had to.

They awoke on the deck of a tramp steamer of Liberian registry somewhere in the North Atlantic. The crew appeared to be mostly Chinese and only a couple of the merchant officers spoke good English, one mate with a pronounced British accent. He was in charge of their drop.

"We'll be in position to drop you sometime tonight," he told them. He walked over to a chest in their cabin and opened it. "Here, try these on," he told them, handing out some clothing.

They were military uniforms, obviously tailored for each of them. Since they were supposed to be part of the Air Force personnel team at the alternate

Pentagon, they made Suzy a master sergeant and Sam a tech sergeant. "Enlisted personnel are never scrutinized as closely as officers," the mate explained. "But don't forget to salute."

They wouldn't. Knowing they were to be in the Air Force, they had memorized an awful lot of material they would be expected to know.

Next came the identification cards and orders. They were supposedly Security Police, formerly with the 1334th SP Squadron at Shaw AFB near Charleston, South Carolina. Their orders, papers, IDs and the like were perfect. Being SPs, they would be expected to demonstrate a lot of technical knowledge, and, as military cops, they would carry a lot of weight, particularly as regulars in a military occupation force composed primarily of reservists, guardsmen, and draftees.

They had suitcases with other uniforms and some civilian clothes and toiletries as well. Sam was particularly impressed by the used look of them, even to a worn bar of soap and a partially coiled tube of toothpaste.

A little before 2:00 A.M. they, their equipment, and the mate were lowered into a large rubber raft with two enigmatic Chinese seamen doing the paddling. About an hour later, they were met by an elderly-looking crab boat and transferred aboard.

The crabber was for real; he'd worked Pamlico Sound in North Carolina for almost ten years since retiring, he told them, as a drug smuggler. His folksy reminiscences of raiding small pleasure craft, murdering all on board, then using the boats to make drug runs before scuttling them, were eaten up by an admiring Suzy. Sam was much less enraptured, thinking of all the lives lost for no cause but profit. But, he realized, a lot of his friends and associates used the substances men like this had brought in without thinking of how they got there or asking to see their pedigree. Smuggling remained a romantic pastime older than America, and its grisly side was never played up.

They turned in, past dangerous reefs, to the sound. A couple of times Coast Guard planes and helicopters looked at the old crabber, but it was a known ship with a long history and Suzy and Sam were well concealed. The familiar wasn't checked very much by the authorities; they were looking for the unusual and out-of-place. Since the crabber had already radioed that he had engine trouble and was heading in, it wasn't thought unusual for him to be on this course.

"I was supposed to go up to Virginia to help out some friends," he told them, "but, of course, I was supposed to have a partial breakdown and turn back. Nothing odd. There really is a bad clutch in one of the engines, too."

"Why not just take us to Virginia?" Suzy asked him. "After all, it's closer."

He frowned. "Hell, Norfolk's a naval base and shipyard. Wall-to-wall checks of just about everything. And the Chesapeake and James are just crawlin' with boatloads of bored, suspicious patrolmen. No, easier here."

He pulled into the slip at his pier without incident. There was nobody around; the watermen were long gone, and the rest of the world still hadn't awakened as yet.

An official-looking military car was parked out front of the crabber's storage shed, and a man in his early fifties with more stripes than they could count on his Air Force uniform was sitting in front drinking a Coke and smoking a cigar. They stopped fearfully when they saw him, but the crabber called out, "Hi, Mike!"

The old sergeant smiled and got up. "Hello, Joe. These my two recruits, eh?"

The crabber nodded. "All yours now." He turned to the confused pair. "Joe's as genuine as you are," he assured them. "See you all."

They were dubious but had little choice. "Joe" put their luggage in the trunk of the staff car and told them to get in, which they did. In minutes they were away.

"I hope you two have eaten," he called to them. "No way I can get us anything until we're well into Virginia."

"That's all right," Sam told him. He was nervous. Joe didn't fit at all the image of the conspirators he had built up over all this time, and the car had an awfully authentic look to it.

"Is this car stolen?" he asked the driver.

Joe chuckled. "Hell, no. I signed it out at Shaw and I'll turn it in at Andrews. You steal one of these and they have you in ten seconds. Nothing but military and truck traffic to hide in."

Even Suzy was intrigued now. "Then you really are an Air Force SP?"

Again the older man chuckled. "No, ma'am, definitely not. But I was, once—before they caught me with my hands where they shouldn'ta been. Sweetest smuggling racket ever done, all on Air Force equipment. I had twenty-seven years in, so they didn't throw me in jail, just reduced and booted me."

That seemed to answer the motivational questions, and even tied him in with the likes of the crabber and the underground drug trade. But they would get no more information out of him about himself, just reassurance.

"The sergeant's for real, he's just somewheres else," Joe said. "All of the procedures are perfect. You can do almost anything in the military if you got the right orders and the right forms." He chuckled. He seemed to find everything slightly amusing. "That's what got me in the end—one form. A real form, perfect signature and everything —and the damn ninnies lost it in the bureaucratic shuffle. Lost it! Military inefficiency defeated me. There was no way to duplicate the signatures on the spot, this drew attention, and that was that. You remember that. Depend on nothing but yourself, and keep it as simple as possible."

They passed a large number of military checkpoints. It was easy. All they had to do was pass over their orders and ID cards. Joe had his and the proper authorization for the car which was real and therefore would withstand even a check with Shaw. Their own IDs had their photos, and their orders said they were proceeding to Thurmont with transfers to the 2794th SP Squadron, Headquarters Command. It was true that a check with the 2794th wouldn't reveal that anybody knew they were coming, but that was so normal in military circles that it wouldn't even be wondered at.

For the first time they saw how tightly the government was gripping the country. Military were everywhere; in a small town in southeastern Virginia they saw several ordinary-looking people pull over others, flash IDs, and randomly check papers. The roads themselves were ghostly not only for their lack of auto traffic but for the graveyards of motels, eateries, and tourist traps ruined by the restrictions.

Outside the towns, where public transportation was the only way to travel, school busses, trucks, and anything else that would do had been pressed into service as shuttles for the people. Those who lived too far out even for that could phone for service; farmers were allowed to use their tractors to get to shuttle-serviced routes.

Two things amazed Sam and Suzy: the apparent ease with which the majority of the population seemed to be coping with the tremendous inconvenience, and its almost casual acceptance by the people.

"Oh, there's been a lot of trouble," Joe told them, "but once you clamp down martial law and use it publicly, consistently, and effectively, you get obedience. Acceptance comes from the isolated cases of terrorism that manage to penetrate the security screen, and the occasional shootouts when they find one of our safe houses. The government controls the press, radio, TV, everything very tightly, and they use them to best effect." Again the chuckle. "Hell, they've caught and killed more of our organization that we ever had! And crime's down to just about zero."

It was Sam's turn to smile. "You mean they fake big victories?"

Joe nodded. "Sure. And, remember, for every really heavy-handed guy in uniform who gets power-drunk there are hundreds of ordinary folks in uniform. The power-drunks get short shrift; report a really bad actor to the local commander and you nail him. Congressmen are also keeping close watch for abuses in their districts." His voice grew grim. "And the real bad abuses, they get covered up. Lots of people just disappear in the night, never to be seen again. They got big concentration camps all over the West, too, guarded with the best elite troops. Americans weren't any different than any other population once they started living in constant fear."

Suzy seemed to like the idea. "So our 'different breed' is just the same after all. It won't be difficult to remold them, with the proper guidance."

Sam was silent on that one, but he didn't believe it. Revolution looked exceptionally unlikely under these conditions, and a lot of human misery was being perpetrated, and perpetrated not by some dictator in a poor and starving country or one with a long tradition of dictatorship, but by a government with its finger on the nuclear trigger and growing increasingly fascistic.

This quickly, too! he thought. He found it hard to accept. Maybe American society was truly as rotten as he'd pictured it—and maybe it was also the most totally politically naive society on earth.

Speed limits were something for the distant past; they filled up several times at military stations, grabbing food at the same time, but mostly they kept going. From Mann's Harbor in North Carolina to the Catoctins was four hundred fifty or so kilometers; they made it in the early afternoon.

"It's Saturday," Joe told them, turning off a road and passing through the checkpoint at a little town called Thurmont, then up a small, winding road where the signs read *Catoctin Mountain Park*. The scenery was beautiful, wild and isolated; it was amazing that there was so quiet a wilderness this close to so many millions.

They turned off on a road where a sign directed

them to *Cunningham Falls State Park,* then got backed up behind three olive drab school busses full of people. Finally they turned; went past a beautiful lake, and down to an enormous parking area.

"Put on the SP armbands and strap on the pistols under the seats," Joe told them. He was already doing so himself. "We're going to be three cops—me the old hand and you two being introduced to the area. All of these people are military having some fun in the water here. Just act new, poke around, and use that phone box over there to make your calls. You have a little money, so get something to eat if you want in the snack bar. Then just wander around, and wait."

They pulled in near the snack bar just up from the bath houses. Hundreds of men and women were here, playing games in the grass and woods, and making use of the man-made beach to swim and play in the beautiful and large man-made lake.

Joe wandered into the snack bar, and for a few moments, the first in a long while, they were truly on their own.

"Now what?" Sam asked her.

"I'm going to take a shit," she said. "You get what you like from the snack bar and make your call. I'll do it later."

He nodded and she went off. He didn't feel like eating. What he felt like was getting a bathing suit and joining those people having fun down there on the lake. Still, he was also conscious that this was the place for them to get out of as quickly as possible, and he fumbled in his pocket, found a quarter, and went over to the phone box.

He stared at the phone for a moment, then reached back into his pocket. Yes, he had two quarters. He sighed, put a quarter in the phone, heard the dial tone, then dialed the number that was supposed to bring the next stage of people here. It was an interesting number, unlike any he'd ever heard of before. One-500-555-2323. What was a "500" number, anyway? And wasn't "555" information?

The phone clicked several times, then rang once, and he heard another picked up. For a second he was confused, somehow conditioned for a response, but now he realized that there would be none. It was probably a recording anyway. "Twenty twenty-five," he said "Two-oh-two-five." There was a click, a dead silence at the other end of the line, and, even before he hung up, his quarter came back.

He remembered suddenly his first encounter with this organization, the TV mail-order switchboard, and realized that this number was probably tied to something like that. A perfectly public toll-free number for subversion, he thought. It was somehow ironic; it said something else about the culture.

He considered whether or not to make the other call. He put the quarter in, then hesitated for a long time. Did he, in fact, want to use the FBI signal?

He thought about fascist America, now actually what he'd always claimed it was. He thought of the camps, of the terror, and of the people in this new organization. Most of all, he thought of Suzy.

Did he *want* to betray them? Deep down? He had to confess to himself that he did not, although those pictures of the Wilderness Organism victims were never far from his mind. Most of all, it was Suzy. She would never be taken alive, he knew that. He couldn't. Not now. He just couldn't.

He hung up, got his quarter back, and turned. Suzy was coming toward him.

"God! I feel better!" she enthused. She drew close to him. "Did you make it?"

He nodded.

"Okay, then, go buy us both Cokes. I'll be with you in a second."

He turned and walked into the snack bar. He didn't see Joe around and figured that the older man must have come out while he was on the phone. Almost at the same time as the Cokes came, Suzy was there as well, smiling and nodding to him.

"Let's go outside. May as well look the place over," he suggested, and they walked outside.

The staff car was gone.

They walked around a while, looking officious, and talking with some of the people, particularly some of the lower-ranking MPs and SPs on routine patrol. Both bluffed extremely well, and were extremely well briefed for the job, but it wasn't comfortable. Parading in front of the enemy when one slip could ruin you wasn't the most pleasant fun in the world; Cornish was only happy that it was hot enough that heat perspiration masked the nervous type.

"I wish they'd come," he muttered between clenched teeth.

"They're looking us over good first," she whispered back. "Want to make sure."

The hours passed, making it all that much worse, and since their cover had them on duty they couldn't relax. Suzy almost had a problem when she failed to salute a first lieutenant in uniform but it was glossed over quickly with apologies. Afterwards she swore that one day she'd kill the son of a bitch.

Finally an official-painted green station wagon with the logo of the Maryland Parks Service pulled up next to them. A young woman in park ranger garb and Smokey the Bear hat leaned out the window and peered at them through dark sunglasses.

"Hey!" she called to them. They went over to her.

"One-500-555-2323," she said softly to them. "Get in."

They got in, still sweating, and moved off.

"I thought you'd never get here," Sam said, relieved.

"Only the first step," the woman replied. "Remove the gunbelts and armbands and put them in that first aid locker back there." They did as instructed, although reluctant to part with the weapons.

The car turned off onto a dirt road in the middle of the forest. It was marked *Official Use Only—Keep Out.* At the end of the road was a maintenance shed of some kind, but no people.

"Go into the shed, get rid of your military clothes, and put on the clothing you find there. You also will have new IDs identifying yourself as Maryland State Police undercover."

They went in and did as instructed. Now they both wore shorts, tee-shirts, and sandals. The new IDs, with badges, looked impressive, and their photos again matched. The clothing fit perfectly.

They walked back out to the ranger, who was leaning against the side of the station wagon.

"Over there you'll see a trailhead," she told them. "Take it. Walk a kilometer and a quarter until you reach a small road. You'll be picked up there. Don't rush. Your contact will go by several times."

They started walking. The woods were beautfiul this time of year, the air warm and the shade of the giant trees invitingly romantic.

"I could stay around here forever," Sam told Suzy. "Sort of like Vermont. You know some of those trees back at the lake were maples?" He looked at her, seeing that she was sharing some of the same feelings.

"If we had a blanket it'd be real neat," she whispered sexily. They kissed long and hard there, then, after a while, arms around each other, they continued down the trail to the road.

The reason why their contact passed here several times was that he ran a shuttle bus. He was a teenager, no more, in an Army private's uniform. His bus was empty.

He pulled up to them as they sat by the roadside. "Hey! You the state cops?" he yelled.

They got up, went over, and boarded the bus. "That's us," Suzy told him. "Want to see our IDs?"

The kid laughed. "Naw. Too much of that now. Just take a seat. I got a long run here."

They wound up, down, around and through the woodlands, often picking up people and dropping others off. Once they passed a gatehouse and Sam whispered to Suzy, "Look! That's Camp David!"

She stared at the sign and at the strange network of walls, fences, and sophisticated electronics detection gear atop them. It *was* Camp David; they were passing right by the getaway White House.

"Boy! How I'd like to spray some pixie dust in *this* neighborhood!" Suzy breathed. For once Sam agreed with her. If the President were in, he suspected, millions of Americans would applaud him for it.

They finally rolled into Thurmont, and the bus

driver stopped near a small parking area now crowded with official cars.

"I was told to tell you that the keys were in it," the kid said. They got off and he rumbled off. They stared after him for a minute. "Do you think he knew what the hell he was doing?" Suzy wondered.

"I doubt it," Sam replied. "Just asked to do a favor, I think. We'll never know for sure."

They started looking over the dozen or so cars. Six were State Police cars and they found one, a brown plainclothes-type vehicle with a flasher that popped up through a roof opening. It had the keys in it.

They got in. Sam decided to drive, and he turned to her. "So where do we drive to?" he asked her.

She rooted around the glove compartment and other places but found nothing. She shrugged. "Start the car. Maybe there's something . . ."

He started the car and the police radio sprang to life, startling them. They were now at a loss as to what to do next, and sat there for a minute or so, wondering. A uniformed man looking like state troopers of all states had looked since they were invented came out of a store, looked over, stared, then started running for them.

"Oh, oh," Sam muttered. "Wrong car, maybe?"

Suzy looked around. There was a shotgun in a case in the door, and she reached for it. The trooper was there first, immediately saw her fumbling for the shotgun, and drew his revolver.

"Okay. Don't make a move," he told them. "Get out of the car and spread 'em!"

They had no choice. Sam had the sinking feeling that this was the ironic ending to their spy-novel odyssey. All this to get pinched in the wrong car. He cursed the spy-masters inwardly, remembering Joe's admonition: keep it simple. They had gotten so cloak-and-dagger they'd gotten tripped up.

Suzy was different. "Wait a minute!" she told the trooper. "I'm Sergeant Fearing and this is Corporal Woods. We're working for the same people you are. Check our IDs!"

The trooper looked dubious. He pulled Sam's wallet from his hip pocket and flashed it open. Then he carefully got Suzy's.

A police van pulled up, driven by a trooper who looked like the first's brother. The side door was unclocked, pulled back, and revealed a bench seat and wrist and leg irons in an inset cast-iron cage. The two troopers had them exceptionally covered, and got help from a couple more. Despite Suzy's protests they were both placed in the leg irons in the van and the door was slammed shut.

The van lurched into motion.

TWENTY

John Braden was nervous. He'd had to use his real ID to get Sandra O'Connell from the RCMP ahead of the Buffalo office; he was now very hot and he knew it. There had been very little choice in the matter, though; when the RCMP request for information had been trasmitted to Washington, it went through a long series of chains of command and, at one point, came up on more than Edelman's computer. Braden had gotten the call with very strict orders: get there ahead of the Buffalo office or else. With the aid of a helicopter and direct information, he'd managed it, but he had no sense of victory.

Just a hundred kilometers or so southwest of Buffalo were a series of small islands in Lake Erie. The helicopter put down on one long enough to get Braden and O'Connell off, then took off again.

Sandra O'Connell still had no idea that she hadn't been rescued. She stood there on the island watching dawn come up and wondered why she was there.

"This is what, in the FBI, is known as a 'safe' house," Braden explained, and it was the truth. "That means the place has a reputable non-government cover and an official owner who pays property taxes and uses it for recreation. Nothing odd or unusual, just an old family resort gone to seed. Nobody can be traced here, and only inspectors and

above can even find out where it is, and then only on
a need to know basis. No computer files, nothing. A
small list. It's the kind of place we take witnesses
against big crime figures to hide 'em out, and to pre-
pare them for new identities."

She looked around. She was feeling much better,
more in control. Things were coming easier for now,
and she felt that she was working out the aftereffects
of the drug.

"But why am *I* here?" she persisted.

He sighed. "Dr. O'Connell, somebody had you
snatched. Somebody really high up. That somebody
now knows that you're alive, that you've escaped
from Martha's Lake VA Hospital, that your story is
now on file with the RCMP. They didn't want to kill
you, you know. Just keep you out of the action until
whatever they want to do gets done. Now they probably would."

She accepted that, and they walked up to the
house.

It looked old, semi-Victorian, and not in very
good repair. It was sheltered from view from the
lake, but you could tell it was there, the upper story
roof peeking through the trees.

The place was a lot nicer inside. Nice rugs, early
American furniture, a modern kitchen and a large
number of neatly made bedrooms. The place had at
one time been a resort; the kitchen and dining
room were truly huge, and the living room could
seat almost two dozen people.

There was a staff, too. An ordinary-looking
bunch of what appeared to be hotel-like personnel,
except that they all obviously wore pistols. Sandra
guessed that there were a half-dozen total, four big
men and two women with strong, serious faces, all

no more than in their late twenties.

"You're the only guest at the moment," Braden told her. "You go upstairs, take a shower, freshen up, whatever you want, before we have a big breakfast. Meg, there, is close to your size I think, at least for casual wear." He called to the women. "Hey! Meg! See if you can find something to fit our guest."

The woman smiled, nodded, and said, "Follow me," to Sandra O'Connell. She followed the woman up the big old oaken staircase.

Braden walked back into the living room, then to the dining room, where he spotted one of the men. "Alton!" he said.

"Sir?"

"I'm going into the office and call in. You make sure she's watched at all times."

The big man nodded. "We're well prepared. You know that."

Braden should have felt secure and satisfied, but he couldn't. This prisoner had gotten away from them once, and now his career was going up the creek because of her.

A small den was off the dining room. He entered, closed the door, and went to a phone on a desk there. He picked up the receiver and dialed. One-500-555-2323.

There was a click and a ring, then silence. "Braden," he said into it, hung up the phone, and waited.

The phone rang inside of a minute. He picked it up anxiously.

"Braden? You have her?" asked a man's voice on the other end.

"Oh, yes, sir. Tight as a drum. She still thinks she's been rescued. Want us to just wipe her?"

There was silence for a moment, as if the man on the other end were thinking hard. Finally he said, "No, not exactly, anyway. We have the medical information from Diefenbaker, as much as they did, anyway. Is she improved?"

"Yeah, pretty good," Braden said. "She still stumbles over some big words and she can't seem to read, but otherwise you'd hardly know it."

Again the silence, then, "Okay, I'm going to send Conway over to run some tests on her. We can excuse it as a routine physical exam. I think she'll be cooperative. He'll have several alternatives depending on what he finds. We may just have to zap her and be done, but we had pretty good reasons for icing her. We weren't going to do it until the sixteenth, but maybe we can advance it a bit. Just sit tight."

"Ah, sir?" Braden said hesitantly. "Ah, what about me? I mean, I can't go back, not now."

"You'll have to ice yourself until after the sixteenth," the man told him. "You know that. Cheer up. There are worse places to be iced. We won't forget you, Braden."

"Thank you, sir," was all he could say, and he heard the other end click dead. He hung up himself and considered it for a moment. There *were* worse places to be iced, and worse ways. He ought to know. He got up and went back into the dining room to join the others for dinner.

Late the next afternoon Dr. Peter B. Conway arrived by small boat, along with some equipment. They helped him unload and used a hand truck to get it to the big house.

Sandra O'Connell had slept most of the day, and was feeling as good as she had since her kidnapping. She was, as the man on the phone had predicted, delighted to take a physical examination and discover just what had, in fact, happened to her.

The equipment was of the relay type. Conway could conduct a complete physical here by using phone lines connected to his monitors and to big medical computers in Cleveland.

"I'm not going to kid you," he told her. "You're a doctor yourself, so I'll give you nothing but the facts."

The exam was thorough and took over two hours. It included blood tests, trace injections and monitoring, everything. They also did a psych profile under mild and proven medication, the best way of determining just what was wrong and where. Not incidentally, it gave Conway the additional information he needed on her present state of mind.

Finally, it was finished, but it was the next morning before everything had worn off enough for her to meet with the examining physician over a breakfast of eggs, sausage, and pancakes.

"Mitoricine," Conway told her. "Ever hear of it?"

She shook her head. It sounded similar to hundreds of other names.

"It's a synthetic and a powerful hypnotic," he told her. "It was all the rage several years ago among the drug counter-culture, but it didn't last too long. For one thing, some of the chemicals involved are hard to get, so manufacture was limited. Also, while just exactly the right dose will produce almost any pleasing effect you want, that effect is determined by the programmer, the person who gives it to you. If you underdose you'll be awake but in a trancelike state, open to every single suggestion. That was popular among the wealthy for its orgy potential. Overdose, however, causes the same thing as long-term usage. There is *always* some minor brain dysfunction. In the usual counter-culture uses, it took months of use to show up noticeably. It affects different people in different ways at first, of course, depending on age, body weight, dosage accumulation, whatever. But, slowly, it was obvious to people that users were getting slower—motor, nervous system, memory, basic skills, all deteriorating. You had three or four heavy doses, and that's what you felt and still feel to an extent."

"But it *is* reversible," she said hopefully. "I mean, I've already gained back a lot."

He sighed. "Well, it is and it isn't. The more you have, the longer it takes to get rid of the effects. The brain works around the problem areas, forges new linkages. I think you got out just in time. Two or three more doses like those they were giving you, or one big overdose, and it might have been beyond your body to repair."

That shook her up. "What—what would be the result if that had happened?"

He shrugged. "As I said, it varies. But let's say you woke up much like you did originally, only slightly worse. No reading, no math, no significant use of vocabulary, unable to tie your own shoelaces, but, locked inside, you'd be at least dimly aware of what happened to you. But, unlike now, where it's wearing off faster and faster, this one would never wear off. You'd be like that for the rest of your life."

It was a sobering thought. In fact, she felt slightly sick. She remembered her inability to tie those knots in the woods, her frustration at the still-effective reading skills block, her inability to even order a hamburger by name or count and recognize the change. It was a horrible thought to be like that, or worse, forever.

Forever.

A living death.

"Excuse me," she said nervously, and got up and left the room. Alton rose to follow her but Conway said, "No, let her be. She's just going outside to think about it." His tone left no doubt that that was what he wanted.

Braden's voice lowered. "Okay, I can see you working on her. Mind telling me what this is all about?"

Conway hesitated a moment, then said, "You saw how she took to the horror story when she thinks she's safe. Suppose it came true? At least, suppose she thought it had?"

"My god! She'd kill herself!" Braden's voice rose slightly, and Conway put a cautionary hand to his mouth.

"No she wouldn't," the doctor said. "She's had a good, strong parochial Catholic upbringing. She might hole up and barely exist in misery, but she would not kill herself. And that, of course, is what she must do."

Braden was intrigued. "You mean fake it? Then why . . . ?"

Conway shook his head. "No fake. A cumulative combination of things. There must be no question of her suicide so they will not question the incomplete suicide note."

Braden had it in a minute. "Oho! But—she's hot. She's going to start asking questions about Edelman, about NDCC, everything. Particularly when we don't get her clothes and effects to her."

"We managed to get some of her stuff," Conway said. "I'll brief you and the others before leaving. Now, you keep her happy as long as possible, but never let her forget. I'm going to leave some pills which contain small amounts of mitoricine. This will keep her slightly off, inhibit recovery but very slightly. Hold her until the fifteenth if you can. If you can't, well, whenever it becomes impossible, do it."

Braden nodded. "You want her found on the sixteeth."

It was now the first of the month.

TWENTY-ONE

"Bingo!" shouted Bob Hartman. He almost ran up one flight and down the hall to Jake Edelman's office.

Edelman was looking over some reports when the excited younger agent burst in. "What's up?" he asked.

"John Braden. He is in fact with the Bureau, the Chief Inspector of the Syracuse office. Lots of time in, an old pro."

"You're sure it's the right man?" Edelman asked. "Remember, I'm supposed to have kidnapped O'Connell and Bede."

"Dead on," Hartman assured him. "Prints, hand-writing, physical description all match. They had to move fast to get there before we did and they used him."

Edelman assumed his thoughtful pose. "Syracuse, huh? Not much for an old pro."

The younger man nodded. "It's fairly new. He was shifted up there replacing Ben Waxler just after the emergency was declared. His own office said he was out most of the time at the Martha's Lake VA Hospital about twenty, thirty kilometers west of the city."

"That would figure," Edelman noted. "Okay, then, so we have an old pro switched to a nothing post so he can oversee security at a VA hospital rather than the GSA who's supposed to. You know what that means."

Hartman nodded. "Hot potatoes. So? What do you think?"

"Raid the son of a bitch," snapped the Chief Inspector. "I want the staff and the doctors involved. Bury 'em at Whiteoaks. And run a check of plane drops in the Syracuse area."

"Ahead of you," the younger agent said. "I already got one. He landed there the day after the snatch. Courier plane, unscheduled. We've run it down."

"You get up to Martha's Lake," Edelman ordered. "Take care of it personally. I'll take care of the crew on this end."

"I've got a plane waiting," the excited agent said, and left quickly.

Jake Edelman called Internal Security. It was his base of power, this counterespionage section, and it was both cleared of questionables and secured in its conversations.

"Billy? Pick up on Bob's rundown of an unscheduled courier drop in Syracuse. I want the crew in the IS tank yesterday, get it? Then call me."

He hung up and sighed. For the first time he seemed to be getting some breaks. More than he expected, he admitted, looking at the papers in front of him. Plants in the terrorist organization had now tipped him to nine locations. Nine. Now this was breaking, too. *They* had to know. Had to at least suspect that he was starting to break it open.

Why were they letting him get away with it? he wondered.

*   *   *

Bob Hartman got to Syracuse in what he believed was record time. The sleek Air Force jet had used more time taking off and landing than it had in the air.

The rest of the team was all ready and waiting for him at the airport. He didn't ask if they were all cleared; he knew that Carlos Romero, the agent in charge, was and Carlos had picked the others.

They sped off in a five-car caravan to the West. There was one military checkpoint, staffed by a bunch of green kids. For a moment he considered drafting them, then decided better of it. These people wouldn't be gang chiefs or terrorists.

Twenty-two highly trained and experienced agents walked into the hospital and simply took it over. Hartman, authoritative, rounded up the staff and separated them by occupation and classification without trouble. A small green cigar box was producued, and a calculator-like device, and a call was made.

Less than three-quarters of an hour passed before military busses from Whiteoaks Air Force Base started rolling up. General Kneiss had been prewarned and ready, one of Jake's good guys.

It took more than three hours to evacuate the staff and "patients" at Martha's Lake, and Hartman's team left it an empty shell, lights still burning.

Special staff flown in on Edelman's orders were already arriving at Whiteoaks by the time he arrived. The severely drugged patients were placed under guard in the small hospital they had on the base; the others were billeted in spare barracks. Hartman recognized quite a number of the patients. They were all scared shitless, he thought, but to an absolutely frightened and beaten person authority is authority and force is force. They had no idea whose side anybody was on, or if in fact there was another side.

The staff proved different. They knew they were in the wrong hands; most demanded to make phone calls or see various government personnel. A few demanded lawyers. The names and numbers of everyone they wanted to talk to were dutifully recorded, but messages were left unsent.

General Kneissel's trained, cleared, and hand-picked Intelligence boys tapped eight officers and nineteen noncoms trying to make interesting phone calls. Again the numbers were recorded, and these people joined the staff.

The doctors broke first, of course. One little Iranian doctor who said his citizenship was on the line finally admitted all and told the story of Sandra O'Connell. Crofton, the attendant who'd let her escape, was hauled in next and informed that he was in for highly unpleasant treatment for the kidnapping and possible murder of O'Connell. He broke, blaming Braden for everything.

"Where is Braden now?" Hartman demanded.

Crofton shrugged. "I dunno. An Army helicopter came and got him a couple of days ago and we haven't seen or heard from him since."

This was also noted. A circle was drawn around Martha's Lake, and the Army helicopters capable of getting to Braden within the time frame were catalogued. Flight logs and orders were run through computer networks.

Not having to play by the rules made life a lot

simpler, Bob Hartman had to admit to himself.

The helicopter, and the name of the captain who had flown it, was quickly isolated. A Bureau helicopter then took Hartman to a National Guard unit just outside Syracuse.

The Officer of the Day and CQ were surprised and startled by the FBI visit, but the OD had been a used car salesman until the emergency and the CQ had been a supermarket clerk. They weren't about to argue with the authoritative agents.

In an Army car Hartman travelled in the early hours of the morning to the home of one Captain Irving Wentzel, getting him out of bed. His wife's protests and shrieks were a bit too much; they had no kids, so they took her, too.

The whole thing had been done under tight security, and yet too many people were involved, too many bystander types and buck-passing types to keep it completely quiet.

While Captain Irving Wentzel was being harshly interrogated as to where he'd gone in that helicopter after leaving Diefenbaker Hospital, somebody called somebody who called sombody else.

Finally, somebody dialed 1-500-555-2323.

TWENTY-TWO

Sam felt relieved by their uneventful capture, and both amazed and grateful that Suzy had been taken so completely unaware and so unable to do anything at all that she was still alive, whole, and hearty. It eased his conscience a great deal.

Suzy had been silent for most of the ride, but now, suddenly, she was getting curious.

"Sam, look at this road," she said.

He couldn't see as well, being shackled farther from the tiny barred and screened window, but still he could see what she meant.

It was a glorified, slightly paved cowpath.

They had travelled a long time—an hour or more, they guessed—stopping only briefly for occasional roadblocks, which held them up not a bit. No roadblocks out here, though. This was a combination of farm country and rich people's homes, the kind with an acre or more of lawn.

Now the van slowed to a stop. Suzy craned her neck to see out the window.

"Anything?" he asked, getting both curious and apprehensive.

"Cows," she replied, echoing his feelings.

There was a key in the side lock, then a pullback of the van door. The trooper produced a second key and unlocked the cage, climbing in.

"Sorry to put you folks through this, but it frankly was the easiest way to get you through the blocks and into open country like this," he said.

Both their mouths dropped. "You mean this was *planned?*" Suzy asked.

He nodded as he unlocked their manacles. "Yeah. Sorry about the lack of warning but your expressions and manner made it all the more convincing back there. Most of those folks were real cops. Sorry we couldn't make it easier, but Charlie was taking a crap and I was getting a candy bar. Hell, we didn't know *when* you'd get there."

"I wouldn't use this again, though," Sam cautioned him. "Hell, Suzy almost blew your head off, and we could easily have gotten ours shot in by some of those real cops."

He shrugged. "Fortunes of war." They were free and he helped them out of the van. They stretched and massaged their legs.

"Okay," continued the phony trooper. "Maybe a thousand meters around that bend is Route 30. When you get to it, make a left and cross the road. About a kilometer up you'll see an unpaved road on your right—it's the last road in Maryland. If you go under a sign that says 'Welcome to Pennylvania' you've missed it. Ten or so old but nice homes up there. You want the last one in, a big old house maybe a century old. It usta be the farmhouse for the place before they subdivided it."

Suzy was all business again. "Ten houses? Won't that attract attention?"

He shook his head. "Nope. Don't worry about it. Most of those folks moved into apartments up in Hanover because of the transportation problem, and others got called out in the emergency, down to

Baltimore and D.C. and whatever. If anybody's in any of those houses now, it's one of us."

"Somehow I can't bring myself to thank you, but it's been a long day and still there's a long walk ahead, so good-bye," Sam said.

The "trooper" smiled. "Okay, good luck and all that. Five got in ahead of you, so things seem to be going well."

With that he got back in the van, did a three-point turn, and headed back along the way he'd come.

"Back to the wars," Suzy said brightly.

He was thinking the same thing, only for a far different set of reasons.

The neighborhood was on the edge of a deep woods, and the other houses, as they'd been told, were empty now. Mt. Venus Road had at one time been paved, but not for thirty years.

There was a phone installed, with a funny sort of gadget attached which they guessed was a scrambler circuit. All they knew was that there had been a note under it in computer typewriter characters telling them to call in to The Man at midnight each night. If there was no call, then it would be assumed that they had been taken. There was also a caution that any attempt to tamper with or remove the funny box from the phone circuit would trigger a nasty explosive charge.

Nobody wanted to touch it.

The next couple of days were spent just exploring the area. They had no orders or assignments, so they spent the time walking in the woods, doing light housekeeping, and discovering the shuttle bus, a standard yellow one, that made hourly shuttle runs between the state line and the county seat of Westminster perhaps twenty-five kilometers southwest. From there you could get regular busses to the other towns in the county and Greyhound to Baltimore, from whence you could get just about anywhere you wanted—if you had the proper papers to even board the big bus.

They had clothing and money and good fake IDs, so they weren't too worried, but Suzy was the leader and she ran a tight ship. It was four days later, and all but one of their team had arrived, when they ran out of groceries. Sam volunteered to go, but two others were sent, and he went back to just relaxing, enjoying Suzy and the nice countryside, his conscience fulfilled. He'd tried and failed. Suicide was not in his makeup, not when life was like this.

The next day the phone in the house rang. It startled them; Suzy answered it, half expecting to hear a pitch for storm windows or something.

"This is 1-500-555-2323," a clear announcer's type voice told her. "Now, listen carefully, for this will only be said once. Your team is complete, I repeat, complete. The missing member was killed by security forces but did not have the opportunity to betray you. The things you will need and all instructions are buried in a chest in a grove approximately eight hundred meters due north of the house in the woods. It is marked by three white-painted stones, is about two meters down, and has been there since before the emergency. Understandably, the things are still the standard blue, so be careful when transporting them to the house. A single stray individual seeing people carrying blue anything will get you lynched. Anticipating this, materials in a sub-basement of your house have been left to change the material into more unobtrusive form, along with instructions. When the transfer is completed, call this number again and report it so. The sub-basement is reached by trapdoor under the coal pile. That is all." There was a click and the line went dead. She stood there a moment, thinking, while the others clustered curiously around. It had obviously been a tape recording.

Sam and two of the others who were muscular made their way into the woods with shovels found in the basement. It didn't take them long to find the spot; they'd been walking the woods anyway, and most had casually noticed the stones.

"Something's really fishy here," Sam told them.

One of the others, a younger man who said his name was Carl, looked up. "What do you mean?" he asked.

Sam pointed to the ground. "Anything buried here was buried a *hell* of a long time before the emergency. A year at least. Look at the trees and shrubbery. I just find it hard to believe that this could be so well advanced."

The others shrugged. "So? It was 'cause here it is. Come on! Let's get digging! If we don't find it before dark we'll be chopping each other's heads in."

It was at least two meters down, a huge coffin-shaped box four meters long and over a meter deep. It even had handles on it, but it took them until well after dark, with some of the others holding flashlights, before they cleared all obstructions away and brought it up. It took ropes and their combined muscle power to do so; the box weighed over 450 kilograms.

They opened it anxiously but carefully. The clamps had almost all rusted shut and took some nervous taps with a hammer to undo. Finally the top came off.

Inside, packed in cotton, were six baby-blue cylinders with complex valves and nozzles at one end sealed with a waxy compound. To some they looked like single tanks, but they also resembled fire extinguishers with rounded bottoms.

And they were heavy. They weighed almost fifty kilos each.

Also in the box there was an ordinary-looking attache case with a ten-digit touch lock. It was also heavy, but not extremely so, and Suzy took it while the three stongest men each gingerly lugged a blue cylinder back to the house guided by a companion with flashlight, then went back for a second. There was an anxious moment when one was dropped, but there seemed to be no damage and no hissing sounds. They kept going.

Finally they had the worst job. "We have to rebury the box," Sam told them. "Even if sombody came by and saw a freshly dug area, which is unlikely, they'd hardly be willing to dig all that way. If we tamp it down and there's one decent thunderstorm, there'll be no more signs."

The others protested, but Suzy agreed completely, and she was the boss.

It was past two in the morning when they finished, dead tired.

Suzy made the call. To her surprise there seemed to be a live voice on the other end, not a tape. She could hear the breathing. It wasn't the same voice, but they were all being distorted anyway, she knew.

"The combination is the complete phone

number," the voice told her, then hung up.

She went to the briefcase. Suspecting some kind of explosion if she tried and goofed, she'd just left it there. The cylinders were all in the kitchen, stacked like wood and covered with a blanket, and the others had all gone exhaustedly to bed after eating.

She punched the number on the keys. One-500-555-2323. There was a *click* and the lid opened as if on a pneumatic riser.

Inside was a foam rubber insert covering the whole inside. Spaces had been cut out, and small bottles, three of them, holding some clear liquid, were strapped in. A cutout below them held a wooden box which, when opened, revealed two dozen wrapped and sealed disposable syringes, some cotton, and a sealed plastic bottle of alcohol. When she took the box out she saw that under the rubber was a thick Manila envelope, and she reached under, having to pry it up where the foam rubber had stuck, and got it out.

The next morning, when they came downstairs for breakfast, a Suzy too excited to sleep greeted them.

"Guess what!" she said excitedly. "We're the ones who get to hit Washington, D.C.!"

Sam Cornish's heart sank. "When?" he asked her.

"On the sixteenth," she said.

He looked with the others at the wall calendar. It was September ninth. *A week from today,* he thought. *Seven more days.*

Now what do you do, Sam Cornish?

TWENTY-THREE

The phone in Braden's den rang. Alton got it, talked for a few minutes, then called the self-exiled security man.

"Yes, sir?" he said crisply.

"The Edelman team is on to you," The Man told him. "They raided Martha's Lake and have everybody out. They know the whole story. It will only be a matter of time before they're there now. I had hoped for six more days, but we can live with this. Give O'Connell the treatment, get her out, then *you* get out, fast."

Braden nodded absently, fear creating a knot in his stomach. "Yes, sir. At once." Suddenly he heard a whirring of rotor blades and panic rose. "I hear a chopper now. Do you suppose . . . ?"

"That's for O'Connell, from me," The Man assured him. "You get out by boat. Time is short. Move!"

Braden hung up the phone and went out to the dining room. Alton was waiting with two of the other men, Gurney and Stone.

"I talked to him before you did," Alton reminded him. "Gurney and Stone know where to take her, and the bird's down and waiting. Shall we?"

He nodded, and the four of them mounted the stairs. The other agents were also busy around, de-

stroying anything that might be of use to the inevitable raiders, shredding and incinerating papers
and the like. One of the women was hauling out the
firebombs and checking their clocks and fuses.

Sandra O'Connell was in her room, relaxing listening to a Cleveland radio station. She was really
depressed; after so much rapid progress over the
few days after her escape, she hadn't improved at all
in the past week or more she'd been here. She was
beginning to fear that her condition was now at its
best state, and the somewhat clumsy attempts to
cheer her up by Braden and the staff hadn't helped
but just made her dwell more and more on the drug
and its effects. What good was a forty-two-year-old
illiterate doctor to anybody?

The four men hurriedly entering the room surprised and startled her. She looked puzzled. "What
is it?" she asked apprehensively. She'd heard the helicopter, too.

Alton took a briefcase and opened it on a night-
stand next to her bed. Gurney and Stone, looking
grim, went over to her and held her down.

"Masquerade's over, Dr. O'Connell," Braden
told her. "I'm afraid you've been had. You see, *I*
was the director at the hospital where you were kept.
I was the one who drugged you."

The shock was almost too much for her. She
struggled and started to scream, but a gag was in-
serted in her mouth and securely tied. Then hand-
cuffs bound her arms behind her back, and despite
frenzied attempts to keep them off, a pair of
handcuff-like leg irons were attached to her ankles.

"We'd hoped to be able to spare you," Braden
told her, "because you knew so much about
biochemical matters. However, that is no longer

possible. We *could* just kill you, of course, but you've put us to so much trouble for so long that it would seem a shame to do so without you performing some last service."

Her eyes showed horror.

Braden reached over to the open briefcase and pulled out a small pump-spray bottle of sealed plastic. There was some sort of wax seal and a tiny gauge on top of it.

"This is what the newspapers so romantically call the Wilderness Organism," he told her. "As you no doubt know, it is a synthesized bacteria. During its active stage, about twenty-four hours after exposure to air, it is highly contagious. Anyone even remotely in the area will catch it, and it'll happily live in the air, on walls, floors, anyplace an infected person touches. Of course, after that period its own little disease, the bacteriophage, or antibacterial virus, has at it, and it's all over for the poor germ. Except that, since it is a catalyst, the damage has already been done to and programmed into the victim's brain. Three days after exposure, give or take a few hours, and you come down with the nasty symptoms."

She shrank in terror from the bottle he so playfully held and about which he so casually talked.

"What we do, you see, is infect somebody, then turn them loose in a crowd to spread it," he continued, obviously enjoying her horror and comprehension.

"Yes, my dear, we'd like you to spread it," he said. "And you will have a unique honor. So far it's only been small towns. *You* will be turned loose in a major city."

She was obviously trying to say something, and

Braden was giving her the full treatment. "Lower the gag for a minute," he told the others calmly. They looked puzzled, but complied.

"You monster!" she spat at him. "You'll rot in Hell for this!"

"If such a place exists it will be infinitely preferable to a place with naive little saints like yourself."

"You can't make me spread it!" she told him.

"That's true, normally," he admitted. He put the bottle back in the briefcase and brought up another, smaller one filled with a reddish liquid and a syringe. "Know what this is?"

She shook her head, waiting for the next terror.

"It's mitoricine," he informed her.

She gasped. "No, no, you wouldn't . . ."

"A big, *big* dose," he said with relish. "We're going to give you a nice chemical lobotomy, then turn you loose in the big city just sprayed filthy with the Wilderness Organism. But—don't worry. The mitoricine contains a vaccine for this particular strain. *You* won't catch it. You'll go on and on and on . . . as a mitoricine retard." He looked at the others, his expression and tone all business again. "Put the gag back and hold her!"

She tried to shrink from it, tried to get away, but she couldn't move, and she felt that horrible needle penetrate her arm, saw the massive amount of red liquid being pushed into her, and was helpless.

In less than a minute she was out.

Braden looked at Gurney and Stone. "Okay, it's all yours now. Don't forget the note and the knife."

They nodded. "Don't worry," Stone said. "We know our job."

They picked her up, carried her downstairs and out the door to the waiting helicopter. Braden and

Alton stayed in her room, wordless, until they heard it take off. Both men breathed a sigh of relief.

"That's that," Braden told the other man. "Hope it works. Let's set the firebombs and get out of here." He turned for the door.

"One more thing, Braden." Alton's voice came from behind him. "A loose end to attend to."

Braden stopped and turned, puzzled. He saw the pistol in Alton's hand and froze.

"What the hell?"

Alton smiled. "The Man's orders. You're the only one they know about in this end of the operation. Sorry." He shot Braden twice in the stomach. The agent cried out, was pushed back by the force of the shots although doubled over, and then lay still on the floor in an increasing pool of blood.

Alton, satisfied, holstered his pistol and ran down the stairs. One of the women ran in the front door, practically screaming, and spotted him. "Mr. Alton! My god! It's too late! The whole goddamn United States Coast Guard's out there! It looks like an invasion!"

From the direction of the den there was a loud explosion as a special telephone, triggered by remote circuits, blew itself to hell.

TWENTY-FOUR

"I think Sam's right," one of the women, Miriam, said. There were other nods of agreement.

Suzy was furious. "Damn it! What do you want me to do? I say the things don't leak."

"But they've been in the ground for a pretty long time, Hon," he pointed out for the hundred time. "Besides, we'll have to transfer the stuff this week to the spray bottles from the cellar. There's real danger and you know it."

"And Sam's right about things smelling funny," a man named Harry put in. "From the Camp on, a lot of stuff hasn't made sense. I, for one, don't want to come down with the disease."

"Easiest way to get rid of us," Sam said. "Once we've done the job, well, we spread it some more. I remember the one in the papers where everybody lost their memory. It'd be a perfect end for our mysterious chiefs to plan for us. I tell you we *have* to know if that vaccine works."

"It works, it works!" Suzy protested for what she prayed would be the last time. "Look, at the Camp we had a demo chamber to check out the effects of some of the new strains. I had the vaccine, so did all the others working there. It worked then, it'll work now."

"You lose, Suzy," Harry said. "We all agreed.

We're not gonna touch that stuff until we *know.*"

She gave up. "All right, all right—but how can we know? We can't just walk into a chemical lab in Westminster, say, and tell them, 'Pardon me, this is supposed to be Wilderness Organism vaccine, but we don't dare spread it to major cities until we know we're safe!'"

"I think we'd be satisfied to be told it's either a biosolvent or contains dead bacteria," Sam said. "They can do that in a hurry. Just a quick report on what it is, roughly. We don't have to make it, only know it's a complex chemical and not just tap water."

Defeated, Suzy agreed that she and Sam would go into town. They walked down to Route 30 and waited for the bus, a bottle of the stuff in her bag. She didn't say a word to him the whole time, and pulled away when he tried to put his arm around her.

"Look, I'm doing this because I love you," he told her seriously. "We have something going now, something good. I don't want either of us to lose that it we can avoid it."

She melted a little, looking resigned. "I know, Sam. I know. It's just . . ."

"Just what?"

She shifted uncomfortably. "Nothing," she said.

The bus's arrival cut short his argument, and they rode in silence to the county seat.

There were two chemical labs in the city, which surprised them. It was a gigantic small town, really, only a half-hour from Baltimore. It had grown with the county, but never quite to true city status. Everybody went to Baltimore for the rare stuff.

The lab wanted them to leave it overnight, but

they refused, and offered to pay quite a bit for it if
done fast. "We don't have to know what it is, just if
it looks like it'll hurt us," Sam told the woman at the
desk. "It's an additive to our water supply and we're
a little concerned about the well."

Finally she agreed and took it back into the
back room. "Only a real quick check, though," she
warned.

Suzy decided to pick up some things she wanted.
She was particularly interested in a purse and a couple of wigs; the purse she needed would handle a
small spray bottle, and the wigs would help in the
disguise, even if bought off the shelf.

Sam found himself alone in the office. The woman
obviously was part of the lab establishment—it was
a small affair, a second-story place run by a couple
of former college teachers as a sideline. They mostly
handled water questions; a lot of homes in Carroll
County still had wells and septic tanks, and there
was always a demand to test for hardness, pollution,
and the like.

Sam was sitting next to the woman's desk, and for
a little while he stared at the touch-tone phone there.

Somehow, he knew, things were going wrong.
Everything was too easy, too slick. All the little nag-
ging inconsistencies came to the fore.

Somehow, he was certain, they were all being had.

His concern over the vaccine had been genuine, a
part of that feeling. Now, though, here it was, the
final question at last.

What the hell, he thought. A little penance, a pay-
back for those hundreds on the airliner. Suzy had
been taken alive before; that phony trooper, if he
was a phony, might as well have been real. And the
others—perhaps one or two might fight, but most

weren't really willing to die in the cause any more or they wouldn't have backed him on this panic trip.

He reached over, lifted the phone off the hook until he heard the dial tone, and, holding it poised just above the two plungers so he could drop it in a second to rest, he reached over with his left hand and punched a number.

And a lot of numbers.

He'd thought about it a lot, worked it out again and again in his mind, until he knew the numbers by heart.

He dialed the special "500" number the FBI had given him, heard it click over, ring, then stop. He punched the touch-tone keys.

Three-4-7-3-6-8-8-3-6-8-7-3-2-8-4-8.

He slowly lowered the phone back onto its cradle.

He felt no sense of victory or accomplishment; in a way, he felt himself a traitor. And yet, and yet, deep down, something far in the back of his mind seemed to relax and and whisper that he'd done a good thing this time.

The woman returned before Suzy. The speed of it surprised him.

"I can't do any more with this. It'll take days to get a more thorough analysis, but—you say this was in your well water, or was your well water?"

He nodded. "You mean there's something wrong?"

She shook her head from side to side. "No, but as far as I can tell from my and my husband's quick look, I'd swear it was distilled water. I'd love to know how you can get distilled water in a well."

A sense of satisfaction flooded through him. It was the justification for his phone call. All feelings of being a traitor vanished. They—they were trying to kill him, all of them. He'd just caught them at it, and he no longer felt he owed anything to them.

"Well, frankly, we've had an older dry well on the place," he lied, "and I went to check it yesterday and got this out of it with a siphon. It kinda surprised me. I think maybe now I understand. They been dumping the stuff from the dehumidifier down the old pipe."

It was an outrageous explanation, and if only for that reason the woman accepted it completely.

"Forty dollars," she told him. He paid it and walked out to the stairs and down them to the street below.

Distilled water, he thought bitterly. Sure. All those elaborate places to be, places to spray, in the instructions. Bullshit. *They* were to be the primary carriers. Just riding into D.C. on a train would do it, as the orders called for. Mix with crowds. Maybe a special strain, this, that stayed communicable for several days but delayed its effect longer.

As he'd understood it, the bacteria in the body somehow transmitted instructions to selected brain cells, causing them to produce an acidic substance instead of the normal enzymes for a period, an acidic substance that would literally burn out pre-determined centers in the brain.

Anybody who could build a germ that could do that could give it any time schedule, any time frame they wanted.

He saw Suzy coming toward him with a bunch of boxes. She saw his expression and knew at once it was bad news.

"Distilled water," he told her.

She just nodded and didn't say a word. They caught the bus that would take them back to Mt.

Venus Road, got off at the intersection, and walked back up the hill to the house. She'd asked and he'd offered to carry the packages, although he couldn't see to what purpose, now.

They were almost to the front door when she said, softly, "Sam?"

He stopped. "Yes, Hon?"

"You understand I *do* love you?"

He frowned. Now what the hell? "Yeah, sure, but . . . ?"

"But I have one thing I live for, Sam. One thing only. All else pales before it. I *believe* in the cause, Sam. I know you don't, not deep down. Most of them don't. But we all do what we have to do."

The tenor of the conversation disturbed him, and he turned. Suddenly he felt an exploding pain go through his jeans to his rump and felt a needle enter.

He stood there, dizzy and confused, for a moment, then toppled, packages flying. He was out so fast he never saw her put the gas-injector syringe back into her purse.

A couple of people inside the house witnessed it and ran outside.

"What the hell?" Miriam demanded. "Why . . . ?"

Suzanne Martine sighed. "Sam was never a revolutionary. He just was a sort of revolutionary groupie. He *wanted* the vaccine to be just water, and when it wasn't he started talking all crazy."

"You mean it's *really* vaccine?" Harry asked, relieved.

She shook her head. "At least it's a thick egg-based compound with suspended bacteria in it, all dead. All the way back he kept saying as how it'd kill us anyway, that he couldn't go through with it. Many years ago he bugged out when our group downed a plane. He just doesn't have the guts to be a revolutionary."

They were disturbed. "So? Now what? Do we kill him?"

"No!" she almost shouted, then caught herself and softened. "Look, I'm still in love with him. He's just too nice for our kind of business. Solid, though. Even when he bugged out on the plane deal he didn't stop us, and afterwards, when he ran, he never copped or finked. No, he's just not right on the raid."

"But what do we *do* with him, then?" Harry asked. "Hell, it's only the tenth."

"So we change things a little," Suzy said. "I got the word from The Man. We go tonight. We'll do the transfers of what we can this afternoon. Sam? Well, tie him up so he doesn't wander off again and leave him here. We'll be back, let him go, and live happily ever after."

Miriam was suspicious. "When did you call The Man?"

"From town," she lied glibly. "I had to report the uneasiness in this unit and the testing. I was told to go at once." She looked down at Sam, knelt down beside him, and kissed him on the forehead.

"Help me get him inside," she said.

TWENTY-FIVE

Alton stood on the stairway, frightened and undecided. His first impulse was simply surrender to overwhelming forces, but he glanced back up toward where Braden's body lay and knew there was no escape from that. Capture meant death in any case; The Man wouldn't spare anything to keep him and his agents from talking.

"Head for the boat!" he yelled to the others. "It's pretty fast—you might still make a getaway in the dark!"

The woman nodded. "What about you?"

"Don't worry about me!" he called back. "Move!"

The three agents made their way out the back. The mini-invasion was still in progress, but troops and FBI field personnel were already on shore. Some Coast Guardsmen made immediately for the boat landing to secure it, while a small cutter broke off and headed for the pier.

The man and the two women, still cloaked in the shadows, saw they'd never make it. They were about to turn back when two shots came at them from behind. They returned fire, attracting the attention of the beach personnel who also opened up.

Alton, who'd fired the shots at them, now made his way to the shrubbery just outside the house and

255

waited silently. When a group of men, a couple of whom had on suits instead of uniforms, ran by, he let them clear, then bolted after them on the run, catching up to them in a matter of seconds. There were so many people running around now that his action wasn't even noticed.

"There goes one!" he shouted, seeing a form running across from the beach side to a grove of trees. They hesitated, unsure of who was who in the dark, but the figure turned and fired back at the pursuers, and the group Alton had joined poured it into the figure.

It was overkill.

Bob Hartman ran toward the house just behind a phalanx of agents. They entered cautiously, checking out every room on the ground floor first. In the den, a small fire was still going from the phone explosion, but it had failed to ignite much else and was burning itself out. They were able to smother it quickly.

Now Hartman's squad ran up the stairs. He stopped by the body of Braden while the others searched the bedrooms on this and the third floor.

Carefully he turned the blood-soaked man over, saw it was Braden, and was surprised to hear a groan of anguish.

"Hey! Get a medical team—quick!" Hartman yelled. "This guy's still alive!"

Blood was running from Braden's mouth as well as his wounds. He opened his eyes, tried to speak, and coughed.

"Just take it easy," Hartman cautioned. "Medical help's on the way."

Braden shook his head slowly and with difficulty, coughing some more, but managed to speak in a hoarse, blood-choked whisper.

"Don't care," he said. "Sons of bitches shot me. Alton."

"How many were there here?" Hartman asked.

"Six—no, four. Other two . . . helicopter. Took the Doc . . ."

Hartman felt triumph slipping out of his grasp with the dying man. Gone! "Where did they take her?"

Braden was having trouble, fading in and out. Hartman had to yell the question to him several times. Finally he got it, coughed again, and said, "Coney Island . . . 944 Pritchard . . . 3A . . ." Again a cough. "Shot her with mitoricine . . . Told her she had the live germ . . . S'posed to kill herself . . ."

The medical people were there now, but Hartman waved them away. Until he got what he needed, he wasn't going to let Braden go. The younger agent looked up at one of his assistants. "Get that?"

The other agent nodded. "Nine forty-four Pritchard, 3A," he repeated. "Want me to get on it?"

Hartman shook his head. "No. Get Edelman up there—fast. He's the only one she'll trust now. *Move!*"

He turned back to the man whose hatred of those who betrayed him was keeping him alive—that, and a possible hatred of himself, too.

"Who's behind this, Braden?" he pressed. "Give me *names.*"

Braden seemed to smile strangely. "Dunno . . . call 1-500-555-2323. Ask The Man who he is . . ."

Braden collapsed. Hartman let the medics take over, and watched as they worked. "Dead?" he asked.

The Coast Guard medic shook his head. "This guy's got a constitution like a bull ox. But the odds aren't good."

"Do what you can," he told them, and went downstairs. A Coast Guard captain entered, and he asked, "Captain Grimes! How many did we get?"

"Three," the commander of the operation told him. "That seems to be all there were."

Hartman shook his head. "No, Braden said there were four. We're missing one."

"Unless he had a hiding hole someplace, I don't see how," the commander said.

Hartman thought a minute. "Hmmm . . . Braden was with the Bureau. This is a Bureau safe house. Makes sense the other four were Bureau, too. If *you* were with the FBI, Captain, and you were being attacked by your own people, where would you hide? Suppose, say, you were a Coast Guardsman in full uniform."

Grimes saw what he was getting back. "I'd join the hunters at first opportunity."

The agent nodded. "Come on. Let's check out my people."

It took some time to sound them up. Hartman had them in a semi-military formation, and he knew his count. He had only one name from Braden, but it was the right one.

"All right, people!" he called to them. "Now, we can go through processing, or ugly shootouts, or like that—but why not make it simple? Agent Alton, why not just step forward and save us a lot of trouble?"

Alton, several rows back, felt a shock go through him at the mention of his name. Everything seemed to just drain out of him; it was all over now. There was no more use.

He pushed through the crowd and walked to Bob Hartman. "I'm Alton," he said softly.

"Who'd you work for, Alton?" Hartman asked him, an almost casual tone in his voice.

The renegade agent shrugged. "We never knew. Sombody big. Somebody who had access to all the computer files. Somebody who knew where all the bodies were buried on people like me."

Hartman nodded. "Blackmail, huh? Well, Alton, it's all over now." He turned to the Coast Guardsmen. "Take him."

Sandra O'Connell awoke and looked around. She knew the feelings she had now; she'd awakened much like this once before.

It took considerable effort to get up and sit on the edge of the bed. Yes, it *was* a bed. It was a little efficiency apartment, old, with a lot of roaches and bad smells. Outside, all around, came the sounds of people, children mostly.

She tried to clear her head, to think. It was hard. The pictures were there but the words wouldn't come.

She was nude, but some clothing lay draped over a chair near her. It looked familiar.

There was a small table in front of the chair, and on it was a ty—ty—she couldn't think of the word "typewriter" to save her life. She stared at it.

She got up, dizzily, unsteadily, and made her way over to the chair. There was paper in the machine, and some words had been typed on it. At least she thought they were words.

She couldn't read the words. Even the letters, the

symbols, made no sense to her now. Just so many funny lines. Several balled-up sheets of paper were around on the floor. She ignored them, sat down on the chair, and tried to get hold of herself.

That bad man, what was his name? He gave her some stuff to make her dumb. For always, they said.

But they also gave her stuff to make people sick.

She tried to get dressed. It was a simple pair of underpants, a simple bra, a simple button-type flowered shirt and zip-up skirt.

It took her over half an hour to get it on right. She kept getting the shirt sleeves on wrong, and she couldn't fasten the bra and finally gave up on it. It took a long time to figure out how the buttons worked, and she misbuttoned them time and again, finally giving up and leaving them that way. The skirt was on backwards, but she didn't care.

The sneakers were a challenge, too. Try as she might, they wouldn't fit, and it was some time before she realized that she was trying to put the right one on the left foot and vice-versa. When she did get them right, the laces were beyond her, and she finally gave up in frustration.

There was a basin there, and she went over to it, turning handles until the water came on. She grasped an old ceramic cup with both hands and filled it with water to overflowing, then drank from it. It spilled and dribbled all over.

In the cracked mirror above the basin she looked at herself. It was hard to see close-up, and she backed away a little.

It was a drooling, mis-dressed idiot she saw. The sight frightened and fascinated her at the same time.

That's me, she told herself. *That's me for always.*

She sat down on the floor and started crying, and

for the longest time she couldn't stop. Finally she wiped her face on the pillowcase and looked around.

There was some money on the table, too, she noticed. She reached up for it, pulled it down to her, and at the same time knocked another object off. It fell to the floor with a clatter and she stared at it.

It was a big, long, sharp knife.

She looked back at the money. Except for it being green, it made no sense to her. She couldn't tell one bill from another, nor recognize any of the portraits or place them with their proper denominations.

She tried to count how many there were, but she got lost after "five."

She was hungry, and there was nothing to eat here. She knew she was in a city, a place with a lot of people. Out there she could get something to eat. There was this money.

But—she would make people real sick if she did, she remembered. Anybody she saw or touched. She didn't like that. She wanted to make people feel good, not sick.

They said they would make her dumb and they had. They said she'd be so dumb she'd go out and make people sick. Well, she'd fool them. She remembered that much. She wasn't *all* dumb. She would fool them. She would sit right here, that's what she would do.

It didn't take very long at all for her to get bored sitting there, and she finally got up and made her way unsteadily to the window, which was open. She almost tripped over her own feet doing so.

She looked out. It was day time, and there were lots of buildings and lots more people. Lots of shops and stores and people walking all over. Music was coming from somewhere, and it sounded nice. She started trying to hum it, but even as it continued to play she got all mixed up.

She'd drank more water. A lot more. She was soaking wet now, and the water was going through her like a sieve. She had to go to the bathroom and there was no place to do that.

Her eyes went back to that knife. If she wasn't going to make other people sick, she couldn't stay in the room forever. She sank down on the floor, tears welling up in her, eyes on that knife, wishing she knew what to do.

Bob Hartman beat Jake Edelman to New York; a swift Air Force executive jet had sped him from Whiteoaks in under an hour and a quarter, getting him in about 10:00 A.M. He hadn't slept a wink in almost three days and looked it, but he was running on adrenalin. After being frustrated by this case for so long, things were finally breaking all over and he couldn't rest.

Jake came in by shuttle at 10:20; New York police and the local Bureau office had prepared for him. He bounced off the plane and hurried to a waiting black car.

"Hello, Bob!" He greeted his associate and they got in with a quick handshake. The car took off, and Edelman looked over at the younger man.

"You look like hell," he said.

Hartman smiled. "Well, I take after my teacher."

The Chief Inspector got down to business. "She's in there? You're sure?"

Hartman shrugged. "Who knows? We've had

units around the place for a couple of hours. The neighbors know nothing, of course, except that the apartment was rented a couple weeks ago, furnished, but as far as they knew never lived in. They have one john to the floor up there in that project, and nobody's run into anybody else taking a crap. Our sensors heard someone moving in there, but we decided not to move until you got here. Considering Braden, we'd all be the enemy to her."

Edelman nodded. "I checked with Dr. Romans at Bethesda about mitoricine. It's an ugly drug but it *can* be treated. The real question is whether or not she really *was* infected with the Wilderness Organism."

"No way," the younger agent assured him, grinning a bit evilly. "Braden died on the operating table, but we had Alton and probed him—and it was simple to pick up the other two who brought her here. None of them would touch the germ with a ten-foot pole. They're scared to death of it."

Edelman seemed satisfied. They sped through streets clogged with pedestrians but strangely devoid of cars. Soldiers were everywhere, along with a lot of New York police cars. When the emergency had cracked down, this city was one of the few with real resistance, and it still wasn't completely under control. The rioting and arson had been pretty well stopped, though; they had simply shot the legs off anybody violating the curfew. Still, there was more potential for trouble here than almost anywhere else in the country; you could almost smell the seething resentment.

The apartment house was a dingy, ancient, crumbling structure, the remains of some long-ago project for the very poor. The squalor, filth, and smell of the place was more animal-like than human. *People shouldn't have to live this way,* Jake Edelman thought.

Up the stairs to 3A; the door was so warped it looked off its hinges, and there were only the ghosts of where the numbers once had been, slightly cleaner than the surroundings. The other residents had been cleared out by this time; most were grumbling and protesting behind police barricades in the street outside.

Edelman put his ear to the door. There was no sound, and for a moment he feared that she was dead. Then, suddenly, he heard a noise, a shifting of a body.

"Dr. O'Connell?" he called, as calmly as he could. "Dr. O'Connell, this is Jake Edelman. Are you in there?"

Suddenly her voice came back at them, its sound strange, almost terrible to hear, its inflection reminiscent of a hysterical retarded person. "Stay away! Don't come near me!"

"I'm coming in," he told her. "I don't want to hurt you, only help you."

"No!" she screamed. "I'll make you sick, I will!"

"They lied!" he said. "You don't have the disease! They lied to you! Now, let me in!"

"No, no! Keep out! I'll—" There was the sound of someone getting up, moving away, then the sound of something dropping on the floor and the person struggling to pick it up.

Jake Edelman acted. The landlord's passkey was already in the lock and now he twisted it suddenly and pushed open the door.

She screamed wordlessly and ran to a far corner of the room, standing there, a little hunched over, like a cornered and frightened animal. She had the knife in her hand.

Edelman looked at her and found it almost impossible to believe that it was the same woman he'd known. There was a sadness mixed with outrage at the sight of her, but he kept it inside.

"Give me the knife, Doc," he urged gently. "It's all over now. No more drugs. No more pain. No more double-crosses. No more fear. Just give me the knife."

She looked at him wildly. "Go away!" she said. "I'll kill m'self!"

He shook his head slowly from side to side. "No, now, don't do that. That's what *they* want you to do, and you don't want to do anything *they* want you to, now do you?" He slowly started toward her as he talked. Finally he was just two meters from her, but she raised the knife, awkwardly, to her own throat. He was afraid she might do it without meaning to.

"They *lie,* Doc," Edelman told her. "They said you had the germ. You don't. That was to make you kill yourself. The drug was to make it hard for you to think, to figure a way out, and to make it easier for you to kill yourself. *They* did this to you. Don't do what *they* want you to do now." He held out his hand, his voice calm, gentle, and steady. "Let me help you. Give me the knife."

Her eyes were wild, her expression afraid and confused. The knife shook a little, but it touched her throat, scratching her.

"For the love of God, Sandra, give me the knife!" he said, more a prayer to himself than a statement directed to her. She wavered; the knife moved away a little. There was a tiny trickle of blood on her throat.

"I talked to Bart Romans at Bethesda," he told her. "The drug you got can be treated, Sandy. *It can be treated!*"

Again there was that frozen tableau for a few seconds; all seemed suspended in time. None of the people just outside the door moved or breathed; even the street sounds and the air seemed stilled.

Suddenly the knife dropped onto the floor and she pitched forward. Edelman caught her, and she pressed into him, sobbing uncontrollably. He put his arms around her and hugged and soothed her.

Now the others came into the room, slowly, carefully, led by Bob Hartman. He walked over first to the typewriter, looking at the sheet still in it.

I, Sandra O'Connell, can stand it no longer, it read. *I became part of the conspiracy to destroy the United States many years ago, while still in college. The deaths I have caused* It broke off.

Another agent reached down, picked up a balled-up piece of paper, flattened it out and handed it to Hartman.

I, Sandra O'Connell, can no longer stand the burden of my sins, it read. *I killed Mark Spiegelm—*

Jake, still gripping the sobbing woman, walked out with her as they uncurled more of the balled-up papers. There were lots of them, each apparently a false start on a suicide note. Joe Bede, who'd been abducted with her, was implicated in some, in others there was an almost insane mixture of leftist radical rhetoric and Catholic moralizing.

"*I* woulda been convinced," one of the agents said to Hartman. "But the autopsy would have showed the mitoricine, wouldn't it? Made it obvious she couldn't write these notes."

Hartman nodded. "I'd think so. But they must

have prepared for that somehow. Find out how long traces remain in the body, and also check with the city medical examiner's office. An autopsy shows only what a coroner says it does."

The agent nodded. "Okay, we'll work on this end. You?"

Bob Hartman sighed. "I think it's time for me to go back to D.C. and get a good twelve hours' solid sleep, then see what your field boys came up with."

Counting the hour on the plane, he managed to get seven hours' sleep before they called him back in.

TWENTY-SIX

"Three-4-7-3-6-8-8-3-6-8-7-3-2-8-4-8," said the computer technician. "I wish there'd been a better, more effective code. Do you know how many combinations that makes? And most of these sons of bitches used non-standard abbreviations like mad."

Jake Edelman was sympathetic. "Remember, these people have risked more than their necks for us," he said. "And this was the most unobtrusive manner of getting information to us. So—what have we got on this one?"

She sighed. "Well, of all the ones the computer flashed past we think we have it. It came in on the number for a Sam Cornish. The back-billing on the 800 exchange gave us a small chemistry lab in Westminster, Maryland. As far as we can tell, the lab's clean." She handed him the paper.

The general idea was to assign each plant a separate 800 number, so when he or she called in they could immediately tell who it was—and by that also know who *not* to shoot, if it came to that. Since the 800 numbers were toll-free only to the calling party, the recipient had the long-distance record of what number and area made the call, which made it easier.

The code was simplicity itself. You just used the letters still on most phone dials to spell out your message. This meant three possible combinations per number, unless it was a "Q" or "Z", which were not on the dial, in which case the "1" was a "Q" and the "0" a "Z". So the first three letter combinations were punched and run up and down until they made some kind of sense, then the next was added, and so on. The problem was in abbreviations and strange geographical expressions.

Jake Edelman looked at the paper. FHSE MT VENUS DC TGT, it read. He looked up at the technician. "F-H-S-E?" he asked.

She shrugged. "Firehouse, farm house, something like that," she guessed. "Believe me, it could be anything. Those first four are the big questions."

"What's this 'Mt. Venus?' " he asked. "Couldn't it be something else to go with the first four?"

"It could be," she said, "but I punched up the Carroll County atlas for Westminster and started looking. There's a Mt. Venus Road #1 and a Mt. Venus Road #2 in Carroll, although they're a ways from Westminster. Still, it checks. And no firehouses on the roads. I'd say they're in a farmhouse on Mt. Venus Road in Carroll County, about twenty kilometers northwest of Westminster, Maryland. There's an emergency shuttle service from there through Manchester and then to Westminster. I'd say it checks out."

He nodded approvingly. "Well done." He looked back at the paper. "D.C. target, huh? How many does this make?"

She didn't hesitate. "Fourteen now, with the batch that came in in the last day and a half. We have the locations for most of the major cities. Of the tops, we're only missing Chicago, the Bay Area, Houston, St. Louis, Detroit, and New Orleans."

The Chief Inspector gave her lavish praise and she left, but inwardly he was disturbed. He called for Hartman, who saw his superior's concern.

"What's the matter? I thought you'd be over-joyed," he asked, stifling a yawn.

"It's good, all right," Edelman said. "It's *too* good. If we got results like this on a routine counter-espionage case or a syndicate plot, I'd smell something there, too." He looked up at the sleepy younger agent. "Don't you see, Bob? How many plants did we have? All told?"

"Thirty-five or forty, I think," Hartman said. "Want me to check?"

Edelman dismissed the offer with a wave of his hand. "So, let's say forty. Now, they're going to hit the twenty top U.S. cities—maybe the top twenty-five, but the ones we have are all in the top twenty so let's stick to that." He shifted, looking directly into the eyes of the other man. "Bob, even if the impossible happened and all of our plants got through undetected—an incredible result for a makeshift organization like this—what would be the odds of us getting plants on fourteen *different* teams out of a possible twenty? Or fifty, for that matter. See what I mean?"

Hartman was awake now, and his mouth opened a bit in surprise. "So that's the answer," he said.

Edelman nodded. "That's right. It all ties together now. All of it, a hundred percent. I don't think we have to hold off on those raids for fear of warning the others any longer. Let's hit them."

Hartman nodded. "And then what?"

Edelman's face was grim, his tone of voice more chilling than Hartman could ever remember.

"Bob," the older man said, "I came into this

agency when it was rocked up and down by abuses of power. In reaction, they weakened it beyond its ability to function, lots of nasty things happened, and we got a compromise that lasted until the emergency. Secrecy was the rule, yes, and we played by the rules. Absolutely. Or we got tossed in the pen ourselves. Besides, I believed that my grandparents had been gassed to death by a system that abused its absolute power, opening up the worst in human beings. I was never going to let that power rule me, never let the temptations of abuse creep up on me, for that would be a betrayal of the principles for which my grandparents died." He sighed. "And now, after all this time, I realize that when this crunch came it was a cage, a prison. It was one of the reasons they put me on this investigation. Hell, Bob, the Nazis of my grandparents' Germany arose in a democracy, and took over and dominated an enlightened and educated population. That was because the Nazis didn't play by any rules, Bob—and in opposing them, you had to debase your principles or you would be debased by them. My ancestors didn't, and they died."

Hartman, who had no such connections to the past and no particular feeling for it, still saw the older man's point.

Edelman's fist slammed down on the desk, making papers and objects jump. "Damn it! I've been used—we've all been used—by the spiritual children of those Nazis! I'm mad, Bob. Damned mad. They set up this emergency, they created this crisis, and all so they could play by these rules, gain this absolute power. Well, by damn, I'm not going to be another good Jew who's marched to the ovens! *We're* the authority, too, for a while—as long as they let us.

And we've got all the powers they gave themselves for the emergency. Well, now we're going to use them! I'll still play by the rules—their rules! Let's see how they like it!"

The last was said with such bitter acidity that it made even Hartman uncomfortable. "Easy, Jake. You know your heart—"

"Heart be damned!" he said. "That's the other reason it's me in this chair, Bob. When they don't need me any more, a little syringe filled with air and —*zap!* The old man's ticker went out. Hero's burial." He calmed down a little. "What about our mysterious phone number?"

Hartman's eyebrows rose. He was taken aback by the sudden change in tone. "Well, the 500 exchange is the overload from the 800s," he replied. "A lot of it's legit business. The 555 exchance, however, is strictly Executive Branch, White House. The number goes into a centrex computer inside the White House and is routed according to a preprogrammed codex. No way to trace it specifically unless we were inside the computer with somebody who really knew what was what, and that's out of the question."

"Not Health and Welfare?" Edelman was genuinely surprised.

Hartman shook his head. "No, that's 517. This is White House."

Jake Edelman sighed and assumed his thinking pose. Hartman knew better than to disturb him, and, frankly, he felt like hell and didn't want to, anyway. Finally the senior agent broke out of it, lit a cigar, blew a big cloud of bluish-gray smoke into the air, and said, "Bob, I'm going to take a gamble. It's a big one, but solid, I think. If not, it won't make much difference anyway. I'm asking you to handle it, so the initial hot potato is in your lap. It can kill you, Bob. Are you game?"

The younger agent was puzzled, but nodded. "You know I am, Jake."

"You know Allen Honner?"

Hartman whistled. "The Chief of Staff? By reputation. I've never met him."

"Well, I have, many times," Edelman said. "He's the President's man on the crisis committee. I checked out a lot of that committee, Bob. Several of them are fans of Mickey Mouse. But Honner—hell. He could do anything—program that centrex computer, get the goods on anybody blackmailable, even rig the assignments of Secret Service. And, if *I* were running a plot as elaborate as this, I sure as hell would be on the committee to solve my own crisis, wouldn't you? It'd be the only way to know whether the plan was working, developing cracks, whatever. I'm betting on him, Bob."

"Logical," Hartman admitted. "So?"

"I want you to put the snatch on Honner, Bob," Edelman said icily. "I want him snatched, then stashed at a safe house so secure even you don't know where it is. I want Bart Romans from Bethesda brought in, and I want a complete mind probe. A hundred percent. I want names, dates, places. When you get him established, call me on the green box line and I'll get there. Clear?"

Hartman shook his head slowly from side to side. "You don't want much, do you?" he sighed. "Wow! Kidnapping and mind-probing the Chief of Staff!" He looked up. "Where'll you be until my call comes in? Here?"

"An even better alibi," Edelman said. "I'm going to personally lead a raid on the D.C. target team over in western Maryland."

The younger man yawned again, got up, and stretched. "Well, okay. Have fun. I'm going to go run some Mickey Mouse fan names through the little computer. We'll see just what the hell is going on here."

The house was easy to spot; there wasn't anybody living in the others and hadn't been for some time. Although the target showed signs of occupancy, it still looked as if no one was home.

They had it ringed and targeted, and were ready for just about anything when they delivered the utimatum through bullhorns.

The lack of any response worried Edelman. Soldiers and agents finally rushed the place, and got no response, either. The door was blown open and they ran inside, quickly fanning out all over the house.

The only human they found was one handsome, muscular black man bound and gagged in one of the bedrooms. In the kitchen, though, they found the remains of the paraphernalia used to administer the vaccine and a number of blue cylinders. None of them were leaking, but the gauges on three of them showed them to be partially empty.

Edelman had no trouble identifying Sam Cornish; he had a photo and prints to settle his plant's identity.

Cornish was upset. "You the head man?" he asked the Chief Inspector. Edelman nodded. "Good! They're crazy! She's the craziest of the bunch!"

"Did they make you?" Edelman asked. "And, if so, how come you're still breathing?"

Cornish shook his head almost in disbelief. "No!

At least, I don't think so. I got them to check out the vaccine, though. I had this feeling all along we were gettin' played for suckers. And we were! It's water— Plain water! And she knew it! Knew it and still sent 'em out, after icing me to make sure I wouldn't tip 'em! Water!"

It took a little pressing to get the full story from the distraught man, and when they got it they were all a little upset.

"She must have decided they couldn't wait for the deadline," Edelman said. "Not unless she wanted to kill you. So they're gone. In action with what they could take. The mean of the true fanatic, I guess."

Sam Cornish still couldn't believe it. "But—we were had and she knew it! Those phony Air Force and State Troopers—they weren't phony. Camp Liberty—hell, I bet those jets I saw so regular overhead were official flights. I bet it's in Nevada or something!"

Edelman smiled. "You guessed a lot, didn't you? I think maybe you'd better give us what you can on the other people so we can stop them if possible. Then you're coming with me."

"Hey, inspector!" one of the agents called. Edelman turned. "You won't believe this, but in this briefcase is everyplace they're going to strike!" the agent said. "God! They didn't even bother to take the stuff with 'em or destroy it."

Sam Cornish nodded slowly. "Wasn't any use," he said. "Suzy knew they weren't long for this world after the mission."

For the next hour and a half they went over descriptions while the place was dusted. Before Edelman and Cornish reached Washington again, the bureau's computers had already made eight of them.

Edelman stopped only long enough to call in. There was a message from Hartman, but he could only tell the other man to take it on his own. Somewhere in or nearing Washington right now were ten terrorists armed with the Wilderness Organism, nine who thought they were immune and a tenth who was so fanatical she would go on with it anyway.

"She's spent her whole life in the revolutionary movement," Sam explained. "One of the tenets of the faith was that you induced a repressive fascism as the setup for revolution. I guess if you really believe that shit you might do what she's doing, even though you know you're a fascist tool."

Edelman nodded agreement. "She just was too much of a true believer in her own peculiar brand of religion. But—she loved you, Mr. Cornish. Loved you enough to save you when she knew she had to die."

Sam Cornish's face was sad, and there seemed a distant look in his eyes. He turned slowly to Edelman and said, "Can I go with them to Suzy's target? I—I'd like to be there. Maybe I . . ."

Edelman nodded. "I'll take you there. She's to board the Metro at Connecticut and Calvert, and ride it out to Glebe Road in Arlington. She has only the one spray, and it's got to look like hair spray or something to get by the checkpoints. She'll spray the train and station. The best time would be just before rush hour, or possibly during it. After four—which gives us a little over fifteen minutes." He paused, a thought rising in his mind. "You don't suppose she'll vary the plan? Get on elsewhere?"

Cornish was positive. "No, not Suzy. Once the plan was made and rehearsed, she followed it to the letter, always."

By the time they made the station, several other

things had been accomplished. The partial prints
and Sam's descriptions had been computer-matched
and they knew the identities and general ap-
pearances of all of them now, along with their
targets. Additionally, while the station was open,
Metro trains were ordered to skip it. The crowds
were backing up, but the soldiers at the station
checkpoints looking at ID cards had kept things
even slower.

"If she sees you she might not use the spray,"
Edelman said hopefully. "We'll see. We have to take
the chance. Too many people down there to do a
general shoot-out unless it's the last resort."

"Worth a try," Cornish said, his nerves tensing,
stomach tight.

Behind them, special Army trucks were pulling
up, and men climbed into strange-looking suits like
spacesuits and checked out nasty-looking tanks with
insulated hoses terminating in what looked like
single-barrelled shotgun housings.

Now Edelman and Cornish joined a group of FBI
and DC police personnel for the walk down into the
station.

The well-lit station was spacious and clean under
the monitors of Metro security. The station itself
was a distinctive work of architecture, cool and efficient. While the field agents continued on into the
gathering crowd, Edelman pulled his charge over to
one of the security booths. "Let's see if we can pick
her up on the circuit first," he said, adding ominously, "If it's clear she's already started any spraying or
is about to, the flamethrowing team will come in full
force. Remember that." Cornish nodded but said
nothing.

The cameras started their sweep, the technician

adjusting so that the faces of many of the people could be seen. They were looking for lone female figures of small stature, and they found several, but Cornish shook his head "no" to each as they looked. Finally they reached all the way down to the end of the platform, where, off by herself, a slight female was reading a paper, a standard shoulder purse suspended from a strap around her neck.

"Hold that one!" Cornish ordered. "Can you blow it up a little more?"

They tried, but as long as the newspaper was up little could be seen but the top of long, reddish-brown hair. Suzy's was short and jet black, but she'd brought wigs while in Westminster. The big man stared hard, praying that it was she, not quite understanding his own feelings at this point, nor even why he'd insisted on coming along, participating in the trackdown. He wasn't sure what he'd do it if *was* Suzy behind that paper. He could only wait and hold his breath, while the other cameras continued to pan and the security and police teams mingled below, trying to get a make on her.

Two figures walked, hand-in-hand, along the sidewalk next to the Congressional Office Building. They looked like two lovers out enjoying a break from whatever routine they normally followed. They turned a corner, and someone with a walkie-talkie in the part just across the street whispered, "It's a make. Go!"

Men and women armed with automatic weapons seemed to pop out of every place at once. A bullhorn barked, "You on the corner! Stop and put both hands in the air!"

The couple broke apart, and the man reached into the woman's bag for something as both dropped as one to the sidewalk. It wasn't good enough. From all over hundreds of rounds poured into them, making in split seconds an awfully bloody mess. Now figures in the white pressure-suits moved up, a confirmation was made on what remained of the dead, and it was noted that there were several holes in the leather purse. One of the suited figures reached in and pulled out a metal object looking much like an ordinary can of shaving cream complete with brand name and trademark. There was a nick in it, but it looked unopened and undamaged. A bomb-disposal truck was called, and the can was placed inside. They were about to clear the mess when they noticed a slight bulge under the man's coat. They opened it to see two small pressurized cylinders strapped to his underarms, and long, thin plastic tubes running down the sleeves. There was no way to tell quickly if the stuff was on.

They stood back and bathed the dead bodies and most of the street corner until it was ablaze with white-hot liquid fire.

The National Visitor's Center used to be the train station when trains were the chief mode of transportation; it still was for some, a center for commuter trains and high-speed megalopolis runs. Out of one train from Baltimore stepped a hesitant young woman, looking nervously around. She got three steps off the platform when figures moved in back of her, grabbing her arms while one shot an injection that knocked her cold. The jets, fed by two small cylinders worn under her blouse and shooting downward to the ground, had obviously not been activated.

A young-looking officer, an Air Force captain in full uniform, got off the bus at the Pentagon and showed his credentials. He was carefully checked by the first team and waved on, making his way, courier-style briefcase in hand, across the inner parking area toward one of the entrances. A checkpoint sergeant, after waving him on, lifted his walkie-talkie and said a few words.

As the captain neared the last rows of cars, figures popped up all around him, weapons pointing directly at him from all directions. He stopped, looked completely around, saw there was no way out, then smiled, shrugged, and put up his hands, the briefcase, unopened, still in his right hand.

The frail, elderly woman in the wheelchair being pushed by a younger man up to the entrance of the Sheraton Washington looked terribly harmless. The man, however, met all but one of the criteria the personnel on guard had on the people they were looking for; he was clean-shaven, but moustaches are easily removed. They decided to take no chances. Armed men and women popped out of the bushes and nearby cars.

The man looked confused and let go of the wheelchair. The old woman started rolling downhill, and, as she did so, a couple of the cops moved to stop her. Quickly the blanket fell, revealing a submachine gun with which the "old woman" opened fire. Also unmasked were two bologna-shaped modules on either side of her in the chair, aimed slightly down.

Two men in white pressure-suits suddenly popped up just in front of her and, as she tried to shift the submachine gun to them they opened up with liquid fire. Back near the hotel entrance, the younger man stood frozen, then slowly raised his hands in the air. There was fear on his face and panic in his voice as he screamed, "I haven't triggered it! Don't burn me! *For God's sake, don't burn me!"*

And so it went across the city. Some were uglier than others, needing extensive flamethrowing, then sanitizing and scientific teams from the Bureau of Standards to determine that none of the Wilderness Organism were loose, and a few innocent bystanders were caught in the mess as some of the terrorists surrendered and others resisted to the death.

"It's Suzy," Cornish said softly as the woman lowered the newspaper a bit. There was no mistaking her now.

He and Edelman walked down to the platform, and were joined by several others as they made their way toward the far end. Calls were already going out to stop all westbound trains, and slowly soldiers moved in to start clearing away the people already down there.

Suzanne Martine was a survivor. She smelled the wrongness and felt the danger even before she saw anything to justify it. Still, she was calm, folding the newspaper and putting it on the bench carefully before casually looking up and around.

She made her hunters easily; they were the only people moving toward her. She went through the various options quickly as she continued to pretend that she hadn't seen them, picked the one that seemed most likely to provide some sort of chance, and walked slowly over to the edge of the platform.

Pistols came out, and the men and women of the authority she hated so much started running toward her.

"Suzy! No! Don't!" she heard a familiar voice scream, and for a split-second she hesitated, seeing Sam. Then, suddenly, as the first shots started, she jumped down onto the trackbed, managing somehow to keep her balance, and ran into the tunnel as shots ricocheted around and near her.

Sam Cornish got to the edge, turned to Edelman, and said, "Please! Let me go!"

The Chief Inspector thought for a second, then nodded. "Okay, son," he said, "but flame squads will be at both ends. Talk her out or I won't be able to stop them." Again the split-second hesitation, then he reached into his jacket and brought out his .38. "Take this."

Sam stared at the pistol for a second, as if he'd never considered the possibilities before. Then he took it, turned, and jumped down onto the track bed. "Watch that third rail!" somebody shouted, but he was gone into the darkness.

TWENTY-SEVEN

He was a tall man of about forty-five, in a brown suit and yellow shirt with brown-and-yellow striped tie, horn-rimmed glasses, and the look of a successful business executive.

He'd received a call from one of Edelman's team on some breakthroughs, and since actions were still in progress they'd requested that he come over there to get the information. He needed and was entitled to it; Allen Honner was the President's Chief of Staff.

A sleek, black car passed the east gate checkpoint at the White House and rolled up to the entrance. The two men inside looked like what they were: career FBI types. One got out, nodded to Honner, and opened the rear door for him. He got in without hesitation, and the agent, picking up a briefcase from the front seat, switched around and got in next to him.

The car started off, passed back out onto Pennsylvania Avenue, and turned right toward the FBI Building.

Honner was confident and interested. "I'll be having a late dinner with the President," he told the agent beside him. "I'll need all you've got. You know there'll be a meeting on the fifteenth on the status and need for the emergency, and a speech on the conclusions reached there on the sixteenth."

The other man nodded. "Don't worry," he said. "I expect we'll have most of this case wrapped or on the way to cleaning up by late this evening."

Honner glanced around. "Hey! Wasn't that the Hoover Building we just passed?" he asked, suddenly disturbed.

The other man shrugged it off and reached into his briefcase. "Don't worry about it. We're not going to the Bureau. Too many leaks there. We need absolute privacy for this."

The Chief of Staff seemed a little upset, and he started to press the matter when the agent's right hand came out with a small pistol with silencer attached and pointed it at him.

"What's the meaning of this?" Honner demanded. "Who are you?"

The agent's left hand fumbled in the case and emerged with a gas-powered syringe. "I'm a fan of Mickey Mouse," said the agent, and, pushing the injector against Honner's buttocks, fired the drug through the Chief of Staff's expensive brown pants.

A few blocks down they switched to a D.C. police van, which roared off, lights flashing. None of the patrols, sentries, and the like checked it. They turned and headed back along Pennsylvania Avenue, reached the circle, turned onto Wisconsin, and headed into Georgetown, turning the lights off now. Down into the old but fancy original section they drove, finally reaching the spot they wanted, turning into a back alley, and pulling up behind a particular house.

The agent fumbled in Honner's pockets, got a key ring, and got out. Quickly and efficiently they got the unconscious man out of the van and through the back door of the house. Four other agents, two male and two female, walked down the alley from opposite directions and, one by one, entered the house. The van drove off, to be replaced in the D.C. police garage.

It was a safe house nobody knew, all right.

Allen Honner awoke, bound hand and foot, in his own bed.

"What the hell is this?" he demanded. "Who are you that you *dare* this?"

A thirty-ish man in shirtsleeves, looking tired and serious, came up to him. "We're the FBI, Mr. Honner," he said dryly. "The part you don't own."

Honner's face showed panic. "You have no right to do this!" he almost yelled at them. "No right at all! Do you realize who I am?"

Bob Hartman nodded slowly. "We know, Mr. Honner. And, yes, we *do* have the right. You gave it to us. You and whatever others are involved in this. Preemptory arrest of citizens whenever an officer believes there is cause, suspension of *habeus corpus,* suspension of civil rights. Yes, Mr. Honner. We *do* have the right. And, thanks to directives coming out of your office, and those of the Justice Department, we may use any and all means of questioning if it is in the interests of internal security. My boss thinks you're a traitor, Mr. Honner. That gives me the right to break every damned little bone in your body, stuff you with any and all mind-probes, drugs, and other devices, and do whatever I feel like to get the truth." He smiled evilly. "And I'm not even responsible, Mr. Honner. I'm just following orders."

Allen Honner was scared to death. His face was white, and he was sweating profusely despite central air conditioning.

"Look," he said. "I'm powerful. One of the most powerful men in this country! Anything you want! Power, money—you name it. Anything. Just—don't hurt me."

Bob Hartman gave a dry chuckle. "All right, Mr. Honner, I'll make you a deal. The truth. The complete and full story, no commas and periods omitted. That's the price, Mr. Honner. The truth, or we get it our way."

The Chief of Staff looked around at the grim faces staring down at him on his own bed. Fear was mixed with confusion. "I don't understand you people! What's in it for you? What the hell will this get you?"

Hartman shook his head sadly. "I see a brilliant mind reduced to a pathetic pawn. I see men and women afraid to move, to think. Others—who knows how many countless lives wracked by a disease that was engineered by human minds. *Engineered!*" His voice exploded with rage. "Crippled minds, crippled bodies!" Suddenly his tone lowered, became calm and mixed with pity. "No, Mr. Honner, I don't think you and your kind will ever understand what we get out of this." He turned to one of the women, nodded, and she brought up a huge case filled with, it turned out, medical gear and monitors. Honner's eyes fell on it and went wide with terror.

"All right! All right! What do you want to know?" he cried, then seemed to sink down in the bed, resistance gone. And yet, as they stared at him, a curious half-smile crept into his expression, and his eyes seemed wild. "I'll tell you what I can," he said. "It won't matter. It's too far along. Even if you know everything now, there's not a damned thing you can do to stop it."

Hartman didn't like the switch in the man's manner; that last was spoken not with bravado but out of conviction. He began to have the creepy feeling that Honner just might be right.

He reached over, got a chair, and sat down in reversed position, leaning forward on the chair back. Recording devices started.

"Whose phone rings when I call 1-500-555-2323?" Hartman asked.

Honner chuckled. "One of mine—if I'm there. If not, one of my assistants'. The coder on the phone makes the voice identical no matter who is speaking."

Hartman nodded. "Where was the Wilderness Organism developed?" he asked.

This, too, amused Honner. "At Fort Dietrick, at NDCC, of course. A private foundation we helped endow started the work based on the Cambridge stuff long ago. A couple of solid scientists felt they knew where both we and the Russians had made our mistakes, and saw the total ban on research as dumb. They, like we, were convinced that other nations were working on the recombinanat DNA problems, and that we would be vulnerable, wide open in fact, if that were the case. It was good defense and good science. The work was there; you couldn't wipe it away. It was inevitable that it be pursued. When President Wainwright was elected to his first term, we arranged for that and a number of other projects to be transferred, funded, and masked by NDCC, supposedly as cancer research—which it was, too, among other things."

"Where are the remaining blue cylinders and Wilderness Organism cultures?"

"Some are at Camp Liberty, some are at Dietrick, in a special bunker, and the rest—most of it—is with the poison gas stores at Dugway in Utah," Honner said. "Except, of course, for the stuff already distributed. We didn't want some of it out very long. It's subject to easy mutation, and that lowers the effectiveness of the vaccines."

Hartman took a deep breath. "Who are 'we', Mr. Honner? Who, besides you, is involved in this?"

"Patriots," Honner said. "Men and women of vision. This isn't anything that's just grown in the last couple of years, you know. It began, in fact, before I was born—a group of patriotic, concerned citizens who saw how this country was going to hell. We were weakening ourselves and retreating from the world in a slow, steady erosion of power and authority—matched by the same disintegration of society inside the country. Open sex, the breakup of the family, the discarding of old values without gaining or adding any new ones. These people deplored this, organized, worked long and hard to set this up, to stave off the eventual collapse either by external attack or from within until they were in a position to control this country and reverse the declines. It was a long time coming—I doubt if a single one of the original people is still alive. But they did their work well. Younger people, bright, ambitious people were raised and nurtured and came up slowly within the system, aided by political maneuvers to place one key person here, another there, working, waiting, until the seat of power was also ours, occupied by one of our own people."

"President Wainwright," Hartman said. "They always said that he was the type of man you'd invent for President. Now you're telling me he *was* invented?"

Honner nodded and laughted. "And, you see,

that's why you can't win. It isn't one guy like me in a power position, or a dozen. It's hundreds and hundreds, all in the right places. We control the Executive Branch. We control five Supreme Court positions—thanks to some timely and easily arranged natural deaths. We already had two seats anyway. Some top senators and key congressmen. And, most important, a lot of key civil service bureaucrats."

Even though Jake had guessed it and Hartman had suspected it, the sheer scope of the conspiracy staggered him. And, once in those positions, those key people had unlimited access to information on most Americans, including others who worked for government. The IRS could tell them just who was spending what on what. The Treasury had a record of every check anybody ever wrote. Blackmail, pressure, and outright power bought the others—and, in many cases, bureaucracy did it of its own accord. If the proper codes and the proper signatures were on the proper forms, you could get away with anything.

Honner talked on and on, and the more he talked the more confident he became, and not without reason. After all, what could Bob Hartman and Jake Edelman do with all this? Go to the press—which was totally controlled and censored? Get powerful political help? Who was who? Even Honner wasn't sure of everybody; they needed a computer to keep track. And on the sixteenth President Wainwright would announce that the plot had been smashed, that it was in fact internal, and launch a massive purge of government. He would eliminate—literally —those he needed to, consolidate his power, so that only his own people held the reins in all three branches of government. Scapegoats would be trotted out and shot, some after giving drug-induced confessions. The takeover would be absolute; within one to two weeks after the address, the last echoes of democracy and freedom in the United States would be gone, probably forever. Even the radicals—the products of schools, universities would be purged. A new generation would be raised under different standards according to government edict. Conformity would be enforced by merciless pressure; the price of not obeying would be too great.

The plot was cracked, all right—but not in time, not in time at all. Honner, Hartman thought with a sinking feeling, was right. They were discovering the evidence of a *coup d'état* weeks after it had already taken place.

Sam Cornish walked into the darkness of the subway tunnel. He suddenly felt a little foolish and out of place, and he looked at the pistol in his right hand and thought, *What the hell am I doing here?*

It was not complete darkness; signal lights and occasional bulbs planted for emergency use every ten meters or so made it possible to see without breaking his neck. Once or twice he came close to the third rail, the source of power and current for the trains, but managed to avoid stepping directly on or leaning into a hot section. He frankly wasn't certain what was hot and what was not.

The next station was some twenty blocks or more away; there was no sign of it in the ghostly-lit tunnel whose bulbs spread out before him almost to infinity. He knew what lay at the next station: a squad of riflemen and a flamethrowing team, the same as was in back of him. *She must know it, too,* he thought, still surprised and still not understanding why he was still surprised. His mind kept going around and around like that.

Either he would find her or he would miss her. If he did the latter, well, the next group to come in sure wouldn't. And if he found her?

Why had he taken the pistol? It was *Suzy* out there, *Suzy* running and hiding in the dark, not some mysterious ogre.

There was a dripping sound, some leak or something that reverberated up and down the empty tunnel.

Yes, it was Suzy out there, he told himself, but not the Suzy of the camps or the Suzy of the good days just over in the Carroll County woods—just over? It seemed years ago—but the Suzy of Kennedy Airport and the marshland near the end of the runways. The Suzy who told them to hold the vertical mortar steady as she timed the takeoff of the great silver bird with hundreds of innocent and non-idealogical people on board, and smiled and laughed as she timed it just right and dropped it in and it had gone *whomp* and torn into that plane and she'd laughed when the explosion littered the sky and found pleasure in the screams, the screams, the screams . . .

Several minutes in, he thought he detected movement. There was some sort of sign up there on the right, and he was sure that some figure had moved near it. Just a shadow, but . . .

The sign marked an escape shaft in case the trains got stalled without power or crashed or whatever. There was also a pumping noise as it became clear that the shaft was also used for providing some ventilation for the stagnant air of the tunnels.

How many between here and there? he wondered.

Would Edelman and his people have them all covered?

But, no, he scolded himself. He was thinking like himself. He would be looking for a way out; not Suzy, oh, no. She had a mission to complete. She couldn't get on one of their fancy big trains now, no, but she could if possible still do a little damage. What would Suzy do?

Air shaft, his mind told him. Not only fresh air down but dead air and exhaust and fumes up. An outlet to the air.

He walked more quickly now, toward that exit sign. And then, there he was. He stopped and listened. There were noises all right, slight and easily overlooked, but there, beyond the exit.

"Suzy!" he shouted, his voice echoing eerily up and down the length of tunnel. "Suzy! It's Sam!"

The sound of his own voice obscured all other sounds for a moment.

"Suzy! Don't do it! It's a plot by The Man, Suzy! We've been suckered by the pigs all along! None of the big boys will die—they got the real stuff! Just you and me and a lot of ordinary people! Suzy! Don't you end up working for the other side!"

Still there was no response. He pushed open the exit door and walked into the shaft. Surprisingly, even to him, he felt no fear at all. He no longer had anything to be afraid of. That, in itself, was a wonderful thing, and he savored it.

There was a wide metal ladder in the center of the shaft, and, looking up, he could see light from the distant street. For a moment he thought he'd guessed wrong, but then he saw her, on a metal ledge not eight centimeters wide, near an access valve for the air system. She was just standing there, looking down at him, but she had opened her shirt to expose the two gas nodules, and had the two long, thin spray tubes out of her pants legs. One hand steadied her on the precarious perch; the other was on the left gas cannister.

He started up the ladder.

"Stay back, Sam!" she warned him. "This isn't any of your fight. I don't know if you finked or what, but it's not your fight, Sam. You don't belong here. Go away."

He continued up at a steady pace. Now he was only a few meters below her.

"Stop where you are, Sam, or I'll just let these jets go right now," she said. Her right hand, which she'd been using to keep her balance, came free, and she grasped the right tube and stuck it in a cavity in the wall behind the air intake valve.

He stopped and stared at her, surprised now at himself as tears welled up in his eyes.

"Stop, Suzy! Please! This is crazy! There's no *reason . . .*" he pleaded.

"Only in blood can come the revolution," she said, eyes not on him but on something distant, something neither he nor most other human beings could see. "The blood of the innocent, though it count in the millions, buys the future of mankind."

"Suzy, if you don't stop I'll have to shoot you," he said, his voice choking up. "I can't let you do it again. Not a second time, Suzy."

Suddenly she seemed to notice him again, and she looked down on him with an expression of mixed arrogance and bewilderment. "Why, Sam?" she asked. "Penance for the plane job?" Her hand moved to the trigger for the cylinder.

He could hardly see her, yet the pistol came up

and pointed at her all the same. "No, baby," he said. "Love." He fired the pistol, not once, but all five rounds in the chambers, and he continued to pull the trigger, clicking away at the useless pistol.

Suzanne Martine stood on the perch, that same expression still there but the arrogance now fading, leaving only the bewilderment. "Sam?" she said, the tone carrying that bewilderment to him as if, for the first time in her life, she questioned everything.

And then she fell, dropping down the shaft, her body striking the ladder once and bouncing, until it hit the cement floor and lay still.

He stopped firing and looked at the pistol again in wonderment, as if he had no idea how he'd gotten there. He let it drop out of his hands and it fell, too, to the floor below.

He started climbing for the sunlight above him.

TWENTY-EIGHT

Jake Edelman looked like he was about to have a heart attack at any moment. He'd aged terribly in the past few days, and he was neither young nor in the best of condition to begin with.

Bob Hartman, who didn't look so great himself, entered, nodded, and sat down in the familiar chair.

For a while his boss said nothing, as if thinking of another world. Finally he looked over at his associate.

"It's the fifteenth," Jake Edelman said.

Hartman nodded. "You're ready?"

Edelman shrugged. "Hell, how do *I* know? Do you realize what a long shot this is?"

The younger man knew perfectly. They had it all now, everything. Everything but a way out except for an outlandish gamble by his weakened boss.

"I visited Dr. O'Connell today," Hartman said. "She's doing pretty well, but it'll take time. A lot of time. She's a remarkable human being, though, Jake. We owe a lot to her."

Edelman nodded. "Pity we couldn't get to Dr. Bede. Dead in LA with those nice little suicide notes."

"Mitoricine?"

"Who knows?" The older man shrugged. "The county medical examiner, who owes his job to

Mayor Stratton, who went to college with Allen Honner, says self-inflicted with some trace of barbiturates and the like but no really funny stuff. He's the ME. Who's to argue? Bede's in Forest Lawn already."

Hartman sniffed derisively. "Well, I dropped in on our doctor after looking in on you-know-who."

Edelman managed a smile. "Poor Mr. Honner still in C.C.U. at Bethesda? That was *some* heart attack! I understand they have to keep him so doped up for pain that he hardly recognizes anybody."

They both shared a laugh over that.

Jake Edelman looked down at the thick transcript of the Honner confessions. "Jesus! The names in here, Bob!"

The other man nodded. "I know, Jake, I know. We'll have a tough time getting them all. A slow process. But everybody in the Mickey Mouse organization has them, knows them, as do the RCMP and MI-5. They're through, Jake, if we aren't."

"Hear about Colonel Toricelli's group raiding Camp Liberty?" Edelman asked. "No wonder that boy, Cornish, saw jets taking off and landing regularly! It was forty-eight kilometers southwest of the Tucson airport!"

Hartman smiled. "Well, there's nothing left now. The papers have been playing up the smashing of the terrorists and the discovery of domestic traitors. All the usual bullshit, except that it's all true. We're heroes, Jake. The President's going to give you the Medal of Freedom and I'm going to get the New York office and all that. Didn't you know?"

Edelman snorted. "You know he wants me to meet with the cabinet and the emergency council tonight. Wants to be sure he has everything. I've been asked to appear on tomorrow's address, can you believe? He told me to bring maps, pictures, exhibits."

Hartman was suddenly bright and alive. "He did, did he?" His expression suddenly feel. "They can't be that dumb, Jake. They just *can't* be. I mean, Allen Honner absolutely did not know what the hell Mickey Mouse was except a cartoon character. They must at least suspect that we're on to them."

"Arrogance, Bob," Jake Edelman said. "Arrogance and conceit. Back in the old days, in World War II, the Germans conquered practically all of Europe and came within a whisker of the world. They did this even though their intelligence apparatus was so lousy the British were almost running it. They just couldn't believe that they could be fooled by some slick tricksters. At the same time, we'd broken the Japanese code yet were so damned dumb we set Pearl Harbor up so it'd be easy for the Japanese to cripple us, and we even court-martialed a general who said we'd get hit by the Japs from carriers there! They've got it made, Bob—and they know it. That's our defense. That and the fact that they are men and women like Honner—they're not used to being on the receiving end. Conspirators and masters of terror are quite often the easiest to terrorize—they *assume* you think like them. You watch."

The tone did not have the full confidence the words conveyed. Hartman knew it, but echoed it all the same. "Go get 'em, Jake. All that can be done has been done."

The old man got up wearily and started packing his exhibits case, then closed it, picked it up, and walked slowly for the door.

"Jake?"

He turned. "Yes, Bob?"

"God be with you," Bob Hartman said.

Jefferson Lee Wainwright, President of the United States, was going over his speech before his cabinet and emergency council. It was a distinguished group: thirty-four men and women who, together, handled much of the top echelons of government and the military.

"And so, my fellow Americans," he was saying, complete with flamboyant gestures, "these radicals of bygone days, defeated and demoralized but not deradicalized, went different ways. Some left the country, some went underground to hiding-holes, but some, the best and the brightest of them, went into normal careers and rose brilliantly in them. Men like Dr. Joseph Bede, who wormed his way into the National Disease Control Center and, there, in a major authority position, secretly used your tax money and your facilities to create what became known as the Wilderness Organism." He paused and looked directly at the crowd, and in a lower, more normal tone said, "And, you know, the son of a bitch really *was* involved in the blowups when he was an undergrad? Man! Will *that* hold up!"

Suddenly he changed back into the Presidential orator.

"These radicals, still dedicated after a decade or two of dormancy, waited for the rallying cry. And it came! It came from those who had wormed their way into government and society and positions of importance! They trained at an abandoned Army test range near Tucson, gathering the scum of the earth from its four corners. And Bede gave them the weapon. The Wilderness Organism."

Again he paused, but remained in his professional charismatic pose.

"Yes, my fellow Americans! But it was not complete. Oh, no. No such beast could be perfect without testing. So they tested it on you. On small-town America, where they could observe its properties and effects. And, when they were ready, they made plans to strike at the heart of our major cities. The tragedies in Chicago and New Orleans are witness to what the whole country could have undergone—and may still. For such elements as these still exist in society!"

He stopped, relaxed, and put down the sheets. "That's all the further Barry got on it. We probably will go through another draft or two, but it's pretty effective. The rest is spelling out the plans and justifying them, and you know all that by now anyway."

Most of them nodded.

There was a commotion at a far door, and heads turned as two Secret Service men entered, flanking a tiny, strange-looking little man with a big nose.

"Chief Inspector Edelman!" Wainwright boomed. "Please come up here so I can shake your hand." He turned to the rehearsed audience. "This is the man who saved the country!"

Jake Edelman came up and accepted the handshake and the polite applause of the bigwigs.

"Inspector, I would like you to brief us all personally on the plot, how you solved it, and how it all worked," Wainwright said. "Barry Sandler, there, is writing tomorrow's speech, and we want to give credit where credit is due and also get the thing a hundred percent accurate." He pointed. "You can take that chair, there. It's Al Honner's. As you might have heard, he had a really bad heart attack."

Edelman's expression was grim, but he smiled slightly at the last and took the plush chair. He was at the corner of the long double conference tables; he could see just about everybody in the room.

"Go on, Inspector. Don't be shy. We're you're biggest fans," said Attorney General Gaither.

Jake looked at the President. "May I have some water?" he asked meekly. The President smiled, nodded at an aide, who got up, poured some from a pitcher on a little table to one side, brought it to Edelman, and resumed his seat.

The audience really was attentive and expectant. Edelman was to be the proof of the pudding; if he gave the official version, then all was well. If he did not, there was still enough time to paper over mistakes.

"Mr. President, ladies and gentlemen," Jake Edelman began. "I wish to tell you tonight of all that my department and its capable staff, with the help of a lot of people throughout government, discovered about this conspiracy against our country. I hope you will bear with me until I am completely through."

They were peering at him expectantly.

"The story starts many years ago, in the turbulent years when Presidents were killed or forced from office, when our enemies made spectacular gains abroad while we did nothing. A lot of people saw this as the end of civilization. Many of these were corporate heads, millionaires, men of influence and power. They formed the Institute for Values and Standards, and endowed it with over a hundred million dollars."

There were murmurings in the room, and a few whispers of "He knows," but they calmed down. They wanted to know all that he knew.

"This Institute endowed research in forbidden areas, masked by the corporation's international operations, and at the same time picked the best young minds they could find in every field. Poor families in particular were targeted, and lavish scholarships were offered. Ideological purity was stressed, as well. These people were young, ambitious, bright, and, of course, malleable. The Institute saw to their philosophical upbringing—wasn't above eliminating those who later strayed or would not stick to the path. This elite, brought up in much the same way the criminal syndicates of America were brought up and replenished, slowly attained position and power in government and industry. All doors were open to them. Their names read like a *Who's Who* in American government, business, and industry. In fact, their names *are* a lot of the current *Who's Who.*"

He paused and sipped some water. Some of the men and women he was discussing stared at him in stunned silence.

"Their eventual goal was to attain enough power, influence, and prestige that they could literally take over the government of the United States of America, take it over, totalitarianize it, and create out of it the nation that their founders had dreamed about. This they did, by hook, ability, and crook. When they had a member President, they felt no compunction about cleverly murdering a sufficient number of Supreme Court justices and other such posts so that they could be replaced with members of the club. But, still, it was far-fetched. You can't become the Congress, for example, not only because of the value of incumbency but also because the voters are damned obstinate. And, of course, the Institute could hardly have a native son in each state and district. And, again—what about Americans used to freedom? Would they respond to a military and governmental *coup* meekly? Hardly—and they have the guns and the geography to make it damned difficult for anybody who *did* take over to ever hold on. So what to do?"

Again a sip of water, and he continued.

"The obvious answer was a popular war, but that's out of style. Wars aren't popular these days, and a war on the scale of a sneak attack means annihilation. So, these bright folks thought, suppose you had a sneak attack by an unknown enemy? Some of their scientific types had continued the recombinant DNA research banned by U.S. law and international treaty. True, the Institute was interested in more than just pet germs—they were interested in designing their own, superior breed of humanity, among other things. There are lots of potentials with recombinant DNA. But what they could make, easily, on the sly, was germs—bacteria, specifically. They made the Wilderness Organism. They did it right here, in the government labs, with NDCC and NIH computers and facilities. The trouble was, they had no idea whether or not their designs worked. Now came the next part of the plan."

He paused again for a sip, and somebody whispered, "Why don't we just shut him up?" She was waved to silence by President Wainwright.

"So," continued Jake Edelman, "friends in the CIA, and those who could be blackmailed—and friends in the FBI as well—combed the files, scoured the world, and plugged into the international terrorist network. The word got around. A mysterious Third World nation with a lot of money and a radical leadership had a weapon to strike at dirty old imperialistic America. They needed volunteers—and they got them, sometimes with the unwitting cooperation of governments hostile to us. The first waves were double tests—first of the engineered bacillus and its properties, as well as the vaccines against it, and second of the network that would be needed for the big job later. Small towns geographically isolated were chosen. The diseases would be studied by NDCC and NIH, of course—including the creators. Modifications could be made, corrections in the biological clocks, degree and means of communicability, everything. Since they also created a bacteriophage, a bacteria-eating virus, they eliminated the evidence as well. Many of the early experiments failed completely, or failed to work as predicted. A terrible plague became a case of the town getting the sniffles. But, after a while, the right combination popped up. They began, by using the bacteria as a catalyst for certain interactions with brain cells, to be able to get just about any effect they wanted. They made a number of strains of the stuff they'd proved out, and they were ready."

There were uneasy murmurings and shufflings in the room now, but these were quieted by the leaders. They wanted to know just how Edelman knew these things.

"A camp was set up and run by radicals for radicals. They didn't even know where they were—they were duped and drugged and thought they were in Africa. There their old-time revolutionary religion was recharged, and they were given lessons in how to release the organisms in major cities. In the meantime, one of their blackmail victims, an FBI agent named Harry Reed, who'd worked on the radical fugitives years ago, was assigned to eastern California and 'just happened' to recognize James Foley, head of one of the early small-town strike teams. We jumped at it, raided the place, and discovered the Wilderness Organism and pegged it to known terrorist fanatics."

They were getting really upset now. Jake Edelman started to feel his one greatest fear, that they would not let him finish.

"Using the idea that we had a mysterious enemy controlling a horrible fate, we scared the American people half to death. They were willing to do just about anything to feel safe from this dreaded disease. It was much worse than soldiers of an enemy. It was silent, invisible, and permanent in its effects. They demanded protection from Congress, Congress gave extreme emergency powers to the President, and we had the military state of emergency called and the mechanics of dictatorship established and tested, and some really embarrassing enemies and problem people vanishing. The American populace was militarized and computerized faster than anyone would have believed, and mostly with its willing cooperation. They were naive and terrified."

He was out of water now.

"So now this radical step had to produce results. There was an early slip, too—much of the Wilderness Organism's model-building was done in NDCC computers, and this was stumbled on by a brilliant doctor, Mark Spiegelman. When taps and monitors showed that he had, in fact, discovered the domestic origins, a minor flunky in the security apparatus at Fort Dietrick panicked and had the security men murder him. It was clumsy and needless, since part of the plot was to show that the thing was indeed of domestic origin. His real crime was that he had discovered the truth too soon; it'd been planted there for later, more carefully planned discovery.

"My own team was charged with solving the mystery. I was chosen because of my impeccable reputation, if I do say so myself, and my heart condition, which would prove a convenient out if I stumbled onto the wrong things or if I followed the script and retired. Now, using the handouts I got from the conspirators, I was to slowly crack the case. Plants I placed in the large body of radicals were spotted and allowed to pass, apparently undetected. They were even spread around, to make sure that I would get word on each team before it was to hit a major city. Of course, some casualties were to be anticipated, but most we got, and the communicability of the strains was kept low. We failed to get word on the Chicago and New Orleans teams, as you know, but seem to have only localized hits. Ten, twenty thousand people in Chicago, less than a third of that in New Orleans. We also almost missed the one for D.C., but got lucky. One assumes that the important people all had their shots, anyway.

"To take the blame, Dr. Sandra O'Connell and Dr. Joe Bede were put under drugs and placed under conditions where suicide would result. We rescued Dr. O'Connell, but not Bede. One assumes that there is now a list of the 'ringleaders' of this conspiracy, that a purge in government and elsewhere will turn these traitors up, and that these will include a large part of Congress and other agencies not under control. Using this as a guise, the Institute personnel will now totalitarianize the nation and hold it in their absolute grip for remolding. Only one thing stands in their way, though, and it's formidible. It's something that will have to be faced here and now, which is why I am here."

He paused and looked around. "Can I have some more water, please?" he asked, holding out his glass. President Wainwright smiled, took the glass, personally refilled it, brought it back and handed it to him.

"Thank you," he said, drinking a bit.

"And what stands in the way of this conspiratorial group?" the President asked him. "If what you say is true, then it would seem that they've won."

Jake Edelman looked up at them and smiled. "The friends of Mickey Mouse," he said.

Most of them met with blank stares, but Attorney General Gaither and Admiral Leggits both looked up in surprise. Wainwright looked at them quizzically.

"An underground group," Gaither explained. "Using the most elaborate codex device we've ever seen. We've identified a number of them, but the codexes are self-destructing and they've been deep-probed and conditioned, all of them. Dig deep enough and you turn their minds to garbage, but you don't get any information."

Wainwright was intrigued. "Why Mickey Mouse?" he asked.

"That's what their leader sounds like over the phone," Leggits put in. "I almost interrupted a conversation in the Pentagon. He was a good officer, too," he added, a trace of sadness in his voice.

"And you are a friend of Mickey Mouse?" Wainwright asked Jake.

The Chief Inspector shook his head from side to side. "No, Mr. President, I am not. I *am* Mickey Mouse."

There was an uproar. It took more than a minute to calm everybody down. Wainwright was still in command here, though, and still confident. After all, Edelman was here. Alone. But that very fact suggested that there were things still to know, things that would make him admit everything openly and sign his own death warrant.

"All right, Inspector, let's play no more games," Wainwright said. "What are you trying to tell us?"

Edelman reached into his case and brought out a blue spray can. It looked very much like the one on the front pages of all the newspapers—a spray aerosol can in baby blue.

"When we first discovered the truth, we created our organization, feeling that if one agency could use government and bureaucracy, then so could the other. Most Americans, even those in positions of relative power, find the current emergency abhorrent. When shown evidence of this conspiracy, they are only too willing to help fight it. My team raided Camp Liberty a week ago, several days ahead of your anonymous tip. We also raided the NDCC bunkers, and we have made a lot of changes at Dugway Proving Grounds, and moved a lot of stuff. Further, *loyal* researchers at NDCC and NIH have been working on a problem for me for a month, since before I even guessed the scope and breadth of this thing. Ever since I discovered the computer models for the Wilderness Organism, from the day of O'Connell's and Bede's kidnap. We worked on it, discovering just exactly the correct sort of radiation necessary to make the Wilderness Organism cultures mutate slightly. And what do you know? They found not only the mutating method, but at the same time the simple, quick treatment killed the bacteriophage! We then wiped the Wilderness Organism clean out of the computers, to avoid making your mistake."

H&W Secretary Meekins was the first to see it, and she was appalled. "You mean that current strains *won't* disappear in a day? They'll continue to live and multiply?"

Edelman nodded. "And they'll be mutated, beyond the vaccine's effectiveness. There will be no defense. Oh, don't worry. It won't destroy the world, I'm assured. There is sufficient radiation from the sun alone to mutate it into harmlessness in a matter of a few days. But, I think, a few hundred strategic releases all over the country will be sufficient to eliminate most human life in North America."

Again they were in an uproar. Wainwright's eyes kept going to the blue cannister in Jake's hand. "That can—that is the new stuff?" he asked nervously.

Edelman felt much better. That question was what he'd waited for.

"Yes, it is. This is the stuff that makes you feebleminded," he told them cheerfully. "Washington wouldn't even notice. This spray can alone is sufficient to, say, infect the entire White House area if I push the little wax-sealed plunger here. See?"

Many were on their feet now. The Secretary of State started for him, angry and panicked, but was stopped by two of his fellows.

When they'd calmed down again, Jake continued.

"The friends of Mickey Mouse have the cylinders.

I don't even know who they are, nor does anybody know them all. We've all been deep-probed and blocked, so I haven't any idea how anybody *would* know. We voted on it—you remember voting, don't you? We decided that we'd rather have death for us and our children than live under your new order. Man will survive. But we won't. And you won't. And if I don't walk out of here, at the proper time, they will know your answer."

Wainwright was shaken, as were the others. None of them could take their eyes off the small blue can in Jake Edelman's hand.

"And you expect us to surrender, to expose ourselves?" Wainwright said. "Hell, man, you might as well push that button. We're dead anyway."

Now it was Jake Edelman's turn to smile. "No, sir, I do not. What I propose is a simple compromise, the art of political expediency. We have the names of all the Institute personnel. It was simple, once we cracked your computer code. We will be watching you. But—here is what I propose you do. I propose you change that speech of yours for tomorrow. I propose that, instead, you outline the plot exactly as you were going to—use the same scapegoats you intended to, except keep it to the dead and those quickly silenced. Then announce that the plot has been completely and thoroughly broken. Democracy is saved, freedom is restored. Slowly you will lift the state of emergency, and all constitutional guarantees are back in force right now. The computer ID system will be phased out. Military controls will be lifted. Slowly, the country will return to normal. Tell the people that Abraham Lincoln suspended constitutional guarantees during the Civil War, and instituted military government to save the nation, as you have. He then ended those measures; now you will, too. Slowly, over the next year, the majority of you in this room will retire or leave for better opportunities. After all, Mr. President, you're nearing the end of your second term. It's natural. You'll retire a hero, an elder statesman. They'll sing songs and write epic plays about you.

"Hell, they'll probably build a giant granite statue of you on the Mall as a hero like Lincoln, and put you on the dime, you son of a bitch."

Wainwright looked thoughtful. His eyes now left the blue cannister for the first time, going to the others in the room.

"Comment?"

"He's bluffing!" one of them said. "We're so close, we can't give in now!" another echoed. But the majority had more pragmatic looks on their faces. Finally Wainwright exhaled and turned back to Edelman.

"We'll have to check this, you know," he said.

Edelman smiled. "Try and find a blue cannister, or a Wilderness Organism," he invited. "Try and find the models. Your five-person team at NDCC are all dead now. They—ah, committed suicide."

Wainwright gulped. "Leave that can there, for analysis," he said.

Edelman shook his head. "Uh-uh. I need it with me. Find your own, if you can," he said, and got up.

"Where do you think you're going?" somebody asked.

"I'm going home, to a wife I haven't seen in two and a half weeks," he said wearily. "And tonight I'm going to wine her and dine her and romance her like there's no tomorrow. And then I'm going to sleep. And when I wake up, I'm going to turn on my television and watch your speech, Mr. President. That's what I'm going to do. I won't be hard to find if you want me."

He placed the can in his pocket, keeping a hand also in the pocket, and closed and latched the briefcase with his left hand. With that, he turned and walked out the nearest door. Nobody stopped him.

He walked wearily down the corridors, then down the stairs, and out the east entrance to a waiting car. Bob Hartman was driving, and seemed to come alive when he saw his boss.

Edelman got in, and they drove slowly off, out the gate, and down the mall, turning right and heading out over the 14th Street Bridge.

Jake Edelman stared at the muddy Potomac. "River level's high," he said. "Pull over to the side, Bob, and stop for a minute."

Hartman, puzzled, did as instructed. Edelman pulled the can from his pocket and looked at it.

"You know, that was cheap spray paint Minnie got," he said. Hartman looked at the can. Coming through the dried baby blue paint were the words *Action Ant and Roach Killer* and the picture of a dead roach, upside down. It was faint, but unmistakable.

Hartman whistled slowly. Edelman got out of the car, looked for a moment at the center of the river channel, and tossed the can into the water.

Slowly, looking very tired, he got back in and they started off once again. Hartman stared at him. "Do you think they'll buy it?" he asked.

"I'm still here," Edelman pointed out. "And so are you. They know there's an organization, they won't find any blue cylinders, and they won't find any trace of the Wilderness Organism at NDCC except five dead traitors. Right?"

Hartman nodded.

"With the founders of the Institute, I think we might have lost," he said. "But with their adopted children? Well, we'll know for sure tomorrow."

They drove on a while in silence, clearing two military checkpoints. Another seven kilometers and they were into the northern Virginia suburbs, and not long after that they were pulling into Jake Edelman's driveway.

Edelman started to get out of the car.

"Jake?" Bob Hartman said.

Jake stopped, turned, and said, "Yes?"

"You're a great man, Jake."

Jake Edelman smiled, turned, got out of the car and slowly walked up to the front door. He fumbled for his keys, found them, and opened the front door.

Bob Hartman just watched him, a tiny little figure, ugly and unkempt, as he disappeared into his small brick house.